A COMPANION FOR THE COUNT

A
COMPANION
for the
COUNT

CLAIRVOIR CASTLE *Romances*
BOOK TWO

SALLY BRITTON

Published by Pink Citrus Books
Edited by Jenny Proctor of Midnight Owl Editors
Cover design by Blue Water Books

This book is a work of fiction. Names, characters, places, and incidents are either products of the author's imagination or are used fictitiously. Any resemblance to actual persons living or dead, events, or locales is entirely coincidental.

Sally Britton
www.authorsallybritton.com

First Printing: May 2021
Paperback ISBN: 978-1-947005-29-7

To Sally's Sweet Romance Fans on Facebook.
You make this whole writing thing a lot more fun.

Clairvoir Castle, the Duke of Montfort's estate, housed over thirty servants, eight members of the duke's family, a governess, and Emma Arlen—who really did not fit in any of the other categories of occupants.

Emma, the duke's ward and companion to Lady Josephine, the duke's eldest daughter, sat in her usual spot in the upstairs morning room. With her legs tucked up on the sofa and an embroidery hoop occupying her hands, she did her best to ignore her friend's pacing from one end of the room to the other.

Despite the large number of permanent residents residing in the castle, the duke welcomed guests in large groups and with great frequency.

New arrivals were expected that very day.

"I cannot like Papa's insistence that I arrange entertainment for the ambassador." Lady Josephine often received a share of the hostessing duties. Usually without reserve. "He reminded me again, at breakfast, to be attentive to the count."

"I was there, Josie." Emma raised her gaze momentarily to her friend's. "His Grace *insisted* nothing. I would say he suggested you would have better ideas for entertainment than most, given that the ambassador is a gentleman closer to your age than your father's."

The duke's eldest daughter did tend toward the dramatic, at least in private. Hers was an emotional nature, but not volatile. She possessed great kindness and compassion and a desire to see all around her happy. But she had also possessed an over active imagination since girlhood.

Josephine glowered at Emma. "I think it has more to do with the fact that the ambassador is unmarried. Papa is trying to play at matchmaking. You know he is."

"I know no such thing." Emma returned her attention to her embroidery and pushed her needle through the cloth of the hand-kerchief. Sometimes, the best way to help her friend get through these moments was to maintain her own composure. "Your mother and father do not believe in young marriages. As you are only nineteen, I think you are safe from them forcing you to the altar."

Age was not the only thing to consider, either. The duke and duchess wanted their children's happiness. They would never force a match that their child did not like. Though they might try to arrange meetings with eligible bachelors from time to time, it was not in their nature to be heavy-handed.

"But he is foreign nobility. That would be a boon to all of England. And Father knows I detest all the men equal to my rank here."

Emma stuck her needle in the work before shaking the hoop at her friend, barely concealing her amusement. "Firstly, Josephine, you have not met all the suitable men in England. Secondly, the kingdom this ambassador represents is new and volatile. Your father would never want you in such an uncertain position. Not after everything that has happened in France."

Josephine sat down with a huff. "The Kingdom of the Two Sicilies is a steady nation, Emma. King Ferdinand has the full support of Britain."

"Which is why the count is coming to visit your father. To

strengthen that support and forge new relationships. That means he will spend most of his time with His Grace and your eldest brother."

As a nearly lifelong companion to Josephine, Emma knew the intimate details of the family's lives. Consequently, she also knew many things about the political state of her nation. Though the war with France had ended years before, Britain still felt the repercussions keenly, as did most of Europe. The reorganization of Italian governments and titles had barely settled, with the Kingdom of the Two Sicilies one of two governments dominating what had once been several city-states loosely held together by European rule.

Napoleon's quick conquest of Italy and its resources had alerted the other large European powers to the importance of securing the city-states into more unified wholes.

Josephine's sigh brought Emma back to herself. "Josie, rest easy. This Italian ambassador is the same as all the others. A political guest, and not at all a permanent one."

"I hope you are right. I have no desire to marry at present, nor to leave my family. I am quite happy as I am." Josephine folded her hands in her lap and lifted her chin higher. "I have more than enough to occupy my time and attention."

Emma pretended thoughtfulness as she tapped her chin with one finger. "What if he is handsome?" If her friend would not be comforted, perhaps Emma could tease Josephine out of her worries.

"If he *is* handsome, you are more than welcome to him." Josephine took up a cushion and threw it at Emma, who caught it while laughing.

"I have no more desire to wed than you do." She thought a moment, then amended her statement with a wrinkled nose. "At present."

When she did decide to marry, she hoped to have the full support of the duke. His place as her guardian, and his acting as a father to her in everything but name, had won her trust and love when she was still a little girl, mourning the loss of her parents.

"You will help me if the count proves overly flirtatious?" Josephine asked, somewhat plaintively. "I have no wish to disappoint my father, or hurt the count's pride, but I will not play the flirt. Even if it is for political relations."

The weight of the moment, the seriousness of Josephine's tone, sobered Emma. "You are not truly worried, are you? His Grace isn't trying to encourage your marriage to a stranger. If he hoped for a match, he would say so directly." She lowered her embroidery hoop to the basket beside her chair.

"But what if this is a test? If the count and I get along, Papa might bring him back in a year or two or give the count hope that there might be a union between us one day." Josephine tangled her fingers together in her lap, as she did when nervous.

Emma rose and came to kneel before her friend, stilling the movements of Josephine's hands by laying her own across them. "Josie, why do you worry so? If the count does not suit you, your father will not press the matter. If you find you do like the count, there would be no harm in seeing him again in the future. I think you are borrowing trouble, nothing more."

"I know what people see when they meet me, Emma." Josephine's voice fell almost to a whisper. "We both do. They see my father's power and influence. Not a woman with her own head and heart. I may be only nineteen, but I know well enough that I am a pawn on the board to most people. A means to an end." She shivered, then clutched Emma's hand in both of hers. "Promise me you'll help as long as you can. I want my freedom a little longer. Please."

Emma stared up into her friend's lovely blue eyes. As children, they had often pretended they were sisters rather than friends. They both had brown curls, were of similar petite build, and liked all the same games. Only their eyes were different—Josephine's blue and Emma's brown. With age, their subtle differences had become more pronounced. Emma's nose was small and turned up slightly at the end, and Josephine freckled easily and was a few inches taller than her friend. And Emma filled out her gowns a little more than the duke's daughter.

But they had stayed as true and as close as sisters, despite any physical changes they underwent or the disparity in their ranks.

Emma made her vow with all the love of a sister. "I will help you, Josie. I promise."

In whatever way she could.

Luca closed his eyes against the bright afternoon sunlight streaming through the carriage windows. Travel in carriages rarely agreed with him. He fasted rather strictly on days when he knew he would be in a wheeled conveyance longer than a few minutes, and on unknown roads. Small sips of tea were all he permitted himself.

Travel on horseback was much easier, but his secretary had insisted that the *Conte di Atella, di Regno delle Due Sicilie,* could not arrive on an English duke's doorstep in anything less than the finest carriage money could buy.

Never mind that he would show up feeling horrifically ill.

Concern about Luca's relative youth had already clouded the opinions in the Italian courts on whether or not he would make a suitable ambassador to England. Surely, eight and twenty years were enough to garner trust for a man of his education and lineage.

Carlo Torlonia, his secretary, sat across from Luca at that moment. Reading.

Next to Torlonia sat Luca's manservant, Gabino Bruno. *Il valletto* in Italian. Valet in English. Of the three of them, Bruno's English was the least capable, and Luca's the most. He had studied English with tutors for several years, along with French during the occupation of the French pretenders.

French had been easier than English.

"Are you reading anything of interest, *Signor Torlonia*?" They had agreed to speak English unless it was absolutely necessary that they revert back to their native Italian. Torlonia needed the practice. Luca still had moments when his accent came out more strongly than he wished. Poor Bruno at least understood a great deal, even if he could not speak more than a few words of English.

"The history of Rutland, *Signore*." Torlonia glanced up from his book. "I thought it best to prepare for conversations which might require more knowledge of the duke's lands." Why did the man always sound smug when he spoke? It was yet another detractor to their relationship.

Luca leaned into the corner of the carriage, looking out as they entered a lane shaded by large trees. Oaks, he thought. There were more oak trees in England than he had seen in the Italian countryside, and their oaks were undoubtedly of a different variety than those his homeland boasted.

His homeland. A place in turmoil, despite the finalization of the kingdom's borders. Already there was talk of secret societies set upon destroying the monarchy, of sowing dissent and rebellion, plunging his land into more bloody conflicts too soon after the war with Napoleon.

He winced when they came out of the shaded lane, turning upward toward a hill. He caught the briefest glimpse of towers resembling the battlements of ancient castles. He blinked. They were turning up a road to go to that castle.

"I thought Clairvoir Castle was newly constructed."

Torlonia glanced up from his book. "Ten years ago, I am told. On a site as old as the Norman invasion, where *three* castles have existed before." He shook his reading material toward Luca. "I told you this book would prove useful, *Signore*. You are also saying the name wrong."

Luca folded his arms over his protesting midsection. "Wrong? Is it not French?"

"As with everything else the English do, they adapted it to suit themselves. I believe they pronounce the castle name *Clee-ver*." As Torlonia had performed nearly all the meetings and tasks necessary regarding their invitation and travel to the duke's country seat, Luca trusted his secretary. Still. "Why ruin a perfectly good French name that way?"

The secretary shrugged, then elbowed the sleeping manservant beside him. "Bruno, we are arrived. Wake up."

Bruno jolted awake. Though he neared the age of fifty, he usually had as much energy at hand as Luca. "*Mi perdoni, mio Signore*." He straightened his coat, then leaned forward in the carriage to adjust Luca's cravat. "You did not sleep?"

Luca lifted his chin, keeping his eyes on the window. "No. You know how I feel about carriages."

The servant nodded once, sharply. "Since you were *bambino piccolo*." Bruno had been with Luca's family for as long as the ambassador could remember, proving a loyal servant despite the upheaval of the nation and the noble class.

Though Torlonia had advised Luca to find a British valet, Luca kept Bruno with him. Loyalty was far more important than a fashionably knotted cravat. No matter what the secretary said about it.

Torlonia tucked his book into a large leather bag he kept at his side, its long strap perpetually over his shoulder. "Remember, *Signore*. You are not to overtax yourself with politics. This is a respite from the politics of our nations, unless the duke extends an invitation for such discussion."

Luca shifted, and the pounding in his head began again, more vigorous than before.

He represented the Kingdom of the Two Sicilies, even though he was of Northern Italian descent and education. His family's holdings, and the title granted him by the king, made him a man of Sicily despite his birth in a northern city-state.

"I hope you will not forget your duties. Your plans for courting the duke's daughter—they will only distract you," Torlonia reminded him, somewhat stiffly.

Luca narrowed his eyes at the other man. "*Sua Maestà il Re* said it would be a good thing to take an English bride. To strengthen our ties to their nation."

Another reason his stomach refused to behave. Political discussions and responsibilities were one thing, but thus far, flirting with the daughters of English noblemen had proven less enjoyable than Luca had hoped. Not only did he have Torlonia's disapproval to reckon with, but the women he had encountered had not impressed him to make any overtures. The young ladies he had met, cousins to the royal family, children of titled men, were all too eager to pounce on him. Many had attempted to speak Italian, with varying levels of success, and still more had made him uncomfortable with their pointed ploys to capture his attention.

More than one unmarried woman had called him *exotic*.

Perhaps he did not look exactly as their gentlemen—fair-skinned and fair-haired as many of the noblemen he'd met had been—but given that he had seen men and women with as many variations in hair and eye color in his own country, he knew no one could tell his origins by looking at him.

Yes, he had dark hair. Yes, he had dark eyes. And no, he did not freckle in the sun, he bronzed. But surely there were plenty of Englishmen who did the same.

The carriage rolled to a stop, and Bruno handed Luca the tall black hat they had acquired in London for formal occasions.

A servant in the duke's livery stepped up to the door, and Luca's chest tightened.

"Time to make a good impression," Torlonia murmured.

On both the duke and his daughter. Luca's king wanted him

to take an English wife. Courting Lady Josephine was a certain step in that direction. Though he had never expected to wed for king and country, Luca would do his duty to both.

Luca stepped out into the shadow of the duke's castle. Castle Clairvoir. A masterful construction, with four levels of windows visible from where he stood and make-believe battlements crowning towers and top floors alike. Though he had seen many ancient castles in the Italian cities, and onhis journey through Spain, where he had served as an ambassador for the previous six months, this castle had a charm of its own.

Servants waited along the drive, dressed in livery and uniforms which proclaimed the wealth and status of their employer.

Head up, Luca approached the doors as they opened to reveal a long corridor—a tall hall lined with ancient shields and medieval weaponry.

And a cannon at the other end, positioned as though it might fire down the corridor to defend the castle at a moment's notice.

The duke and duchess waited inside, standing so as to grant him an unrestricted view of the room stretching into the distance. In a row next to the ducal couple were the people he presumed to be their family members and important members of the household.

Luca stepped inside, removing his hat and gloves and handing them to a waiting servant.

The duke's black hair turned silver above the temples, and he boasted broad shoulders despite being in his mid-fifties. His duchess, the very picture of sophistication and elegance, greeted Luca with a warm smile.

Luca bowed deeply before the duke, and the Englishman's deep voice echoed off the tall ceiling and hanging shields.

"Welcome to Castle Clairvoir, Count Atella. We are honored to host the ambassador of the Kingdom of the Two Sicilies and look forward to strengthening the ties between our countries.

Allow me to present to you my wife, the Duchess of Montfort. My mother"—an older woman with graying hair and a nose remarkably similar to the duke's held her hand out to Luca for him to bow over it—"Sarah, Duchess of Montfort."

Next in line was a tall man near Luca's age. The duke's heir. "My eldest son, Lord Farleigh. My eldest daughter, Lady Josephine." The woman next to the heir took after her mother in appearance, tall and willowy in stature, with a sprinkling of freckles across her nose. Brown hair, blue eyes. Pretty. But young.

This was the woman to whom his secretary objected, and his king would likely approve, if Luca wished to pay her court.

A movement behind Lady Josephine drew his attention to another young woman, a woman with dark hair, an impish nose, and brown eyes that met his briefly before her gaze dropped to the ground. She was a few inches shorter than Lady Josephine, dressed as finely, with a smile hiding at the corner of her mouth.

"Lord Atella, allow me to introduce my companion, Miss Emma Arlen. She is my dearest friend and has helped me devise all manner of entertainments for your stay with us."

Miss Arlen curtsied, her smile disappearing completely, and her gaze did not raise to his again.

"It is a pleasure to meet you, Lady Josephine. Miss Arlen."

The duke spoke again, his deep voice commanding. "My younger children, two daughters and a son, will meet with us in the garden for refreshment after you have recovered from your journey."

Luca bowed again. "Of course." He gestured to his secretary. "Allow me to introduce *Signor* Torlonia, my personal secretary. He will assist me in matters of state and correspondence with my king and His Royal Highness, Prince George."

All the introductions made, the duke called the butler of the household to show Luca to his suite of rooms. Luca cast one last glance at Lady Josephine, determined to offer her his most charming smile, but she looked behind her at the same moment.

His gaze skipped over her shoulder to Miss Arlen, who peered back at him with one eyebrow raised.

He forced his attention away, following the butler up a staircase, then another, and through a hall dominated by a painting of the duke.

Torlonia quickened his step to walk beside Luca, whispering so as not to be overheard by the butler. "The Lady Josephine. *Che bella*. And such eyes. She will be a distraction if you are not careful."

Luca nodded once, sharply. But rather than think of blue eyes, he remembered a pair of brown beneath a skeptically raised eyebrow.

CHAPTER TWO

Emma continued to feign reading while Josephine fretted at her side. The beautiful weather and scent of the last blooms of summer were not enough to deter the duke's eldest daughter from her concerns.

"He is *so* old. At least a decade older than I am. What is Papa thinking?" Josephine asked, keeping her voice low enough that it would not carry to the other side of the terrace where her father and the Italian count sat in conversation.

Glancing up from her book, Emma first took in her friend's deep frown and then the foreigner in their midst. "He is not yet thirty, I would wager." Emma looked back down at her book and bit her lip to keep from laughing when Josephine groaned.

"I am *nineteen*, Emma. He is too old."

"I am twenty, dearest Josie. He is *not* too old. You are simply determined not to like him." Emma turned another page. She was rereading *One-Thousand and One Arabian Nights*, one of her favorite story collections. "You could give him a chance."

"Stop teasing me." Josephine sat down at last on the stone wall around the fountain, folding her hands tightly in her lap. "I haven't any desire to marry at present. Especially someone who will take me far away from my family. Even if the count were the perfect man, I cannot think I would want him."

"No one is making you do any such thing," Emma reminded her, giving up on reading her book. She closed the pages and put it down on the stone beside her. "Your father asked you to help keep Lord Atella entertained. That's all you must do, and I am here to help you."

Isabelle and Rosalind, Josephine's younger sisters, were sitting politely on a couch brought out to the garden for them to practice behaving themselves in company. Their mother, the duchess, and Miss Sharpe, their governess, sat in chairs on either side of the girls.

"Do you remember when your mother and our governess used to hover over us like that?" Emma asked, nudging her friend with a shoulder. "As though they were afraid we would start spouting nonsense or stand on our heads the minute they looked away."

A brief smile appeared on Josephine's face. "They had good reason with the two of us. Remember when the Swiss ambassador visited Papa, and we made all those horrid faces at his secretary?"

"The secretary was an ancient goat." Emma did not bother hiding her gleeful grin at the memory. "He kept telling the ambassador, in French, how lovely we were. I am fairly certain he should not have noticed that girls of thirteen and fourteen were lovely."

"I quite agree." Josephine picked up Emma's book. "Oh, are you reading this again? How can you like this story? I find the sultan horrid."

"I find him rather amusing." Emma didn't bother hiding her smile. "And it isn't just one story. I like them all. *Arabian Nights* is one of my favorite collections. Thank goodness your father has all the volumes. Even if he insists on hiding a few."

The duke had purchased every volume of the Jonathan Scott translation for Emma and Josephine years before, thinking them something his children would enjoy. Of course, after he read the stories himself, a few of the volumes disappeared from the schoolroom. Apparently, the tales were not all appropriate for young readers.

"Do you think he's handsome?" Josephine asked, idly turning the pages of the book in her hands.

"The sultan? Or the goat? Or your father?" Emma asked, leaning back enough to trail her hand through the cool water of the fountain. "You know I have always thought the duke quite refined."

Josephine scowled at her. "The ambassador, Lord Atella."

"It doesn't matter what I think." Emma glanced in the direction of the duke and ambassador again. The duke sat at his ease, while the ambassador, dressed all in black except for his white cravat and green waistcoat, sat stiffly.

When Josephine had made introductions an hour before, Emma had studied the man closely. He wasn't so tall as the duke or Simon, but his average height still made him taller than her. His eyes were striking, too. They were brown, but darker than hers. And his hair was as black as his coat and hat.

His angular jaw and wide-set cheekbones made his face rather interesting and, yes, handsome. But there was something about him, and it wasn't just how stiffly he sat on the terrace. An air of seriousness enclosed him. He hardly appeared capable of smiling, let alone laughing. Were all Italians so somber?

At that moment, he looked up toward the fountain, his gaze meeting hers. Catching her scrutiny, his eyes widened a moment before his eyebrows knitted together.

Emma, not one to allow anyone to intimidate her, tilted her chin upward and smiled. Not a flirtatious smile, but an expression of easy happiness. Then she pointedly turned her attention back to Josephine. "He caught me looking."

"Oh, bother." Josephine shoved the book back into Emma's hands. "And now he's coming this way."

Indeed, the man had excused himself from the duke's

company and now walked across the short-cropped grass and paving stones to their perch on the fountain's edge.

They rose when he came within bowing distance, returning his courtesy by slightly bending their knees.

When the Sicilian ambassador spoke, his words had a lilting quality to them that made them charming. "Ladies, I have told His Grace that I find the gardens quite beautiful. I understand there are some statues here that are excellent copies of the ancient statues in Rome. I hope it will be possible to tour the gardens soon."

"Yes, of course." Josephine hardly smiled, wearing her most polite social mask as she always did when she entered an uncomfortable situation. "I believe we planned a tour of the gardens for tomorrow afternoon, after you are rested from your journey."

"That would be excellent, yes." He glanced briefly at Emma before focusing his attention on Josephine again. "I must express my gratitude for your efforts on my behalf. The duke said there are many entertainments planned."

The man did not smile even once, though he was all politeness.

What a shame such a handsome man, with such a charming accent, would prove so excessively dull.

Josephine suddenly hooked her arm through Emma's and started prattling. "Yes, my dear Emma and I have spent a great deal of time planning a welcome for you, my lord. If you like, we can present you with a full itinerary tomorrow morning. I know my father will need some of your time to discuss the relationship between our two countries, but between those important conversations, we will ensure that you do not grow bored."

"Thank you for your kind consideration, my lady." He bowed again.

Emma had the distinct impression that he actively avoided looking at her. Poor Josephine. If the man dedicated such focus to her in a simple conversation, Emma had little chance of distracting him should his attentions grow too pointed.

Nevertheless, she had promised her friend to try.

"*Conte* Atella, what is something you hope to accomplish during your time in England?" An ambassador would show an interest in discussing politics, surely.

He tore his stare away from Josephine to meet Emma's bright smile, and she saw the way his eyes widened slightly again. Was he not used to young ladies smiling at him? It was no wonder, given the way he kept his expression as inscrutable as a sphinx.

"Besides the betterment of the relationship between our nations?" he asked, his black eyebrows lifting.

Emma clasped her hands together at her waist, refusing to look away from his deep brown eyes. "Yes. Let us assume that goal is achieved, thanks to your great talent at negotiation. What more would you like to do?"

He stared at her another moment, then put his hand to his chin as he considered her. It took a great deal of control to maintain her patient smile before he answered, "I should like to see a play by William Shakespeare. I have read his work in Italian translations and the original English, of course, but I have seen none of his plays performed in his native language."

Emma's lips parted in surprise. She had expected him to say something more about trade negotiations, or meeting an important member of Society, or a dozen other things that would fall under a political classification.

"Oh, there is at least one performed every Season in London," Josephine said airily. "Emma and my mother always attend them. What did you see last spring, Emma? All of his plays blend together for me, except for that horridly long tragic one wherein everyone dies."

"*Hamlet*, you mean," Emma said, somewhat absently. Then she returned her gaze to the count. "Last year we attended a performance of *The Tempest*. Are you familiar with that one?"

"Ah, the one on the island. Yes. It is one of my favorites."

And then he did something that quite changed Emma's initial opinion of him.

He smiled. A small, polite smile. But it changed enough about him, making a brief glimmer of light appear in his dark eyes, to make her reconsider her initial impression of him.

Before she could respond to his words, or the smile, Josephine tugged Emma down into another curtsy. "It was lovely to speak to you, Your Excellency. But you must excuse us now. Emma and I have to see to this evening's entertainment, you see."

The smile vanished, replaced with an austere mask. "Of course, Lady Josephine."

Josephine dragged Emma behind her, walking at a brisk pace for the door into the conservatory. "Quickly, quickly," she muttered in a soft, urgent tone. "I think we slipped away before Papa noticed. He was speaking to Mama." She tugged Emma behind a tall pedestal upon which a large fern rested, then peered around it. "There. I think we made good our escape, and now we needn't see him again until dinner."

Emma pulled at her arm to take the appendage back under her own control. "Josie, that was terribly rude." She peered over the fern but realized she couldn't see the count from that angle. "Even if your father didn't notice, you can be certain he will ask where you slipped away to in such a hurry."

"I'll come up with a good excuse for that later." Josephine grinned and straightened, brushing her hands together as though to remove dirt from her gloves. "Let's go back to my room. We need to put together a copy of the itinerary for the count."

"Very well." Emma followed her dearest friend through the plants into the castle proper; they had reached the bottom of the main staircase when she remembered: "Oh, I left my book on the edge of the fountain." She bit her lip and turned around. To leave a book, any book at all, in such a precarious place was as near to committing a sin as ever she had come. But to leave one of her *favorite* books? Had she lost her wits?

"Oh dear. You aren't going back to get it?" Josephine asked the question with reluctance, then sighed when Emma frowned at her. "I know, I know. You cannot leave a book like that. Fine. You go fetch it; I will wait in my room. I cannot risk being trapped by the count again."

"I understand. I will be quick." Emma turned around, going back the way they had come. At the conservatory door, she rushed in and turned around a large pot containing a large shrub covered in purple leaves—and ran headlong into a sturdy black wall of wool and buttons.

ALTHOUGH LUCA HADN'T EXPECTED AN ENGLISHWOMAN TO throw herself into his arms, at least he didn't topple over when it happened. He instinctively caught Miss Arlen with one arm around her, his hand landing between her shoulder blades, while still keeping her forgotten book in his other hand.

"Miss Arlen." He peered down at her, the angle of his gaze awkward, unable to release the woman given that she leaned heavily against him.

"Oh dear." She looked up, her eyes wide and her cheeks reddening. "I am terribly sorry, but I neglected to look where I was going. I beg your pardon."

Her utterly charming appearance improved with her blush. "No, *signorina*. I am to blame. *Mi scusi*." He tried to offer her a reassuring smile, but her eyebrows had drawn tightly together.

"You may release me now, my lord."

She didn't seem as dependent on him for stability as she had a moment ago, so he dropped his arm and stepped back. Then took another step away for good measure.

"Again, my sincere apologies." He bowed, tucking the hand

with the book behind his back. "You are alone? Is Lady Josephine not with you?"

"As you see, sir." She gestured at the empty doorway behind her. "Lady Josephine had a—erm—pressing situation to see to for this evening's entertainment." Her blush had faded, and the engaging smile she had worn before suddenly reappeared. "I am to join her, but I realized I forgot my book by the fountain. I must retrieve it."

Luca relaxed, rocking back on his heels. "That is not necessary. You see, I have your book here." He produced the volume from behind his back with a flourish. "I see we have similar tastes in books as we do in plays, Miss Arlen. *Arabian Nights*. It is one of my favorites." He held it out to her with a bow.

Miss Arlen reached for the small volume with both hands, and one eyebrow tilted upward again. "You've read it? In Italian, I presume?"

"Yes. The work is stunning, is it not? I particularly enjoy the tale of *Ali Baba and the Forty Thieves*. Though the voyages of Sinbad also entertain me."

Her mouth fell open as she accepted the book, then folded her arms tightly over it, as though hugging the volume to her. "I agree. Sinbad's travels are exceptional. I do wonder who wrote all the stories, originally. They cannot all have the same author."

The spark of interest he had seen in her warm brown eyes when they spoke of Shakespeare returned.

"I have thought the same. It would be like trying to ascribe all the myths of the Romans to a single person. Doubtless the stories were known for centuries and someone finally thought to write them down."

An idea flickered in his mind. The woman standing before him struck him as clever, and obviously she was close to her mistress. Perhaps if he could win the companion to his side she would help further his cause with Lady Josephine. Befriending the lady's closest confidant might gain enough of Lady Josephine's favor to allow him to court her. Surely, even the daughter of a duke could be won by someone as single-minded as Luca. If he courted, wooed, and wed her, that would fulfill his duty to his king and strengthen the fragile bond between nations.

Miss Arlen peered up at him with a charming tilt to her head.

His idea appealed to him more.

What had they been discussing?

"I haven't read all of them yet," she said. "I am afraid the duke has hidden several volumes from us, because there are things in some of the stories not fit for an unmarried woman's consumption. At least, that is what His Grace said." Her smile turned mischievous. "Someday, I'll find where he hid them. Or obtain my own copies."

Luca coughed and covered his mouth with a fist to fight back a smile. He had to maintain formality, given his position as an ambassador. "A worthwhile pursuit, though I must say, I agree with His Grace to some extent."

"I suppose most gentlemen would, as it falls to your sex to protect mine from all the unpleasant things in life." She batted her eyes at him in such a way that made Luca wonder if she mocked him, or perhaps the role of men as protectors of innocent maidens.

"I would not put it that way." He folded his hands behind his back and studied her, uncertain enough of her temperament not to risk saying more on the subject of protecting female sensibilities. "Perhaps you would be so kind as to recommend other titles to me during my stay. As we have similar tastes, I can only hope you have discovered some works I have not yet found. Would you do me that very great favor, Miss Arlen?"

Those lively eyes of hers narrowed, and she briefly chewed her bottom lip before speaking with vivacity. "I would be happy to introduce you to my favorite library shelves, my lord."

"*Grazie.* I will be in your debt."

She tapped her fingers on the book she held, studying him as she spoke. "Excellent. I enjoy collecting on debts and favors." Then her smile reappeared. "You must excuse me, sir. Lady Josephine is expecting me."

"Of course." He bowed more deeply. "It was a pleasure to speak with you again."

She curtsied. "Until dinner, my lord." Then she took her leave, glancing over her shoulder only once at the door. He noticed the curiosity in her eyes, somewhat at odds with the mischief in her smile.

Then she was gone.

Luca relaxed, but hastily reminded himself of where he was. Whom he represented. Luca drew himself up to his full height, then went back to the gardens and the duke. Every discussion he had with the powerful nobleman would benefit his people. He had promised his king, and himself, to represent their nation.

Winning over the ducal family was of great importance. If he bent his will to that end, Luca's time in England would prove fruitful indeed.

CHAPTER THREE

Distracting the Italian *conte* might not prove as difficult as Emma had originally thought, given the interest he showed in her reading habits. When she reported her conversation with him to Josephine, the duke's daughter appeared delighted and agreed that Emma might easily keep the man too occupied for him to attempt a courtship.

In Josephine's room once more, Emma held the sheet of paper with their list of planned activities. She sat at Josephine's dressing table while her friend dressed for dinner with the aid of her maid.

That evening after dinner, Josephine, Emma, Isabelle, and Rosalind would each perform something musical. A simple way to pass an hour, then fill whatever remained of the time before midnight with conversation.

"Tomorrow, we tour the gardens in the afternoon." Josephine held still while her maid tugged the hem of her gown into place, then smoothed out the silk overlay on the skirt. "Mr. Gardiner and Miss Sharpe will accompany us, to answer any questions the ambassador might have about our plants."

Emma grinned as she made note of the betrothed couple coming with them on the *conte's* copy of the itinerary. "If we get the two of them talking about flowers or bees, they will happily take hold of the conversation and never let it go again."

"Precisely my hope." Josephine approached the dressing table and shooed her friend off the chair before taking it herself, giving the maid access to Josephine's hair.

Emma had already dressed for the evening, so she did not mind taking a seat at the foot of Josephine's bed. "The next day, your father is going riding with the ambassador. It looks as though they are occupied most of the day. We sent the invitations for dinner that evening, which is all we have planned."

Meeting Emma's gaze in the mirror, Josephine widened her eyes theatrically. "That suits me. The Hepsworth sisters will do all they can to keep the count's attention. You and I might have a brief respite from him."

The memory of the *conte*'s arm going around Emma to steady her came to the forefront of her mind, as did the intensity of his eyes as they had spoken about her book. "I cannot think it particularly kind to leave him to those two."

Josephine turned in her chair, causing the maid to squeal. "My lady, your pearl pins!"

"Pardon me, Liza." Josephine turned back to the mirror. "But Miss Arlen startled me." She gave Emma an accusatory glare in the mirror. "You cannot show him mercy, Emma. It will only encourage him."

Though tempted to laugh, Emma pressed her lips together and went back to the itinerary. "On the following day, your father has guests arriving, and we are to walk with the *conte* to Lambsthorpe during the afternoon."

"We shan't escape him there." Josephine giggled. "Oh, I do sound terrible, don't I? I am sorry. I cannot like my father hinting so heavily that he wishes for me to take an interest in a man. As it is, we know my options are limited. But I should much prefer to *have* options. Perhaps marry someone in London next Season."

"All finished, my lady." Liza curtsied, then tidied up the dressing table.

"Thank you, Liza. It looks lovely." Josephine stood and ran her gloved hand down the front of her gown. "What do you think, Emma?"

Emma pursed her lips, taking in the high neckline and overly fluffy sleeves of Josephine's least favorite gown. "I think there is a reason you have not worn that dress since last autumn. It truly does not suit you."

"I know." Josephine grinned triumphantly. "I have no wish to appear to my best advantage." She retrieved her fan from the mantel and snapped it open. "After the Lambsthorpe outing?"

Emma looked down at the paper again, shaking her head at her friend's dramatics. "We have invited your father's guests to the lake for the afternoon. The boathouse is prepared, along with all the fishing equipment. Your mother is the official hostess, of course."

"Of course." Josephine paced the room, wafting the air before her with her fan. "And then a quiet dinner that evening with only the occupants of the house in attendance."

"Then we have nothing to worry over for a few days, given that your father will wish to discuss politics with all the men, and Sunday we have the wedding after services in the family chapel."

"Miss Sharpe's wedding to Mr. Gardiner." Josephine's pacing came to a halt, and her expression softened. "Theirs is a beautiful love story."

The moment of wistful longing took them both, as Emma could not deny how she felt about what their two friends had found together. Yet Emma was as unlikely to marry for love as the duke's daughters, given her place as ward, and her substantial inheritance.

Josephine collapsed into a chair with a sigh. "That is as far as we have planned, isn't it?"

"Hm? Oh. Yes. That is all we have at present." Emma easily

found her smile and folded up the itinerary. "Shall I give it to the *conte* after dinner?"

"Do, please." Josephine looked up at the clock above her mantel. "We have to go down soon."

Emma rose from her place and held her hand out to Josephine. "Why not now? There is no use sitting here imagining the worst when we could simply get on with things."

"Must you always be so wise? If you didn't laugh and tease so much, I should think you a woman of fifty rather than twenty." Josephine took Emma's hand and allowed her friend to drag her upward.

"I am remarkably wise, and a great deal older than you are."

"Ten months older," Josephine said, playfully bumping her shoulder against Emma's as they walked out of the bedroom into the corridor.

"Yes. But those ten months make all the difference." Emma flipped open her fan ahead of her and put her nose in the air, making Josephine giggle.

Even when Emma came of age and obtained her inheritance, she could not imagine leaving Josephine. They were loyal friends and sisters by choice, though not by birth. After Josephine married, things would change. Emma would have fortune enough to live comfortably in a cottage for the rest of her days, if she wished. If her parents hadn't been in that carriage accident, had lived to raise her in their home instead of the duke's, no doubt they would find that a sorry ending for her.

The idea of settling somewhere in the country, alone, held little appeal. If she wasn't careful, she'd end up a busybody spinster in Bath, gossiping at the water pumps. Emma preferred the cities of England to the countryside. If the duke and duchess did not entertain at the castle as often as they did, things would be rather dull.

Few members of the British upper classes and nobility had reason to host parties and political gatherings as frequently as the duke. His position in Society and in Parliament kept him busier than anyone else in the kingdom. Once Emma left his household, her life would most assuredly turn quieter.

Unless she married someone of political or social significance.

Emma snorted, making Josephine turn to her.

"Is something wrong?"

"No. I was only thinking." Emma waved her friend's concern aside and tried to do the same for her thoughts. Few gentlemen looked twice in her direction, given they thought her position with the family one of employment. Which she preferred, if only to keep fortune-hunters at bay.

Josephine nodded somewhat distractedly and went back to her own thoughts.

Once Emma gained her independence, her time in the duke's circles would dwindle. She would settle firmly in the middle classes and be lucky to marry a gentleman who leased a house in London every other Season.

They had come to the drawing room the family frequented before meals. When Josephine hesitated on the carpet, her eyes darting to the footmen waiting for her signal to open the door, Emma gently prodded her forward.

"Come on, Josie. Let's see if the *conte* is the sort of man to arrive early, promptly, or last of all." Then Emma gave the nod to the servants, and they immediately drew the doors open.

They entered the drawing room, and the *conte* with his secretary stood up the moment they saw the ladies.

"Early," Josephine muttered from the corner of her mouth.

Emma smothered a smile as they curtsied to the Italians.

THE FIRST EVENING IN THE DUKE'S CASTLE PASSED SLOWLY and somewhat uncomfortably for Luca. Despite his work in politics, finding himself in a new place with new and unknown people always meant a period of adjustment. He had yet to properly determine the motivations of the people around him, or to understand the things which they held important and in esteem.

While his peers might think politics dull, Luca never tired of sharpening his mental acuity through discourse and debate. The trick was to engage in conversations, even with those who disagreed with him, in a way that made the topics interesting rather than inflammatory and lively rather than heated.

Before he could enjoy that aspect of his time in the duke's castle, he had to understand the other players in the game of political hospitality.

Over dinner, he sat at the right hand of the duchess.

"You were in Spain before you came to England, were you not?" the duchess asked him, her sharp blue eyes taking his measure. "I have not visited the Continent in some time, but I still have friends in the Spanish court."

That opened the first conversation, giving him insight into the duchess's world. They discussed his acquaintances there, found several in common, and then the duchess confessed her love of architecture.

Luca brightened at that change in topic. Here was a chance to speak on something personal to the duchess. "Ah, yes. I understand that much of the castle's current design is owed to your creativity, Your Grace. The outer structure is especially magnificent."

Genuine delight touched her features. "The duke's late father had drawn up the initial plans, but I was quite pleased when His Grace put the finalization of the design in my hands. Aside from my family, this castle is my greatest work."

Some would deem her emphasis on family sentimental, but the warmth in her eyes as she looked down the table to her husband wasn't something easily feigned.

Across the table from him sat the companion, Miss Arlen. She chose that moment to speak, one corner of her mouth turned upward. "I love the little touches other members of the family contributed over the years. For instance"—she gestured up to the ceiling—"His Grace is responsible for an entertaining tradition in this room, with the tiles above us."

Luca politely turned his attention upward to the gold-painted ceiling, noting that someone had sculpted each tile into an intricate floral design. "They are fascinating, and quite beautiful. What is the tradition, Miss Arlen?"

"I am not permitted to say; it is something of a game with His Grace. There may soon come an evening that you learn of it." She shared a knowing glance with the duchess. The higher-ranking woman returned the smile with an affection Luca could not help but notice.

The companion held favor with more of the family than Lady Josephine.

Lady Josephine sat quietly most of the evening at her father's left hand. *Signor* Torlonia sat on her other side, and between Luca and his secretary sat a younger daughter of the household. Lady Isabelle. On the duke's right hand sat his son, Lord Farleigh, the youngest daughter Lady Rosalind, then Miss Arlen. That made the table unbalanced, but Luca's first evening meal was informal. At least by ducal standards. Which meant not requiring an additional male guest to even the numbers.

The family had an easiness about them, a kindness in the way they spoke to one another, that he hadn't found common among the upper classes in England. It almost set him at ease. As a stranger, however, he maintained his reserve.

After the meal ended, the ladies left to prepare for the musical portion of the evening. The duke gestured for Luca to take the vacant chair on his left, where his eldest daughter had sat.

The men spoke of inconsequential things. The meal, the roads from London, and the wine they had enjoyed with dinner. Lord Farleigh, though younger than Luca, held himself with the same confidence his father possessed. As heir to the title, Lord

Farleigh would be an important person to come to know, too. The duke represented the past and present of England and English sensibilities, but his son would carry England into the future one day.

"Do you ever tire of traveling, Lord Atella?" the young man asked during a lull in the conversation. "You and my mother were discussing Spain before. I have never visited that country."

"It is a beautiful land, wherein many cultures have mixed to create cities of vibrance and color." Luca had seen mosques and cathedrals with histories of being built and destroyed and rebuilt every time one force or another conquered Spain. "I grew up in the Kingdom of Naples, which then joined the Kingdom of Sicily after the wars ended." He waved away the turbulent history of his people before anyone could remark upon that disturbing history. "All I ever wanted to do, as a boy and as I grew into adulthood, was travel outside of my land. When the opportunity finally came, I was fortunate that someone in His Majesty's court knew of my desire."

The duke sent his son a significant glance. "And that is the duty of those who regularly attend court functions. Know the people around you, their talents and desires, to fit them properly for service to king and country."

They rose from the table shortly after that conversation; the duke led the way to the music room where the women in the family waited to perform. The governess for the younger girls was present, sitting in a chair near the instrument to help her charges turn pages. The younger daughters both played pieces written by Italian composers, a nod to Luca's homeland.

They were quite proficient for girls of their age. The melodies were bright and cheerful. Then Miss Arlen went to the instrument, showing the skill befitting a young lady of her standing in the household, and finally Lady Josephine played a piece by an Austrian composer. .

When the duke dismissed his youngest daughters for the

evening, the rest of the party adjourned to a sitting room already lit with candles and lamps.

The evening passed in conversation regarding Luca's travels, with the duke and duchess as the primary audience. Lady Josephine and her companion said little, though Luca caught the eyes of the latter upon him. Measuring him, perhaps, for her mistress.

That evening, in the sitting room adjoining his bedroom, Luca sat at the writing desk at his disposal. He rehearsed all he had observed about the duke's family. He made notes under each household member's name in a little book he kept on his person. He had filled other pages with notes containing English idioms and phrases with which he was unfamiliar and notes about English sentiments regarding trade with his kingdom—and dozens of other things he needed to remember or learn.

At the top of one page, in his native tongue, he wrote: *The Courtship of Lady Josephine.* Then he tapped the desk's surface and lifted his gaze from the paper to stare out the window into the night.

He had never courted anyone before. Despite his age.

At eight and twenty, he could look back in time and remember the girls and ladies he had met who stirred some interest in his mind if not his heart. But he had never acted on any of those fleeting moments of curiosity. His homeland had been volatile, his place within it uncertain, for too long.

His father and mother had sent him to a monastery when he was fifteen, when Napoleon had crowned himself king and his stepson the viceroy of Italy. Luca's sisters had been sent to a nunnery, tucked away safely from the political strife his parents faced alone.

Their family had held important positions in the Duchy of Basilicata for over two hundred years, and the world at large had been uncertain what Napoleon would do with those who held high places in the governments he usurped.

Upon the darkness outside, Luca's memory painted a scene from his youth, when his father had woken him in the darkest hours of the night.

"*Sbrigati, figlio mio. You must away, quietly.*" *His father's words guided him through their shadowed house in the country.* "*There will be a summons from the viceroy. You mustn't be here when it comes.*"

Luca closed the book, the snap of the sound breaking him out of his memories. He dropped the slim notebook into a drawer, then twisted the supplied key to secure it. During the day, the book would stay with him.

He rolled the pencil in his hand, marveling at the simple instrument. The machine-made wood-cased pencils had been impossible to get hold of during Napoleon's reign, and in the years to follow, as trade negotiations faltered because of Italy's uncertain future. He examined the sharpened end, then the exposed graphite core of the other side. He twirled it in his fingers, a smile upon his lips.

The Kingdom of the Two Sicilies had stabilized under King Ferdinand's rule, and Luca would be as this pencil. A simple tool, an implement in the hand of his monarch, writing a new future for his people. Less uncertainty, more growth. The end of unrest, the beginning of modernization.

If he performed his duties well in England, he could accomplish much. An English wife with the backing of a powerful father would strengthen his influence and open doors for his people.

He had time. Rumor was that Parliament would not open again until January, after the Twelfth Night celebrations ended. He was a guest in the duke's home until the family quitted the country for London. Three and a half months was plenty of time to court a young woman.

Luca stood from the desk and rubbed at his lower back, his muscles still aching from the carriage ride. A good stretch of the legs was in order for the next day. The walk through the gardens with Lady Josephine, Miss Arlen, and the naturalists ought to help.

He went to bed with a barely formed idea of strolling through gardens and dazzling Lady Josephine with his sophistication and charm.

Gaining a lady's favor couldn't be too difficult.

CHAPTER FOUR

Emma walked through the garden a step behind Josephine and the *conte*, while they walked several steps behind Mr. Rupert Gardiner and Miss Sharpe. With the most animated gestures, Mr. Gardiner pointed out the different species of flora in the Clairvoir gardens, noting which were native to England and which had been imported to the duke's lands.

The late September afternoon, verging into October, boasted more sun than usual for that time of year. The breeze rustled through the leaves, now changed from green to yellow and orange, with reds and browns scattered throughout the gardens, too.

Mr. Gardiner stopped beneath a particularly bright-hued tree. "Here you can see this maple, imported from Norway, thrives in the garden. I noted in the summer that the magpie moth favored this tree, despite its lack of ability to disguise itself among the leaves."

The ambassador frowned up at the tree and asked a few polite questions about tree and moth both before they continued on their walk. He appeared far too serious every time he spoke, which made Emma wonder if she had imagined his smile from the day before when he had returned her book.

He held himself too stiffly, though perhaps his posture had something to do with walking next to the mostly silent Josephine.

The scene they made, Emma reflected to herself, would likely be a pretty one if put on paper or canvas. Here a gentleman and lady walking, with obvious affection for one another. Behind them a man and woman not touching, dressed elegantly, and uncertain of one another.

Of course, the picture would not be complete without Emma bringing up the rear of the party in her smart rose-hued walking gown and pelisse.

Traditionally, when a lady walked with a gentleman, the companion's role kept her several steps behind. Given that Emma didn't receive financial compensation for her role and acted out of long-standing friendship and sisterly affection, she rarely confined herself to what others expected.

Today, she thought only to observe the *conte* and give Josephine an opportunity to form an opinion of him.

Thus far, Josephine appeared unimpressed.

Josephine had cast several glances over her shoulder during the quarter-hour of the walk, ostensibly to check that Emma remained well walking behind them. In reality, she had sent Emma many subtle signals only the two friends would understand.

The overall message was quite clear. Josephine was not enjoying her time with the Italian nobleman, and her patience wore thin.

Emma quickened her step enough to come to the *conte*'s free side. When he acknowledged her with a dip of his head, she smiled up at him. "Are you interested in the study of botany, *Signore?*"

He wore a diplomatic, unemotional mask that afternoon, giving no hint of his thoughts. "I enjoy learning of the natural world, Miss Arlen."

"I quite enjoy the gardens, but I cannot say that I wish to

know as much as our friends." She gestured to Mr. Gardiner and Alice, both of whom had wandered off the path to peer down into a bush, likely forgetting for the moment that they had others with them. "His Grace is an amateur naturalist."

The *conte* glanced at Josephine, his tone far too formal when he spoke. "Do you share that interest with your father, my lady?"

Josephine blinked, appearing momentarily confused by the question.

Oh dear. Emma bit her lip to keep from laughing. *She wasn't even listening.*

"I beg your pardon; I am afraid my mind was on other matters." Josephine did not even blush when she admitted her inattention. "Upon what subject are we speaking?"

Emma gestured to the *conte*. "His lordship wonders if you are interested in the science of naturalism."

"Heavens, no." Josephine laughed airily, wrinkling her nose. "I love flowers and gardens, of course, but I am content to appreciate them informally. Once you start bothering with the scientific terms and debating the merits of introducing one sort of plant over another to a garden, I am decidedly *uninterested*."

Though not the most diplomatic of answers, given Josephine knew nothing of the ambassador's feelings on the subject, at least it was honest.

Emma watched Mr. Gardiner and Alice step further away, still studying the plants with interest. She couldn't help her amusement as she noted, "Those two could spend all day discussing flowers and butterflies in terms most of us would not understand."

"Indeed. Thank goodness they found each other." Josephine grinned in their direction and then pointed down the path. "Let us continue. Perhaps they will notice and rejoin us, but I rather think they will like being left to themselves."

The *conte*'s eyebrows raised as he looked from Josephine to

Emma. "They are unmarried. Is it done, to leave the two of them alone?"

"You will find all manner of rules in English Society are only followed when it is convenient," Josephine answered primly, her eyes twinkling. "And they are to marry this coming Sunday. I imagine a few moments to themselves would be appreciated."

The *conte* appeared to think on this for a moment, though he continued walking with them. "You are pleased by their match, true?"

"Yes." Josephine kept her hands at her side as she walked, her chin up and posture regal. "They complement each other nicely."

They said nothing for a time, the man walking in silence between the two women. Emma tried to study the *conte* from the corner of her eye. If he hoped to catch Josephine's interest, he did not appear to know how to go about such a thing. Over the years, Emma had seen a number of admirers seek Josephine's approval.

None had ever held themselves quite so stiffly in her presence.

Though the duke's daughter held no interest in the ambassador as a suitor, the duke would wish their guest to be comfortable. With her promise to assist Josephine foremost upon her mind, Emma took it upon herself to guide the conversation.

"Does your estate have gardens, *Signore*?"

Conte di Atella's eyes momentarily brightened, though he kept his gaze on the path ahead of them. "Yes. Though they are not like this. They are smaller. Along the hill where my house looks over the valley and the city, Atella. The gardens are walled in, with trees along one side and a fountain in the center. There are more vineyards on my family's land, all along the hills. It does not rain there so much as in England."

Emma watched him speak, noting the careful way his lips formed the English words, and that his tone softened somewhat when speaking of his home. As an ambassador, he likely would not see it again for some time. That put her mind on another question.

"Have you family still there, *Signore?*"

"*Sì*, I do." His shoulders relaxed, and he turned to look at her rather than Josephine as he spoke. "My parents are both still there, at the villa. As are my three sisters."

Emma tried to make eye contact with Josephine. But her friend appeared lost in thought again, not attending to the conversation. "Your parents are both living?" she asked, not bothering to hide her surprise. "I assumed, since your title is *conte*, that your father had passed it to you."

His shoulders stiffened again, and his expression closed once more. "My father holds no title. I am the first of my line conferred the great honor, by the king himself, when he gave me the role of ambassador for our people."

The stern tone he used had apparently roused Josephine from her thoughts, and she cast a swift, confused look to Emma before speaking. "The first to bear your title? Really?"

Emma glowered at Josephine. Her response did nothing to soften the man, who likely found the question impertinent. Emma hastened to speak. "That is a very great honor and responsibility. Titles are so rarely conferred in our modern era. At least here in England."

The ambassador nodded tightly. The newness of his rank appeared to make him uncomfortable, and Emma could not blame him. Bloodlines and ancient nobility were everything in the courts of Europe. A newly made nobleman didn't have the pedigree most expected of one in his position. But then, most of Europe's monarchies had changed or been challenged during Napoleon's reign. Establishing new noble lines in many old countries had likely occurred out of necessity.

Josephine shrugged one shoulder. "My family has possessed Montfort and its titles since the fourteenth century." She apparently caught the somewhat aggravated glare Emma sent her direction, as she hurried on to say, "But they were only earls at first, and the title passed through one female line."

Why had Josephine allowed herself flights of fancy in the *conte's* company? Emma knew well enough that Josephine possessed a great deal of finesse in social matters, if not political, and usually wielded her status as a duke's daughter with grace.

Emma's glare must have pulled her friend back to her senses.

Josephine tilted her chin upward and made a stronger effort to keep her attention on the man standing between them. "That is all ancient history, of course. Lord Atella, you must tell me about your sisters. Are they all younger than you? Are any of them my age?" She laughed and put a hand to her chest, perhaps wishing to remind the Italian lord that nearly a decade separated them in age.

Emma barely kept from groaning aloud. The next several weeks—nay, the next three months—would prove challenging if the *conte* had any romantic intentions toward the duke's eldest daughter.

CHAPTER FIVE

The day after the disastrous walk through the gardens, which had ended shortly after the ambassador revealed he had three younger sisters, Emma entered the library alone.

Every morning, Josephine kept her grandmother company in the dowager's apartments. Though Emma accompanied her friend to most of her lessons and entertainments, she did not mind missing the opportunity to sit beneath the dowager duchess's eye for an hour or more for instruction. In recent years, she and the dowager had learned they had a common taste in reading, and little else. So, Josephine read to the duke's mother, and skipped the etiquette lessons.

Rather than peruse the shelves for a book—she had quite a few in her room she had yet to finish—Emma threw herself onto the most comfortable couch in the room. The large velvet couch, cream colored with dark green pillows heaped on each corner, had always proved a perfect place to pass the morning.

The windows of the library lined one wall, their Gothic arches bearing stained glass *fleurs-de-lis* bathing the room in colored light. The duke had covered the walls in bookshelves twice her height, with busts of eminent historians and playwrights atop them. A table and practical chairs, along with comfortable high-backed chairs, and a writing desk furnished the room most comfortably.

Emma stared up at the ceiling, enjoying the quiet.

Until the hidden door between the duke's personal study and the library opened behind her, the click so soft that most would not even notice the sound.

Hastily, Emma sat up, correcting her posture.

Men's voices drifted into the library, and she belatedly remembered that the duke had scheduled an early meeting with the ambassador.

The duke's deep voice came from within the room, not the doorway. "I will think on what you have said, Lord Atella, and send for the requisite documents from London."

"Thank you for your attention to this matter, Your Grace." The *conte*. He stood in the doorway.

"We will meet you for the ride this afternoon, Your Grace." And that was the secretary, Mr. Torlonia. "If you would excuse me, I will compile the notes of our meeting for you both."

"*Grazie*, Torlonia."

The secretary walked through the room at a fast clip, papers held to his chest, not even noticing Emma sitting in the couch's corner. She relaxed. Perhaps the ambassador wouldn't see her, either.

The door between the library and study clicked closed, and the *conte* took a few steps into the room, then stopped. "Miss Arlen?"

Emma rose from her place and turned toward him, making brief eye contact before bending her knee in a polite curtsy. "Good morning, *Signore*."

He wore a dark blue coat over an ivory waistcoat, colors rich and well suited to him. His hair had been combed to one side, but the wave at his forehead suggested it would not hold in that strict style for long.

He bowed to her, then his gaze swept the room before settling on her again. "You are alone? Did you wish to see His Grace?"

"No, I have no need to bother him at the moment." She gestured to the couch. "I am enjoying the quiet. The duke took care that this room is always silent, for reading and contemplation, when he and the duchess built the castle."

For a long moment, the man said nothing. At last, he nodded. "It *is* near silent in this room, isn't it?" He gestured to the couch behind her. "Please, do not let me disturb you. I know too well the value of quiet thought." He almost sounded sad at the admission.

Retaking her seat, Emma studied the *conte* with interest. "I suppose a man in your position needs time to organize his thoughts." She gestured to the chairs. "Would you like to enjoy the quiet for yourself? I am perfectly capable of sitting without saying a word, so we may both enjoy a moment's peace."

Rather than turn down the silly offer, the *conte* surprised her by taking one of the empty chairs situated several feet away from the couch. He did not look at her, but instead took in the room itself. "It amazes me how this castle and its rooms appear so old, when they have not stood even so long as I have lived."

Part of the charm of Clairvoir Castle for the duke and duchess had been filling the entire castle with ancient artifacts from other family holdings and the Continent.

As the castle had been Emma's home for half her life, she took pride in the building, too. Which meant she could not resist the topic. "The first day I stepped into the castle, it already had suits of armor lining the entrance passage."

"When did you join Lady Josephine?" The ambassador appeared as impassive as ever in his expression, but she noted the way he tapped the arm of his chair with his fingers—the only sign of possible restlessness. "I confess, I know little about the practice of introducing a lady's companion to a household."

Emma studied his eyes, unabashedly attempting to read him and his interest in her. Did he make conversation with her out of politeness? Boredom? Or only to find out more about Josephine or the family? Her first loyalty always fell to the Duke of Montfort. He had acted as a father toward her almost as long as she could remember.

"I first came to the castle directly after the builders finished work, a decade ago. I was ten years old to Lady Josephine's nine." Of course, she had been a part of the family since her sixth birthday, when a tragic accident took her parents away forever.

Had she not been paying attention, she would not have seen the slight widening of his eyes and the way his chin came up just a fraction. Most people either thought of companions as glorified servants or conveniently impoverished relatives.

"I have surprised you, *Signore*." Emma smiled at him and had the pleasure of seeing him shift in his seat when he dropped his gaze from hers.

"You were very young when you began your work. The family has treated you well?"

If she told him of her position as the duke's ward, would that explain things to him? Not that it was any of his business. Best to answer his question and nothing more. "They have treated me with the best of care and understanding."

He nodded once. "Good." Then he stood and went to one of the bookcases with an abruptness that made her blink.

Hesitantly, Emma came to her feet again. "Do you need help finding something to read?"

"You said you would introduce me to your favorite shelves." He pivoted to face her again. "Are you available to do so now?"

Emma narrowed her eyes at him, and when she did so, his lips curled upward at last. The man wore propriety like a mask, and any break in that mask made him instantly more attractive. Or, Emma corrected herself, more *approachable*. She gestured to a set of shelves on the opposite side of the room. "My favorites are on that side of the room. The classic literature."

She crossed the room, skirting the enormous globe and a small table, and the ambassador followed on her heels until she stopped before a bookcase with rows of her favorite old tales.

The ambassador leaned in to inspect the titles, his shoulder nearly brushing hers. "Ah. Shakespeare, *Arabian Nights*, and what else do you consider a classic?"

"Oh. Well." She pointed up near the top. "They are in order by author. Here is Daniel Defoe—*Moll Flanders* and *Robinson Crusoe* are both here. John Dryden's books." She pointed lower on the shelves. "Milton. Pope. Swift. Oh, and *Pamela,* by Samuel Richardson." She let her gaze linger on English translations of the *Iliad* and *Odyssey.* "There are other books I enjoy, of course, but the more modern novels and poetry collections are in other rooms."

"I see." He bent to examine a lower shelf and removed *Pamela.*

"If you read that, you will need to read a later book by Richardson. You see, in this one, a moral woman reforms a rake. He wrote another later in which a good man does the same for a woman."

He blinked at her. "A rake?" He straightened with the book in hand. "You do not mean a garden tool."

Oh. He didn't know that word? Emma's cheeks warmed as she contemplated how to explain. "A—a bad man?" When his eyebrows pulled together in a frown, she realized her wording was too simplistic. "He tries to take advantage of her—she is lower than he in Society, and without protection, so he attempts to make her his—" She winced. "But she doesn't—that is, she maintains her virtue." Her cheeks positively burned as she realized how the book sounded. How *she* must sound, admitting she claimed a book with scandalous subject matter as a favorite.

"You enjoy this book?" he asked, his words slow and his tone giving away none of his thoughts. "Even though a man approaches a woman dishonorably?"

Releasing a nervous laugh, she shrugged helplessly. "I am

explaining the story very poorly." She rubbed at her temple, ordering her thoughts. "Pamela defends herself in a way that was —is still—somewhat revolutionary. In the end, she wins a place in the world above what most would deem appropriate for her station. It is not a perfect book—I do not think such a thing exists. But I believe it is one people ought to read and discuss."

He stared at her, his dark eyebrows lifting at last. "You enjoy it for the controversy and discussion it inspires."

She put a cool hand to her cheek and turned back to the shelves. "Yes. That is precisely it. I enjoy vigorous conversation and debate."

A touch on her forearm had her turning her head to look at him, her cheeks still warm.

His dark brown eyes glowed with interest. He tipped his head to one side as he spoke. "I enjoy those things too, Miss Arlen. That is how I gained my king's notice." His smile reappeared, larger than before. "I will read this book if you promise to discuss it with me later."

A knot in her chest formed and then tightened. "Yes. Of course. But if you would prefer to read something lighter—"

He shook his head, dislodging a lock of hair so it fell across his forehead, instantly giving a touch of boyish charm to his expression. "No, this will do." He held the book against his chest. He appeared thoughtful a moment before speaking again. "Tell me. Does your mistress enjoy the same books as you?"

He meant Josephine. Emma had to laugh at that. "No. I am afraid not. Lady Josephine prefers adventure novels or love stories. Mrs. Radcliffe is a favorite of hers, and of late she is enamored with the books *Persuasion* and *Rob Roy*. If you wish to read those, I will find them for you."

The ambassador's smile tightened, then vanished. "Perhaps after I have enjoyed *Pamela*. I have not heard of these other titles."

"They are quite entertaining." She shrugged, then pointedly looked to the long case clock in the room, checking the time. "Oh, you must excuse me, *Signore*. I must prepare for a ride with Lady Josephine and Her Grace." She dropped into a curtsy.

"Of course. Thank you for the book." He bowed, but she did not meet his eyes again as she hurried from the room.

Despite his age, his position in Society, and his reason for being in England, he was just like all the other gentlemen she met: he spoke to her only to gain an understanding of the ducal family, and perhaps to get closer to Josephine, as her friend had suspected.

Not that it mattered to Emma. It never mattered to her. She would be loyal to the family, as always, and not give insult to the duke's guest.

The *conte* wasn't different or special. There was no need to feel insulted or used. This was simply the way things were.

The knot in Emma's chest grew larger, making it difficult to swallow, as she went back to her room to change for her ride.

Luca stood before the long mirror in the dressing room adjacent his bedroom, with Bruno brushing off the coat he'd helped Luca into only moments before. His valet hummed an Italian love song to himself as he worked, the familiar tune and cadence soothing Luca's troubled mind.

Not that anything had gone wrong that day. Quite the opposite. The conversation with the duke had proven fruitful, given the duke's immediate desire to send for legal documents regarding trade between their countries. Luca's literary foray with Miss Arlen had given him another excuse to speak to her and gain her trust, putting him one step closer to earning Lady Josephine's interest.

Torlonia stuck his head through the doorway. "Are you finished yet, *Signore*? Bruno, it cannot take a quarter of an hour to see a man properly turned out for dinner."

Bruno stopped humming and frowned, but he said nothing. He hadn't forgiven Torlonia for suggesting Luca replace him with a younger valet.

Luca spoke over his shoulder, not moving from the spot where Bruno had put him. "If you wish me to make a good impression on a duke, whose shoes likely cost more than my entire ensemble, every moment before the mirror counts." He winked when Bruno glanced at up him, making the old man smile.

Bruno spoke in Italian. "You belong at tables with kings and princes, I promise." The old man went to a short velvet box and opened it, then selected an emerald stickpin for Luca's cravat. "The last touch." He fixed it in place.

With a snort of impatience, Torlonia removed himself from the doorway of the dressing room, backing into the bedroom. "Young men and politics—you are more worried about your appearance than your points of debate."

"You know that is not true." Luca nodded his thanks to Bruno, then went out to speak to his secretary. "And I advise you to remember who, here, is the ambassador and who is the secretary. If the king put his confidence in a *young* man, so too should you." His words lacked any bite. He had asked for Torlonia to accompany him for a reason.

The older gentleman had successfully navigated a hostile court for years, and he knew more about the history of English trade negotiations with the former Italian Republic than Luca did. If only he had as much faith in Luca as Luca had in his secretary.

Torlonia sighed. "Forgive me, *Conte* Atella." He rubbed at his wrinkled forehead. "I know you think part of your work is also to secure an English bride. Care for your appearance is important in this house, at the duke's table and any other in this country." Then he fixed Luca with a curious raise of his eyebrows. "Do you think the duke's daughter has shown an interest in you?"

Luca didn't allow himself to worry. "It is early in our acquaintance. I do not believe she wishes to come to know me yet, but if I can win the favor of her companion, Miss Arlen, that may help me to win Lady Josephine's good opinion."

"I fail to see your reasoning for this, *Signore*." Torlonia, a confirmed bachelor, couldn't possibly understand the way a woman's mind worked.

"I have three sisters," Luca reminded him. "If a suitor for the eldest snubbed my younger sisters, he gained favor with none of them. The man who won fair Angelina, who is now my brother-in-law, always had a kind word for the other two. Women trust other women, their friends and sisters, more than they trust any man."

That bit of explanation did not impress Torlonia, given the way he sighed. "Let us hope you are correct. We must go down to dinner now, *Signore*."

They arrived in the sitting room where the family had gathered the previous evening. This time, the duke's younger daughters were not present. Instead, the duchess introduced him to Mr. and Mrs. Josiah Hepsworth and their daughters, Miss Maria Hepsworth and Miss Hannah Hepsworth.

Lord Farleigh, the duke's eldest son, had one of his own friends in attendance to create even numbers between the men and women. But Luca barely had time to properly greet the guests before Miss Hepsworth and Miss Hannah stood on either side of him, batting their lashes and tossing blonde curls about as they giggled.

Why they were giggling he could not be certain, except that they seemed to think it would somehow please *him*.

When it came time to escort the women in to the table, he experienced a moment of hope that his separation from the overly enthusiastic Hepsworth sisters would grant him peace and sensible conversation.

His hope died swiftly when Mrs. Hepsworth, the mother, sat on Luca's immediate right.

She used one hand to hold her fork delicately and the other to fluff the feather in her turban. "You must tell us all about Italy. Do you go to Venice often? I understand the canals are an incredible sight to see."

"I have never been to Venice—"

"I have always wanted to see the Sistine Chapel, too. How far is that from Venice?"

"The magnificent chapel is in Rome, madam. They are on opposite sides of the peninsula—"

The woman squawked like an irritated hen. "That cannot be too far. If we planned a trip next summer, I should like to see both."

Luca winced. "I am certain such a journey could be arranged, especially by boat, but I am afraid not many are permitted into the chapel itself, as it is part of the Vatican."

"Pish. One only has to make the right friends for such excursions. You have seen the Sistine Chapel, have you not, Your Grace?"

Luca turned to the duchess who sat at the end of the tabled on his left. The regal woman, as beautiful as her daughters with only a hint of maturity in the wrinkles around her eyes, appeared momentarily taken aback. "No, Mrs. Hepsworth. I am afraid I have not had that honor. Of course, I have never ventured all the way to Rome. Monaco is as far east as I have been on the continent."

Mrs. Hepsworth made a noise of discontent. "What a horrid shame. But then, I am sure nothing abroad rivals the beautiful works and buildings here in England. Westminster Abbey, for example, is a marvel." She arched her eyebrows at Luca. "Have you visited Westminster Abbey?"

He had finally managed a small bite of food but hastily swallowed it before having much of a chance to diminish its size. "From the outside, yes. I have not yet entered it."

"And how does it compare to your Catholic cathedrals in

Italy?" She batted her eyelashes with more aggression than her daughters.

Had he been ten years younger, Luca would've squirmed in his seat and abruptly changed the subject. Catholics were still unpopular in England, with several laws in place which removed many of the rights of normal English citizenship. It was something his king had mentioned as a sensitive subject to address where and when Luca could.

Somehow, he didn't think Mrs. Hepsworth would treat the political ramifications of being Catholic in England with any respect.

Luca cleared his throat uncomfortably. "I find that wherever I go, each country and even each city has their own traditions and cultures which make their buildings unique. It is impossible to compare them. That which is beautiful and perfect in London would be out of place in Italy, and the reverse is also true."

A movement across the table caught his eye, and he met Miss Arlen's gaze. She had that one eyebrow raised again, as she assessed his words.

"I see." The woman at his side pursed her lips and frowned. "You are Catholic, I presume?"

He nodded once, a small dip of his head, and her eyes narrowed.

Did his religion disqualify him as a marital possibility? He hoped so, because even he could not have misunderstood the pointed attentions of first the daughters and then the mother. A foreign count, even if he was Catholic, might be a temptation to more than one English mother.

"Lord Atella," Miss Arlen said, bringing his attention to her. "I wonder if you would like to play a game at our table? Mrs. Hepsworth has come close to winning."

Luca caught a laugh-turned-cough from somewhere down the table, and he did not miss the way the duchess feigned disinterest in the turn in conversation.

What was this?

Miss Arlen smiled benignly at Mrs. Hepsworth. "Do tell him about the game, Mrs. Hepsworth."

The matron flushed with pleasure. "Oh, I would not presume to take that honor—I know how His Grace enjoys presenting it to his guests as something of a challenge."

Miss Arlen looked to the duchess, who finally raised her gaze from her plate. "His Grace will not mind, Mrs. Hepsworth, and it is only fair after your unflagging attempts that we allow you to explain the game to another honored guest."

"Thank you, Your Grace. I am most honored." She fluttered a hand over her chest and made a deep bow with her head—the feather in her turban nearly falling into a soup tureen with that movement. "Lord Atella, the game is quite simple. You see the tiles above? There are two that match, but only two. I have tried to find them a few times without success—dinner always ends before I can check them all carefully. Perhaps you will have better fortune."

Luca narrowed his eyes at Miss Arlen, whose expression had turned far too innocent. If the search would prevent the continuance of the previous topic, he meant to devote his time to it. No matter his suspicions.

The plan proved sound. Mrs. Hepsworth did not wish to distract him from his purpose, and he could sneak bites of the delicious meal and immediately return again to matching tiles. The amount of detail in the designs was astounding, considering how rarely most looked upward.

Miss Arlen had told him during their first dinner that the duke played a game with his guests and those tiles. He hadn't thought it so simple a thing as matching, like a child's game.

Except he couldn't find the matches. When the ladies rose from the table to go to the sitting room, Luca had to admit defeat. Mrs. Hepsworth was all kindness and disappointed on his behalf, but she left the room with her daughters and very few words.

The duchess had led the ladies out, but Miss Arlen lingered a moment longer to brush invisible crumbs from her gown. She met his gaze only after the other ladies had withdrawn, and the duke had already called for a stronger drink for the men to enjoy in private.

"I hope that was helpful, my lord."

"The game? It was diverting." And yes, helpful. But he didn't want to admit it with her standing there, wearing that secretive smile.

She nodded, but then leaned slightly across the table to whisper to him, "There is no matching pair, my lord." Then she turned and went to the door, looking over her shoulder once before a footman closed it behind her.

Luca's jaw fell open. The game was a ruse—one which it seemed the whole family took part in. One that Miss Arlen had begun for his benefit. Surely, she would not tell him the truth if she meant to mock him. What had she said before? That the duke had commissioned the panels especially for some sort of amusement...

It wasn't a cruel prank. Instead, Luca thought it incredibly useful.

He finally sat back in his chair and released a relieved laugh.

Miss Arlen had rescued him, and she wanted him to know it. But why?

CHAPTER SIX

A woman skulking outside of a man's bedchamber, no matter his rank or hers, would certainly beget gossip, if not ruin a lady's reputation entirely. Therefore, Emma did not stand outside the *conte*'s rooms. Instead, she sat in a window seat at the end of the corridor, sketching the scene outside the window and *not* staring at his doors.

The ambassador's half-hearted efforts at flirting, painful as they were to watch, left Emma embarrassed on his behalf. She had left a note for Josephine, excusing herself from going down to breakfast with Josephine as she usually did. Emma hoped to obtain the visiting nobleman's good opinion, and perhaps enough trust that she might be honest with him when it came to Josephine. How honest could she be without giving him offense?

After half an hour of waiting down the corridor, she wondered if he would rise as late in the day as his English counterparts. The duke always rose early. Why she thought the ambassador would do the same, Emma could not say.

Surely the man had a great deal to accomplish in a day, even if the months before Parliament convened were more relaxed in the countryside.

A door mid-way down the corridor opened, the sound of the latch's release barely audible from her distant perch. Emma adjusted her posture and bent over her sketchbook while affecting a more diligent expression. At last.

Conte Atella stepped out of his chambers, closing the door behind him. He turned her direction, hands tugging at the hem of his jacket as he walked. His gaze cast downward for several steps before he raised it to the end of the corridor—and caught sight of Emma. She watched him from the corner of her eye, noting his reaction with interest.

His steps slowed, and he dropped his hands to his side before he tucked them behind his back. He came forward a few more steps and cleared his throat.

Emma tilted her head more to the side, enough to meet his gaze with hers, and shared what she hoped looked like a welcoming smile.

"Good morning, my lord." She lowered her feet from the wide window seat to the ground and offered the customary curtsy. "Are you on your way to breakfast?"

"I am. Would you like to join me, Miss Arlen? Or have you already enjoyed a morning meal?"

"Oh, I haven't been downstairs yet." She tucked her pencil behind one ear—a most unladylike habit that always made the dowager duchess sniff. "Only His Grace and Lord Farleigh will be at the breakfast table this early. Usually, I wait for Lady Josephine."

"I see." He glanced at the top of the stair, then down the corridor the way he had come, as though the duke's eldest daughter would spring out from another alcove. "When is it her habit to rise?"

"Not for another hour at least." She grinned at him and gestured to the stairway. "Perhaps I had better join you, or risk wasting away to nothing before she wakes."

A twitch of his lips hinted at a smile, but the ambassador's stoic mask remained in place. He offered her his arm. "It would be a pleasure to escort you."

Emma held her sketchbook against her chest while looping her hand through the crook of his arm. "Very gallant of you, *conte*. Will you defend me against any dragons we meet between here and the table?"

His eyebrows lifted. "Will there be many?"

Though she could not tell for certain if he mocked her or joined in her game, Emma answered with a quick tongue. "Most assuredly. As well as lions, and perhaps a bear."

There went his mouth again, his lips tilting upward on one side, as though he fought the urge to smile away. "Those are not as fantastic as dragons."

They started down the stairs without incident, Emma inwardly sorting through the conversation topics she had considered all morning. "I wonder, my lord, how you are enjoying your time here in the country."

"I am enjoying it very well." His tone had changed; his words sounded less personal and more rehearsed. "The countryside is beautiful. I think the English word for it is *verdant*."

"I think that is what most people have to say about England, those who are not familiar with it. Everything is always very green." She paused on the stair, necessitating he do the same. "And we cannot help but boast of it, I think. See that painting?"

He humored her by glancing at the wall, and then he tilted his head back. "Is that a dragon?"

Emma allowed herself a laugh. "I warned you, did I not?"

The painting on the wall depicted St. George's dragon, sans the sainted knight, asleep between two green hills.

He shook his head, and when he looked down at her, she caught the twinkle in his eyes. "You did warn me. Does that mean we will come upon lions and bears in a similar manner?"

"Of course." She grinned at him as they continued down the steps to the ground floor. The family only had a handful of rooms on the ground floor, as most of it was taken up by the grand entrance and the servants' kitchens and passages. The breakfast room had an impressive pair of glass-paned doors which opened into the rose gardens, where the duchess preferred to take her breakfast in the summer. The rest of the year, the view into the lush greenery was still quite beautiful.

When they stepped onto the black and white stone of the ground floor, Lord Atella pointed to the carving of a lion guarding the top of a doorway. "You have a refreshing sense of humor, Miss Arlen."

"Thank you." Emma kept pace with him, allowing a moment of quiet to lie between them. "Her Grace, the dowager duchess, does not find my humor endearing. She believes that women of rank, including Lady Josephine, ought to be more austere. It is not the fashion in England to be seen laughing or smiling too much."

"It is much the same in our court," he answered, his severe expression returning. "The years of hardship are perhaps to blame, but there is always the thought that one must protect their thoughts from others."

"That might also be blamed on years of political uncertainty." Emma gave him a sympathetic smile. "But I believe we are entering a new age, my lord. Tyranny replaced with prosperity, and uncertainty with light-hearts. We all ought to smile more."

The *conte* regarded her with an unchanging expression, but she detected a hint of something in his eyes. Curiosity, perhaps. "What does your Lady Josephine think? I have been in her company but little, and I cannot say whether she is more of your mind or her grandmother's."

Turning the conversation back to Josephine, to an aspect of her character in particular, confirmed to Emma the *conte's* interest in her dearest friend. She had rather hoped Josephine's suspicions were overdramatic and unfounded. This meant Emma had to keep her promise to distract the ambassador.

They were nearly to the breakfast room. The footmen on

58

either side of the doors had reached for the handles to pull them open.

"Lady Josephine prefers comedies to tragedies, *Signore*. She would always rather laugh than frown." Emma released his arm to precede him through the open doors, though she stopped mid-step not even partway into the room.

The duke sat at the head of the small rectangular table, Simon at his right, and another familiar nobleman on the duke's left. That man stood upon seeing her and came around the table. "Emma! Look at you—you haven't changed one whit."

"How terribly rude," she said with a laugh, hastening toward him. "One ought never to remark on a lady's inability to alter in only a year's time."

Sir Andrew, Simon's oldest friend and Emma's cousin, immediately opened his arms to give her a warm embrace. Then he stepped back and looked her over, eyes narrowed critically. "Ah, forgive me. I forget how particular you are about compliments. What I meant to say is that you are as lovely as ever, of course."

"Reserve your flattery for your admirers, Andrew." Emma stepped back and eyed him critically. "You have changed. You've had a haircut."

He laughed, then looked over Emma's shoulder to where the *conte* stood, likely thinking Emma had lost her mind along with her grasp on propriety. She looked to the duke who had stood along with Simon, and, at his nod, made the introductions herself.

"Forgive me, Lord Atella. Please allow me to introduce my cousin, Sir Andrew Wycomb. Sir Andrew's baronetcy is in Bytham, though he is lately returned from Ireland. Dear cousin, this is His Excellency, *Conte di Atella, di Regno delle Due Sicilie*." When the ambassador darted a glance at her before he bowed to her cousin, Emma saw surprise lighten his eyes.

Perhaps she shouldn't have tried so hard to speak his title in his native language. Her accent might have offended him.

"It is a pleasure, Your Excellency."

"I am pleased to meet you as well, Sir Andrew." The ambassador gestured to the table. "Might we join you for breakfast?"

"Of course, Lord Atella. Please do." Sir Andrew pulled a chair out next to him for Emma, which she took with murmured thanks. The *conte* settled across from her, next to Simon. "Emma, does your mistress not follow behind? I suppose it is still far too early for her to rise."

Emma tsked at her cousin. "No one disapproves of Lady Josephine's habits as much as you do, Andrew. You ought to stop teasing her so." She pointed to a covered platter. "Worry less about Josie and more about filling a plate for me, or I am liable to bite out of hunger."

The duke raised his eyebrows but said nothing about the banter, while Simon snorted outright before covering his mouth and feigning a cough. The *conte* stared at her like she had gone mad.

"You mustn't mind Sir Andrew and Emma," Simon said, before Emma could make her own excuses. "They are as brother and sister, closer than cousins, and torment each other out of fondness rather than any desire to inflict wounds."

"Though they often see fit to inflict the rest of us by making us listen," the duke said, quirking an eyebrow upward. "Miss Arlen, we were just discussing your plans for the day with Sir Andrew. I have other guests arriving this afternoon, but there is no reason for your cousin to wait upon them for entertainment."

"I am not certain how entertaining our plans are, Your Grace." Emma paused to nod in approval as her cousin served a breakfast of cold ham and fruit onto her plate. "But Andrew is welcome to join us. As is Simon. Josephine and I planned to walk to Lambsthorpe with Lord Atella, to introduce him to our village as well as take a little exercise." She turned her smile to the ambassador to see him filling his plate with far more dignified a manner than such an activity deserved. "That is, if Lord Atella still wishes to walk with us?"

He paused, a serving spoon midway to adding a heap of sugared strawberry preserves onto his plate. "I cannot think of a better way to spend the afternoon than in company with Lady Josephine and you, Miss Arlen."

"I can think of a dozen better things to do than watch the two of you buy ribbons," Andrew muttered, but he winced when Emma cast him a glare. "Oh, all right. I'll come."

"Only if you will be nice to Josephine," Emma insisted. "The two of you are far too much like warring cats, forever hissing and spitting at one another. If you were not friends with Simon, I should think the family would cast you out of the castle at once."

"Does being your cousin count for naught?" he asked, placing a hand on his chest as though her words had wounded him.

Emma sniffed. "You might be my cousin, but Claivoir is my home, and I shall defend those inside from the battlements if I must."

The duke's eyes shone with good humor, and perhaps approval, too. "Thank you, Miss Arlen. If ever we must face a siege, I shall know exactly where to place you for our defense."

Simon leaned close to the *conte* again, stage-whispering to him. "It is incredible you went this long without seeing some ridiculous occurrence in our home. I hope we do not alarm you."

The *conte* had apparently arranged his plate to his liking, as he held his fork as though ready to stab at his meal. "Not at all, Lord Farleigh. I only hope, should we fall under attack from Sir Andrew or anyone else, that I should be allowed to fire the cannon in the entry hall. I have been contemplating the idea since first laying eyes upon it."

For the space of a second, Emma gaped at the Italian, then she choked on a laugh and had to cover her mouth with a napkin. She hadn't at all expected him to join in their ridiculous conversation.

Andrew annoyed her by clapping a hand hard upon her back between her shoulders. "Choking, Emma?"

She shook her head, her eyes full of tears as she glared at him. "Contemplating battle plans, Cousin."

He chuckled and turned to the *conte*. "You must tell me more about where you are from, Lord Atella. I visited Rome in my boyhood, but I have not seen much of the rest of your country."

Emma recovered after sipping at her tea, then gave most of her attention to her meal. She had heard Lord Atella's polite answers to the most basic of questions about himself and his homeland. Really, no one seemed all that original in what they asked him.

The poor man would be dreadfully bored of English hospitality in next to no time. Especially if Josephine bent her mind to avoid him rather than make him comfortable, as her father wished. While boredom would not necessarily lead to an international incident, Emma's insides twisted uncomfortably at the realization that Lord Atella would leave the castle with a poor view of the English way of life.

Hemmed in as she was by her duties and Josephine's wishes, there wasn't much Emma could do. She sighed, cut a triangle of cold ham, and popped it in her mouth. Politics, as much as she enjoyed them, were not meant for her. Such a pity.

Luca adjusted his glove, tugging at the dark leather to ensure it stayed put. Then he tucked an unruly curl beneath his hat, before straightening his posture as he waited for the rest of the walking party. He had arrived by the grand doors in the entry hall first, though the waiting footmen holding the hats and gloves of the other gentlemen reassured him that they were not far behind.

A door somewhere above closed, and the echoing voices of men reverberated down another hall before Lord Farleigh and Sir Andrew appeared where the cannon waited at the other end of the hall. They were talking with animation as they approached.

"...finest horse I've ever seen. Spanish stock. Can't think of why I've never purchased one before now," Lord Farleigh said. Then he gestured to Luca. "Our ambassador friend can tell you all about it. We went riding yesterday afternoon."

"If you mean to ask what I think of your Andalusian, I will confess myself most impressed," Luca said, tucking his hands behind his back to avoid fiddling with his gloves. "I cannot think I have ever seen its equal."

Lord Farleigh struck Sir Andrew in the shoulder. "There, you see? I am not a braggart."

Sir Andrew rubbed at his shoulder, then accepted gloves and hat from one of the attending servants. "Perhaps not, but you do seem to dwell on topics which make you appear an expert." He nodded to Luca. "Are you certain you want to wander about the countryside like a rustic, Lord Atella? The ladies might take pity on us and call for the carriage."

Luca's stomach rejected the idea of the carriage more swiftly than his words could, twisting about itself uncomfortably. "I think I can manage the walk, and I should not like to disappoint Lady Josephine or Miss Arlen."

"You needn't mind Sir Andrew." Lord Farleigh had popped his own hat onto his head and taken up a walking stick, too. Though it was obviously for ornamentation rather than practical use. "He hates walking."

"It doesn't strike me as a practical way to go anywhere, especially if one has so much as a mule to spare." Sir Andrew shrugged almost impudently. "Aside from which is the trouble of arriving at your destination perfectly well, then being obliged to return home without half as much energy as you had when the exercise began."

"Lazy." Lord Farleigh cast the accusation over his shoulder.

"Practical," Sir Andrew retorted. "I take exercise in a dozen different ways. Walking needn't factor into my health. Do you fence, Lord Atella?"

The sudden address made Luca take a mental stumble, but his English righted itself quickly enough. "Sì. I fence."

"And row?" Sir Andrew added, lifting an eyebrow at his friend.

"Row?" Luca narrowed his eyes, trying to determine what the baronet meant. "Ah. The sport—rowing. No, I do not."

"Shame." Sir Andrew looked Luca up and down critically. "We have the picnic at the lake tomorrow. I had hoped to add you to my team. You have the shoulders and arms for it."

Luca looked to Lord Farleigh with the hope the duke's son would translate Sir Andrew's meaning. The young nobleman glowered at his friend, though, and missed Luca's confusion.

"You cannot form your team the day before. We agreed we would choose our fellows tomorrow, at the lake, depending on who wished to participate."

A light scuff against the marble preceded Lady Josephine's voice, calling out to them from the end of the hall. "Oh dear. Are we turning the picnic into some sort of competitive event?" She wore a cream-colored gown with a dark blue jacket and a slim-brimmed bonnet tied beneath her chin with a matching blue ribbon. The ideal picture of a lady, of course.

Miss Arlen walked at her side, dressed all in green and wearing a broader bonnet. The two of them together were quite lovely, and so different. The duke's daughter wore yellow gloves and shoes, her companion, soft brown leather of both. They were elegantly dressed, with no disparity that Luca could detect in the quality of their clothing.

Luca stiffened. To appear to best advantage, he squared his shoulders and lifted his chin just so. "Lady Josephine. It is a pleasure to join you on this outing." It was the first time he had so much as glimpsed the duke's eldest daughter that day.

"Lord Atella, good afternoon." She curtsied when she drew near but kept her gaze on her brother and his friend. "I apologize for our tardiness if it meant you had to listen to my brother and Sir Andrew quibble over their boating."

Luca returned her gesture with a deep bow and the slightest

of smiles. "It is of no consequence, my lady, for you are here now."

While the lady appeared too distracted to make eye contact, her companion never glanced away. Watching him. Luca raised his eyebrows at her, wondering what she meant to convey with her stare.

Lady Josephine spoke abruptly, fretting with her bonnet's ribbons. "Do you have our list, Emma? We had better start on our way."

That secret amusement appeared again in Miss Arlen's eyes as she darted her gaze away from his to her mistress. "It is in my reticule."

"How far is Lambsthorpe?" Luca asked, directing the question to Lord Farleigh.

"Not even two miles away." Lord Farleigh gave his walking stick a twirl, then gestured to the doors. Two footmen opened them in unison.

As Luca passed beneath the entry, he glanced back at the men dressed in the duke's livery. What must it be like to have grown up in a way that meant having every whim seen to and every order obeyed? Luca's family, while not poor, had gone through too many lean years for him to take servants for granted.

He looked forward at the others—all younger than him by several years—and experienced a moment of pure envy for their serene smiles and laughter. As he watched, Lady Josephine fell into step with Miss Arlen, their bonnets tilted toward one another as they conversed. The two noblemen followed behind, their many-caped coats teased by an autumn breeze.

Somehow, Luca had already fallen behind, missing his chance to walk next to Lady Josephine unless he ran like a fool to catch up to her. With a stretch of his legs, he managed to come abreast of the other men, at least.

A half hour's walk to the village would mean an excellent opportunity to observe all of them and better determine his course in wooing Lady Josephine. Before long, he realized she cast her gaze backward fairly often, though she made no attempt to join the men's conversation.

She seemed to only look back when Sir Andrew said something which annoyed her.

Miss Arlen kept her bonnet turned forward, until they turned down a dirt path away from the road.

"We cut through here," Sir Andrew explained, falling back a step. "It's narrower than the road but takes a quarter mile off when we go down the farm tracks."

"The walk is more shaded, too." Miss Arlen gestured to the trees above them. "They are not trimmed so much as those which hang over the main roads."

Sir Andrew gestured elaborately to the women. "We must watch over your pretty complexions, ladies."

Lady Josephine sniffed in reply.

After smothering a laugh, Lord Farleigh ducked slightly. As the tallest in their company, his height became a liability as some branches reached the top of his head. "Men, you had better keep hold of your hats. Lest these branches snatch them off completely."

Their order shifted as the ladies fell back, allowing Sir Andrew to hold branches to clear the path for them from time to time. Soon it was Sir Andrew and Lady Josephine leading their group, with Miss Arlen and Luca in between, while Lord Farleigh brought up the rear, his hat completely removed from his head and in his hand.

Miss Arlen gave Luca a thankful smile when he pushed aside a thorny branch that reached too close to her dress. "Thank you. I confess, I did not expect the track to be this overgrown. I suppose the farmers have all been too busy with harvests to give heed to our little shortcut."

"How often do you take this route?" Luca gestured to what looked to be barely more than a game trail to his eyes. Yet it wound its way through farmlands and between meadows, along the paths of humans rather than furry creatures.

Light on her feet, Miss Arlen skipped over a protruding tree root on her side of the lane. "Rarely. We usually have Lady Isabel and Lady Rosalind with us, and Lord James. That means we stay to the road, as Lord James would love nothing so much as to lose himself along the path, collecting insects or frogs, or sticks and stones. The road keeps the children out of mischief."

Luca glanced back, realizing Lord Farleigh had fallen behind enough for the growth to obscure him from sight. He frowned and looked ahead, glimpsing Lady Josephine and Sir Andrew perhaps thirty feet ahead, at the top of a small rise.

Their voices, raised in argument, drifted back. But the words were too broken up in passage through the branches for Luca to make out what they said.

"Is Sir Andrew often at odds with his friends?" Luca asked, trying to conceal his frustration. The man did not even seem to like Lady Josephine, yet he had wound up walking beside her, leaving Luca to escort Miss Arlen.

"Oh, he enjoys a lively argument from time to time. But it's all in good fun between Andrew and Lord Farleigh. I think it delights him that Lady Josephine rises to the occasion. She cannot stand to let him have the last word on any subject." Miss Arlen pushed aside a branch tipped in yellowing leaves.

The change of the seasons had begun, as evidenced by the reds, oranges, and golds in many of the trees above them. Yet enough green leaves remained to hold the memory of the summer sun a little longer.

As though to contradict him, a large yellow leaf flitted down from a tree and caught itself upon Miss Arlen's bonnet. The stem tucked into a small gap between a ribbon and the straw of the broad-brimmed hat.

Miss Arlen kept walking, unaware of her new ornament.

"What of you and your sisters, my lord? Do you never tease one another?"

The implication of her words, that Sir Andrew and Lady Josephine perhaps regarded each other as brother and sister, eased his mind. "Not often. I did not spend much time near my sisters in the years when it would have seemed most natural to tease." His parents had hidden him away in a monastery and then sent Luca to a university in Spain. Every moment spent with his family had been treasured. "I cannot imagine tormenting them with inconsequential arguments."

Miss Arlen's head turned so quickly that the leaf nearly dislodged, but instead waved like a flag in the breeze her movement created. "It is not a torment, I think. Though I haven't had a brother, Andrew has done his best to teach me how to laugh at myself. I think that is an important quality for a person to possess."

Luca ducked beneath another branch to save the top of his hat. Bruno would scold him if he returned with his hat in less than pristine condition.

"Do you often laugh at yourself, Miss Arlen?"

"I try to." She sent another of her amused smiles in his direction. "Please do not think me foolish, my lord. I am not one to make light of those situations which require solemn contemplation or thoughtful responses. I learned in my childhood that so much of what is wrong with the world cannot be changed with a dour disposition. But if I look for the humor in a situation, if I can laugh, then I can bear onerous burdens for far longer than if I dwell on the solemnity of an issue overlong."

Luca silently held aside another branch to clear her path, her words churning about in his mind. "I wonder what members of your parliament might say to such a stance."

Miss Arlen laughed outright, and the leaf in her bonnet trembled as though it did the same. "From what I understand, Parliament is as likely to roar with laughter one day as they are to thunder with anger the next. Our wisest politicians couple humor with hard truths, else no one would listen to them long enough to care what they said."

He had to bite back his own smile at that. "Then perhaps you ought to apply to the House of Commons, Miss Arlen. It seems you would make an excellent member."

"Are you calling me a comic, my lord?" She arched that single eyebrow at him, a trick he wished he had learned given how artful it appeared on her lovely face.

"Perhaps a wit."

She laughed again, and the leaf shivered. Luca reached out a hand and plucked the leaf from its place. His quick movement startled Miss Arlen, so that she took a step back, catching her foot on a tree root.

Luca tried to catch her arm, but the branch above caught his hat, pulling him to a stuttering stop before dislodging the headpiece entirely. Miss Arlen caught herself after a few steps backward by grabbing at a thin branch. They both stood still a moment, the trees around them silent, staring at each other in wide-eyed horror.

An apology formed in his mind, though one of the English words he needed in order to make it proper eluded him—

Miss Arlen snorted. Not a sound he expected from a well-bred woman. But he realized the noise was made as she attempted to quell a laugh. Her eyes danced merrily, and then she put a hand up to point at the top of his head. "You have a leaf—" Then her laughter poured out, like water from a fountain, bubbling with absolute glee.

He put his hand atop his bare head. She was right. When the branches had snatched his hat, and they'd left a leaf in his tousled hair. He narrowed his eyes at it, then paired it with the yellow leaf he'd plucked from her bonnet. "A matched set."

"Perfect." She stepped out of the branches, then bent to

SALLY BRITTON

retrieve his hat from the ground. "Lord Atella." She held it out to him.

He accepted it from her, looking down into her bright, open gaze. "Thank you, Miss Arlen." He tucked the leaves into his coat pocket without thinking. When he realized what he had done, he grimaced and put his hat on. "This is not how I thought this walk would be."

She looked behind when there was a crash in the brush, and he turned to see Lord Farleigh. "Ah, there you are. I began to think everyone had left me behind on purpose."

Miss Arlen went to his side, looping her arm through the earl's. "It is not our fault you are so terribly slow. Perhaps if you actually used that stick, you'd move faster."

Luca sighed and followed along behind them. When they crested the little rise in the land, the path opened at last. The village lay beneath them, and Lady Josephine and Sir Andrew were at its boundary, looking back. They had finally realized how far ahead of their group they were.

Not at all how I thought it would be. Getting near Lady Josephine on a walk to the village ought to have been an easy matter. Instead, Luca brought up the rear of their party alone. How would he ever get near enough to have a conversation with her? Let alone to flirt with her.

His conversation with Miss Arlen had flowed easily enough, in private.

Perhaps Luca needed to reconsider his strategy. Maybe it wasn't enough for Miss Arlen to approve of him. Maybe he needed more from her.

Obtaining an English bride of high connection and rank was necessary to his career. No matter what Torlonia said.

CHAPTER SEVEN

E mma lounged on a cushion beneath an old oak, her shawl loose about her shoulders. Alice Sharpe sat next to her, spectacles upon her nose, sketching. The duke's daughters were playing pall-mall with other ladies, while the men stood along the shore trying to form rowing teams.

All the young gentry—and the not-so-young chaperones and parents—had come at the duke's invitation for what could well be the last outdoor event of the year.

A day at the lake, with country entertainment upon the shore, and sport for the men upon the water. Though the breeze sometimes felt a little cooler than Emma found comfortable, she enjoyed the spectacle of the scene.

"Aren't you going to play?" Alice asked, not looking up from her work.

"Aren't you?" Emma retorted.

Alice peered over the frames of her spectacles with a smirk. "I am the governess, not an invited guest. I am only here to keep watch over my charges."

"That is a fine excuse, even though we both know you were

officially discharged yesterday." Emma leaned further back on her cushion to look up into the tree branches. "You are as much a guest as Mr. Gardiner is."

"And he is at the shore, trying to look like he is interested in rowing when I am certain he is actually trying to find late-season water-skippers." Alice leaned away from the tree trunk to peer out at the men. "I think he only came to be near me, and then Sir Andrew dragged him away. Poor Rupert."

Emma sighed, a touch envious of the couple's happiness. "The two of you are a wonderful pair, Alice. Your happiness is inspirational."

"Thank you." Alice turned her attention back to her sketch. "And what about you, Emma?"

"Hm?" Emma stared up at the snatches of sky she could see through the tree branches. "What about me?"

"Yes. When will you find a similar state of happiness for yourself?" Alice had a way of asking personal questions in a way that made them sound perfectly reasonable. Perhaps it came with being a governess—the ability to make any question sound like a scholarly examination rather than the start of a potentially embarrassing conversation.

Reflection upon the question kept Emma from making an immediate answer, though in the past she would have said something flippant. Made light of the topic of marriage, at least when it came to herself. But Alice had become a friend, and friends who asked serious questions deserved honest answers.

"I cannot know for certain." She watched a little squirrel, red with furry points on its ears, hop from one limb to another. Likely looking for food for its winter stores. "Josie isn't ready for me to leave her, and no man comes courting the companion when the duke's daughter is present." She smiled to herself. "I always thought of that as a bit of protection. A gift of time. I need not worry over courtship and marriage until Josie marries. That seems to be a very long way off."

"You are an heiress yourself, though." Alice did not lift her head; her pencil gliding across her paper in long strokes kept her gaze. "Though I suppose that isn't common knowledge, given how Lady Rosalind swore me to secrecy *after* she blurted that fact out in conversation."

Emma snorted. "Rosalind cannot keep anything like that to herself. I think it must make her feel important, to get attention for saying such things." Emma looked over to the lake again. "But you are correct. My waiting inheritance isn't generally known. I am most grateful to His Grace for that."

Alice bit her lip and leaned closer to her paper, pushing her spectacles up slightly before applying her pencil again. "I have known you only a few months, Emma. Even still, it surprises me to know you haven't given much thought to your future. You have plans for everything and everyone else."

"There is no need to worry over my future. Not until Josie marries. Or declares her intentions to remain an old maid." Emma didn't fear the latter. Josie, for all her declarations of youth and disinterest in marriage, had a romantic nature. She would turn her mind to matrimony when a man caught her interest, if not her heart.

Emma peered across the stretch of grass between the tree and where the men had gathered. She spotted Lord Atella standing with them, his coat removed like the rest, anxiously listening to instruction. He had said he didn't row. How had they convinced him to try? And in front of so many people he did not know?

The man had something deeper than Simon or Andrew's competitiveness to motivate him. As serious as he was, it was hard to imagine him wishing to join in for entertainment's sake. As a political ambassador, he would not want to make a fool of himself, either. So what took him from the comfort of lawn games and picnic food, from the men content to sit and speak of politics on the bank, out into strange waters?

Perhaps he meant to impress Josephine. Or he wanted

Simon's approval. Currying favor with a future duke wasn't an uncommon thing for Emma to see.

Lady Isabel appeared at the edge of their rug, her lower lip out in a pout. "Rosalind cheats," she declared, then dropped onto a cushion. She swiped an apple from the bowl at the center of the cushions and rugs. The bite she took out of it was rather fierce.

"Have you proof of that?" Alice asked, looking up to meet Isabel's gaze.

The girl shifted and lowered her eyes. "Not precisely."

"Then let us withhold our accusations of such." Alice looked to the lake. "It appears the gentlemen have finally decided who will be in which boat."

There were three boats, and each would hold a team of five men. All who had agreed to participate in rowing were young and most were unattached to any particular lady. The older gentlemen who had dared accompany their sons and daughters were scattered about on chairs, watching their youthful counterparts. Likely placing wagers on their sons, too.

Lady Josephine arrived, taking another fruit from the bowl before sitting next to Alice to study her sketchbook. "Oh, that is an incredible likeness, Alice."

The former governess scrutinized the drawing. "Do you think so? It has been so long since I've drawn a portrait, though I think I could draw stems and petals blindfolded."

Emma started and sat up. "Portrait? I thought you were sketching the bowl of fruit."

"I never said that." Alice's eyes glinted with mischief. She turned her sketchbook toward Emma. "I was sketching you."

Emma looked back at her likeness, her lips parted in a protest that died before she could speak it. Alice had drawn her in profile, the way she had been leaning back on the cushions and looking upward. And Alice had caught something in her sketch that Emma wasn't certain she liked. An open, undisguised longing.

Despite the peaceful pose—her form an idea rather than a finished concept—her detailed expression wasn't one Emma wanted anyone else to see.

She swallowed and forced a smile when she met Alice's probing gaze. "Thank you, Alice. I think your skill with portraits is comparable to your botany work. Perhaps better."

Alice's eyebrows raised. "Thank you." Did she know what she had seen? Did she guess at what Emma's true feelings were? Perhaps she had caught that expression upon Emma's face in an unguarded moment, and her steady line of questions had been Alice's attempt to puzzle out what it meant.

The men were marching to the short boat launch upon the lake. Emma stood with a deliberate movement. "Oh, look. I think the race will start soon." She plucked her parasol from the ground and popped it open. "We had better attend to it."

The other ladies playing with their mallet and balls had come to the same conclusion, as they put their equipment down and started walking toward the water. Alice and Josephine stood and brushed at their skirts, then Isabel and Rosalind joined them. The young girls took up bickering over the game as they fell into step behind the three adult women.

Sir Andrew stood at the forefront of one group of men, giving orders and gesturing to where he wanted each man to sit. Simon had his own small crew to direct, and it appeared Lord Atella had been conscripted into the earl's boat. The third vessel was manned by the only married man in the group, young though he was, their neighbor Mr. Whitfield. Rupert Gardiner, Alice's intended, manned an oar for that team.

Simon saw the ladies and chaperones gathering along the shore and waved at them, then shouted. "We are first going to get our boats to the other side of the lake. Once they are in line, we will race back to the dock. The first boat to draw even with the dock is the winning team." He gestured to Lord Addington upon the dock with them. "Our friend, Baron Addington, will wait for us to signal we are ready. Then he will fire his weapon, signaling the race's start."

"Brave of them, to move a university river sport to a lake," one of the matrons said quietly to her daughter.

Emma looked over the pastel dresses and ribboned bonnets, counting seventeen unmarried ladies. They were all neighbors, except for a few guests of the duke she had met the day before at dinner. The castle hosted many people when the duke was in residence. And every guest with single daughters was always certain to bring them, likely hoping to catch Simon's eye.

As of yet, no one had accomplished such a thing.

"The earl is in fine form," Miss Finchley, the baron's daughter, murmured to her mama. "He is so handsome."

Someone agreed, and Emma bit her tongue. Would they find him nearly so handsome if he wasn't the heir to a dukedom? Miss Finchley ought to have given up her pursuit by that point. The previous summer, she had shown she possessed an unfeeling heart when a small boy—her father's ward—had gone missing, and she'd thought it a waste of time to go looking for him.

The duke's family, despite their high birth, were exceptionally compassionate toward others. Someone with a stony heart and an attitude dismissive of others could never impress Simon.

The men climbed into their boats and began rowing across the lake.

Emma picked out Lord Atella among them, rowing with as much vigor as his fellows. "I do hope the *conte* is all right," she murmured quietly to her friends. "He said he didn't participate in rowing as a sport."

"If he elected to join them, I'm certain he will be well enough." Josie shaded her eyes, having forgotten her parasol under the tree. "I only hope Simon trounces Sir Andrew. Your cousin is insufferable when he wins any sort of game."

Alice pursed her lips and turned just enough to look at both of them from the corner of her eye. "I am surprised either of you care about the outcome of the race."

Josephine colored. "I don't care who wins, you understand. As long as it isn't Sir Andrew. Though I suppose I ought to cheer for my brother."

The men had nearly reached the far side of the lake, rowing in unison.

"Lady Josephine?" Lady Addington turned to peer at them. "Where did your brother find boats built for rowing teams?"

"My father had them made, but shorter and more suitable for a lake than the long boats used in the river races." Josephine's benevolent smile, the one she reserved for people for whom she had no personal affection yet knew she must treat with respect, seemed to please the baroness. And act as an invitation to more chatter.

"His Grace is always so thoughtful of others. The invitation for today's event said it was meant to be a welcome for the new ambassador from Sicily. Though I know the baron met him, we have not yet had the opportunity to introduce my darling Elizabeth. Do you think—when the race is over—you might correct that oversight?"

Emma saw the way Josephine bristled, even if it was too subtle for others to notice the way the corners of her eyes and mouth tightened. Josephine's polite smile widened. "I am certain we can arrange that, my lady."

Directing her gaze away, Emma had to bite her tongue. It wasn't enough for Miss Finchley to go after Simon, but she had to pursue a foreign count, too?

"He's very dashing," Miss Finchley said, and Emma could well imagine how the young woman would bat her eyelashes as she spoke. "Though quite old, I think."

Why did everyone think him old? Emma huffed quietly.

"I thought so, too," Josephine said, surprising Emma by agreeing with anything Elizabeth Finchley had to say. "My father informed me, when I asked, that he is eight and twenty. Nearly a decade our senior."

The baroness laughed airily. "A decade isn't too terrible. Not when he possesses such a charming accent, as foreigners usually do. The baron is a dozen years older than I am. I think it a good thing for a girl to marry someone older and wiser. It gives her greater direction."

Josephine's response was carefully neutral. "What an interesting idea, Lady Addington."

Direction? A man, giving a woman great direction? Emma gripped her parasol tighter in an attempt to avoid grinding her teeth into powder. Why did people insist on treating women of her age as though they still needed looking after? She had been looking after Josephine for years. And had managed quite well at it, too.

"Perhaps the ambassador would like to visit us while he is here, Mama. We could invite him to dinner," Miss Finchley said, her voice as pinched as her heart.

"An excellent idea, Elizabeth. Yes, we will have your father extend the invitation today," the baroness fairly cooed.

Emma looped her arm through Josephine's. "My lady, would you like to go nearer the dock so we might congratulate the winners when they arrive?"

Though Josephine blinked with surprise, she hastily followed Emma's lead. "Yes. I think, as one of the hostesses, that would be right."

As they walked down the line of observers, Josephine smiling and nodding to her guests as regally as any queen, she spoke quietly to Emma. "Only think, if we could get all the mothers in the county to invite Lord Atella to dinner, I might not have to see him at all."

Disappointment in her friend stuck Emma like a thorn

through her stocking. It surprised her, and a rebuke rose all the way to her tongue. But she didn't voice it. Her first loyalty was to the duke's family and to Josie. She tempered her response, wording it carefully. "I cannot think it would give him a good impression of England and the English if he dined with certain members of our neighborhood."

"Oh, bother England." Josie widened her eyes, far too dramatic. "I suppose you are right. I'll warn Papa so he can help Lord Atella make his acceptances to the correct houses and leave the rest with his regrets."

Emma nodded once, then looked across the lake. One of the men waved an oar in the air, then sat back with his fellow. "That must be the signal for the baron—"

A shot rang out in the air, startling Emma. She ought to have paid more attention, but with the race underway, her gaze didn't leave the boats or the oars. And her eyes naturally settled upon a dark head. Lord Atella.

Emma barely breathed as she watched, the boats seeming evenly matched.

She hoped his team won.

Though Luca hadn't found himself kindly disposed to Sir Andrew during the walk to the village, the baronet had coaxed Luca into participating in the boat race with a few simple words and a wide, knowing grin.

"Come, Lord Atella. You must race. Think only on how it will impress the ladies."

Thus, he was seated facing Lord Farleigh, with his back to the opposite shore, waiting for the signal to begin. Farleigh would shout instructions which, he assured Luca, were easily followed.

"Rowing is all about keeping a rhythm. If you can play an instrument or dance, you can row," the duke's son had insisted.

Luca ought to have known better. First, how would rowing from one side of a lake to another gain a lady's favor? Especially with Luca untried in the sport. Second, rowing proved far more complex, given how he had to avoid the oars of the other men, dip his starboard-side paddle at the same depth as the rest of them, and then repeat the cycle over and over until his arms burned.

A shot traveled across the water to signal the start of the race, and Farleigh started shouting his commands. "Row!"

Luca rowed. In a moment, Luca received a command.

"Atella, your stroke is early!" Then he yelled to someone else, "Blanding, slow the slide!"

They were moving across the water with such speed, Luca couldn't imagine the others going any faster. He glanced over his shoulder, expecting to see Sir Andrew's boat behind them. Instead, he saw a wake in the water. Luca snapped his gaze forward—Sir Andrew's boat had already pulled half a boat-length ahead.

Gritting his teeth, Luca pushed himself harder.

"Atella," Farleigh snapped, "Stroke slow, or we'll turn port side."

Starboard side, port side—Luca wanted to get ahead of the baronet. He corrected himself, and Farleigh started yelling with greater enthusiasm. "That's it, men! We'll overtake! Keep heads down and arms moving. Stroke! Stroke! Stroke!"

Risking another glance up, Atella's heart lightened. They had pulled nearly even with Sir Andrew's team again.

Farleigh shouted, "Atella, touch it up!"

What the blazes did that command mean? Luca adjusted, trying to fall in line with the other rowers again. Someone at the bow received a rebuke next, and Luca dared not look up or away from Farleigh again. Every time he tried to find the other boats, his team suffered. Keeping his head down and minding his own work must see him through.

They drew near to shore, given that Luca could hear the birdlike cheers of women. Calls for one team or another hit his ears, and then the voices raised louder. A moment after, Farleigh relaxed. "Hold water, men. We passed the finish."

Luca remembered the explanation for that call. He lowered his oar to drag through the water perpendicularly, as did the other men, bringing the boat to a stop. He turned to look at the dock, his pulse thudding with excitement and exertion—

Sir Andrew's team had won, and Mr. Whitfield's team came last.

His heart sank, and his gaze swept the land looking for the reactions of the on-lookers. Everyone seemed cheerful, with ladies clapping gloved hands, a few of the younger crowd bouncing up and down, while gentlemen were slapping backs and likely collecting on wagers.

He found Lady Josephine's dark green spencer, but she had turned to speak to the woman in rose-pink at her side. Miss Arlen. Despite the distance between them, he felt it when their gazes collided. His shoulders fell, his disappointment keen, though ridiculous, he knew. He watched as she lifted one shoulder, tilted her head to the same side. The simple movement conveyed a sympathetic understanding—or so he thought.

No one could read emotion across that much distance. Could they?

He sighed and dropped his head, following the last of Lord Farleigh's instructions to bring the boat back to the dock. When he finally climbed out, someone handed him his hat and coat. Though the day was cool, his exertion left him uncomfortably warm. He draped the coat over his arm and walked down the boards to shore, where the victorious crew accepted congratulations from the onlookers.

Luca added his praise to others, to men he had met only that morning. Then he came to Sir Andrew, who grinned broadly and put his hand on Luca's shoulder.

"An excellent race, Atella. You did well enough that I'm

surprised you thought yourself unequal to the event. I dare say, should we race again, it is your team that would come out ahead." The easy way Sir Andrew spoke, his tone friendly rather than boasting, deflated Luca further.

Good form meant accepting a loss graciously. He knew that.

"Thank you, Sir Andrew. I enjoyed the exercise, though I am not certain I will take up the sport any time soon." He gave a slight bow. "Congratulations on your victory."

Lady Josephine and Miss Arlen appeared, and Miss Sharpe nodded her own greeting before skirting the knot they formed in search of her betrothed.

Sir Andrew's demeanor changed the moment the duke's daughter paused at his side. His grin turned crooked, and he folded his arms over his chest. "Ah, Lady Josephine. I believe you wagered against my win today."

"Of course I did." She narrowed her eyes at him. "I had high hopes of your pride being lost upon the lake." She gestured to the water. "But no. You have prevailed, though that overlarge head of yours should have sunk your boat."

Luca drew back slightly, surprised at the acidic words spoken in such sugared tones. Neither baronet nor lady gave him the barest attention as they lobbed their insults at one another. The noise around them rose as more excited conversation exchanged among other members of the party.

Rather than take offense, the baronet chuckled and spoke louder. "Perhaps it would have, had I not been determined to win merely for the pleasure of you losing a few pence."

Miss Arlen moved closer to Luca, and he bent toward her when he realized her intention to speak to him without shouting. "Lord Atella, would you help me by the tree a moment?"

Though curious, Luca immediately agreed. He did not even bother taking his leave of Lady Josephine and Sir Andrew. They seemed content to amuse themselves with their witty exchange of words for the moment.

He followed Miss Arlen, noting the way she twirled her parasol upon her shoulder, and caught up to her at the edge of a rug beneath a large tree. Cushions lay about everywhere, and a large bowl with apples and pears set in the center of the carpet. He'd seen her there before the start of the race, too, with other ladies.

"Please, won't you sit?" Miss Arlen gestured to the rug. "And take some lemonade. Here, I will pour you a glass." She gestured and a footman appeared, dressed in clothing suitable for working out of doors, though it was impeccably clean. He brought a tray with cups and a large pitcher of lemonade.

The duke's guests need never want for comfort or convenience, it seemed.

Luca lowered himself to a cushion, dropping his coat beside him and setting his hat atop his head. He accepted the cup from her and drank, the drink sweet and refreshing.

She settled across from him, tucking her legs to one side and adjusting her shawl. "We have a moment to speak in private, *Signore*, while the others celebrate."

"Have we a need to speak in private?" he asked, lowering his cup. They had already done so, though quite by accident, a few times already. He sipped at the lemonade thoughtfully.

She pursed her lips and drew her eyebrows down as she studied him. "I think we must. You will forgive me for this observation, *Signore*, but I must make it. Based upon your actions and gestures, I believe you are attempting to win my lady's favor."

Luca nearly choked, lemonade burning the back of his throat, then he forcefully held the cup out toward the servant. The uniformed man hurried to take it, bowing before backing away again. Miss Arlen simply stared at him, one eyebrow arched, not the least distressed by *his* distress.

"There is no need to deny it," she said before he could deny her supposition. "I have seen many a man attempt to win her favor. As you have seen, she is not eager to flirt or even entertain suitors. My lady has no wish to take part in courtship with anyone at present." Miss Arlen appeared most serious and spoke with gentle practicality. "I do not mean any disrespect by telling you this. I only wish to save you the time of pursuing her."

He looked down at the carpet, then over to the dock where Lady Josephine stood speaking with Miss Sharpe and Mr. Gardiner. And Sir Andrew.

"I am certain your words are kindly meant," he murmured, then met Miss Arlen's gaze again. "But I am not dissuaded, Miss Arlen."

She appeared ready to ask why. Instead, her expression softened, and she released a tired sigh. "Very well, then. If your attentions toward her are honorable, I suppose I must do my part and offer my assistance."

He put a hand on his knee and leaned toward her, narrowing his eyes. "Your assistance? Miss Arlen, I am not certain what you mean. You cannot try to warn me away with one breath and offer help in the next."

A bright smile grew upon her face, causing her dark eyes to lighten. She spun the handle of her parasol and raised her gaze heavenward. "Oh, Lord Atella. A woman may change her mind as often as she wishes. Surely, with three younger sisters, you know this?"

Yes. Unfortunately, he did.

"No one knows Lady Josephine the way I do," Miss Arlen continued, her matter-of-fact tone returned. "You know nothing of her likes or dislikes, or how best to approach her with your offer of courtship without frightening her away."

That was a possibility?

"What are you proposing, Miss Arlen?" he asked, lowering his voice. The crowd was drifting their direction. "Nothing dishonorable—?"

Her eyes widened, and she raised one hand and hastened to assure him. "Not at all. Lady Josephine is as dear to me as a sister.

I mean only to help your chances by educating you in how to approach my friend in a way that will gain you positive attention." Given the wide-eyed way he gaped at her, the man wasn't ready to take anyone's advice or admit he needed the guidance. "You may take your time to consider my offer. You will be a guest in the duke's home for many months. Perhaps you will not need me. If you change your mind, do let me know. My lady is my friend, but her tastes are...peculiar." Miss Arlen's smile returned, along with a hint of amusement in her tone. "I hope you enjoyed the lemonade."

She stood and walked away without another word, and the other guests returned and began settling under trees and in chairs once more. The talk was of the race, with men retelling their part of it in excitement.

Luca hardly understood how anyone could work themselves into such a frenzy over rowing a boat. He let out a sigh at the same moment Miss Sharpe sat down next to him, Mr. Gardiner on her other side.

"You did well in the race, my lord," the woman said, kindness in her voice and expression. She glanced around the rug as the other ladies settled. "Did Miss Arlen leave?"

"Yes, I believe so." He adjusted his hat, settling it more firmly in place. Straight. Precise. Very English. He slid his coat on, too.

Miss Sharpe sighed and looked to her betrothed. "I wasn't finished with her portrait." She opened the book in her hands, revealing sketches. "Look, Rupert. What do you think?"

She held the book out before her.

Mr. Gardiner took her book, though he spoke to her with teasing words. "You know I am no judge of human form in art. Show me a beetle or a moth, and I will give you every bit of praise you deserve. Yes. She looks pretty in the sketch."

"Oh, you horrid man." She spoke with obvious affection rather than censure, then she took her book from him. "My lord, what do *you* think? Is it a good likeness?" Miss Sharpe pushed the book into his hands the moment they were through the sleeves of his coat. He caught the book somewhat awkwardly and looked down, his eyes falling upon Miss Arlen in repose.

He studied the lines of her cheekbones, the sweep of her eyelashes, the curve of her jaw. Her profile was perfect, but the look of vulnerability she wore in the sketch had never appeared on her face while in his presence. His gaze rested on the expression, trying to puzzle it out.

Gardiner's voice interrupted his study. "Ah, Alice. The poor ambassador. He doesn't know what to make of it, either."

Luca felt his cheeks burn, as though he had been caught staring at the real Miss Arlen, and he handed the sketchbook back to Miss Sharpe. "No, no. It is most excellent, Miss Sharpe. Quite lifelike. You have a talent for more than drawing insects, I am certain."

Miss Sharpe's smile broadened. "There, Rupert. You see? That is how one compliments a lady's drawings. Thank you, Lord Atella." She stared up at him, her gaze behind her spectacles contemplative. "Miss Arlen is a most handsome woman, is she not?"

Perhaps he had put his coat on too soon. The discomforting warmth made him clear his throat. "I think I need another glass of lemonade." He signaled one of the servants holding a tray.

Miss Arlen's attractiveness was absolutely none of his affair. He needn't speak on it to others. Especially when Miss Sharpe turned such speculative eyes upon him when she asked her question.

The only woman he needed to concern himself with was the duke's eldest daughter. Lady Josephine. Even if she had spent most of the day acting as though he did not exist.

Luca needed to change that—but how? Miss Arlen's offer hovered at the forefront of his thoughts, and he easily pictured the woman's kind smile. Yes, she had been amused by his attempts.

But she had cared enough about her friend to extend her help to Luca.

What kind of man would he be, to accept such a thing from her? Did it make him weak, that he would consider her offer for more than a moment? At the moment, Miss Arlen presented the most attractive offer.

CHAPTER EIGHT

O ne of Emma's favorite rooms in the castle was not the largest or most lavishly decorated, but it possessed a peaceful quality she quite loved. The chapel at Clairvoir, longer than it was wide, had a ceiling which stretched the room upward to two levels. The vaulted ceiling, with woodwork gilded in gold by masters, drew her eyes heavenward every time she entered, as she imagined cathedrals must do.

The chapel was a cathedral in miniature. Tapestries purchased from the King of France lined the wall, depicting the miracles of Christ healing the ten lepers on one side and the Sermon on the Mount on the other.

Padded benches, large enough to hold three, ran down both lengths of wall. Today, for the wedding, the gardeners had brought in boughs of autumn flowers to decorate the small pulpit where the young rector held the service for the ducal family and guests.

Most of the time, when the duke did not have guests, the family took the carriage to Lambsthorpe for services. Today, they sat in the box at the second level of the chapel, looking out over their guests and the betrothed pair sitting near the front of the room.

Emma sat beside Alice instead of in her usual place in the family balcony.

Though several of Alice's far-flung relations had attempted to obtain an invitation to the wedding—in reality, an invitation to visit the castle of the Duke of Montfort—Alice had not extended a welcome to any of them.

"They couldn't be bothered with me before I became friends with the ducal family," she had admitted to Emma the day before. "I am not about to subject Their Graces to any of my family's hypocritical behavior."

Quite right. Emma smirked to herself, then glanced up at the balcony to exchange a triumphant smile with Josephine. They had subtly encouraged Alice's match to Mr. Rupert Gardiner. While neither of them would take credit for the couple's happiness, they certainly enjoyed seeing it first-hand.

Before she turned forward, lowering her eyes from the balcony, Emma's gaze caught on Lord Atella's dark stare.

He sat behind her. Staring boldly at her with his lips pressed tightly together.

She didn't flinch, but slowly lifted one corner of her mouth in a smile.

He frowned more deeply.

The rector called for everyone to join in song to close the sermon, requiring Emma to face forward once more. Alice's hand trembled, so Emma took hold and gave her friend a reassuring glance. Outside, the clouds broke, and the already bright white of the room glowed more warmly. Gold accents on the windowpanes shone, and the candlesticks near the altar did the same.

Alice let out a trembling breath and added her voice to the hymn. Emma nodded her approval, then she faced forward.

What must the former governess feel, moments away from joining her life to another? To the man she loved?

Emma let her eyes wander across the aisle to where Mr. Rupert Gardiner sat with his parents, all three in a row, singing with bright eyes and vigor. None could doubt the happiness of the family when it came to welcoming Alice among them. Given the way the younger Mr. Gardiner kept stealing glances at Alice, respectability alone kept him from crossing the room and sweeping her up in his arms.

At last, the time came for the wedding sacrament. As Alice left Emma alone on the bench, a chill swept around Emma. Someone had likely left a door open somewhere in the hall behind, causing a momentary draft. She reached down to the bench to pick up her shawl, only to discover it gone. She frowned and peered down near her feet.

The shawl settled on her shoulders—along with the brief weight and warmth of a pair of hands.

Emma's breath caught. The shawl had fallen behind her, and Lord Atella had seen her stretching about looking for it. Presuming to cover her shoulders for her, while kind, also struck Emma as bold. She said nothing to him, pulling the Indian wrap tighter about her shoulders. But she sat straighter. Lifted her chin a touch.

The *conte* hadn't spoken to her since she'd made her offer to help him the day previous. Granted, there had not been a lot of opportunity for him to do so. But he *had* glared at her once or twice from across the dinner table. Perhaps he had found her idea insulting. Given that she had practically said he lacked the ability to flirt with Josephine, his offense was fair.

Even if Josephine had an interest in courtship and marriage, a man as solemn as the *conte* had no hope of winning her. Josie had too much vivacity and energy. She needed someone to match those things in her. And as much as Josie delighted in playing hostess to her father's guests in tandem with her mother, the young woman had no interest in politics. An ambassador's wife would never escape the discussion of national laws, tariffs, taxes, borders, and treaties.

Obviously, Lord Atella knew none of those things.

Emma could help Josie by *helping* Lord Atella. Fulfilling her friendly obligation to Josephine without causing an embarrassing incident for the visiting dignitary.

If he'd only let her.

The rector placed Alice and Rupert Gardiner under their wedding vows and pronounced them husband and wife. Alice's pink cheeks and bright eyes swept upward to where the duke and duchess sat with their family, and she offered them a deep curtsy while her husband bowed. Then they walked down the aisle together, arm-in-arm, past all the guests and the small organ in the back. Everyone else rose to follow the happy couple into the dining hall, where a wedding breakfast fit for a king and his bride had been laid out at the duchess's command.

It was a generous gesture from the duke and duchess, bestowing that honor upon a friend and his new bride. It immediately set up Alice, the new Mrs. Gardiner, for great social success. Should she wish it.

Emma walked along behind the other guests filtering out of the chapel, watching the people ahead of her and trying to ignore the man behind her.

Except they somehow wound up seated at the table together. The seating arrangements were informal, with everyone present for the wedding taking the place that pleased them best. Alice glanced over at Lord Atella, watching as he lifted lids off of platters to ascertain their contents.

"Miss Arlen. We have some sort of jelly here, sweet rolls, baked ham...?" He glanced at her, uncertain of something in one of the dishes.

Perhaps he hadn't learned all the English words for different foods. "A little of everything except the jelly, please."

He served her before filling his own plate with a light repast. Then he ate quietly, the elderly gentleman at his other side more inclined to talk to his neighbor than give the ambassador much notice. Emma glanced to her other side to find Lady Rosalind and

Lady Isabella had settled next to her and were talking rapidly to each other about their future weddings.

Though tempted to join in their conversation—as unrealistic as they were in their plans for lace-trimmed gowns of blue and pink—she gave her attention to the ambassador. If she had made him uncomfortable, that would reflect poorly upon the duke's hospitality.

"Lord Atella? I wonder—have I given you offense? I hope you know such was not my intent."

He stared at his plate without making an immediate answer, frozen with his fork mid-stab in a piece of ham. When he spoke, his tone was most subdued. "I have done nothing except think on our last conversation, Miss Arlen." He lowered his fork and kept his eyes trained upon his plate. "And I would like to accept your offer."

ONE OF THE BEST WAYS TO FORGE BONDS WITH PEOPLE OF foreign countries and cultures was to make a sincere effort to learn their ways. If Luca could do that for an entire nation of people, he could take the time to focus that ability to learn of one woman. A young woman, of marriageable age, completely suited to the role of ambassador's wife, and of high enough rank to impress his peers at home and abroad.

He hadn't ever learned how, exactly, to gain the favor of a woman who wasn't already impressed by his title or position. If he merely wanted a wife—without care of her status or suitability for the role—he could have had one long since.

Luca stared down at his plate, his humiliation making his ears burn. Spending years in a monastery and kept close to home, there hadn't been time to learn the social art of flirtation. And English women were quite different than Italian women. The majority of his country remained Catholic, which meant strict observation of maidenly modesty in most circles. Not to mention how desperate families were merely to survive as their fledgling country fell under the rule of another Hapsburg monarch.

He released a deep sigh.

Miss Arlen's hand delicately rested on his wrist, with just the slightest pressure to alert him to her presence.

He let his gaze travel from her fingers up to her warm brown eyes. Rather than appear smug, as he had feared she might, Miss Arlen's expression was gentle.

"I will help you, Lord Atella. Perhaps you would like to meet me in the conservatory this afternoon? Then we can talk."

Luca nodded his acceptance of the invitation, then made himself focus on his meal. Having a little help wouldn't be the end of the world, nor would it result in his humiliation. Miss Arlen struck him as a friendly enough sort, and she would do nothing to give insult to a guest of the family. Trusting her felt safe.

Perhaps all he needed to know were a few little things, like Lady Josephine's favorite flower or book, or her favorite music.

Cheered by this thought, Luca looked forward to his brief afternoon meeting with Miss Arlen. All would be well in short order.

CHAPTER NINE

Luca paced between the potted plants of the conservatory, noting the large basins full of green vines and long-stemmed flowers. He glanced upward at the ceiling which was half-covered in paned windows. The room felt much warmer than the outdoors and functioned as both a greenhouse and salon for the duchess, he'd been told.

He smoothed a loose curl back from his forehead, then adjusted the cuffs of his coat. His plan to grow closer to Lady Josephine through her companion had taken an unexpected turn, but that did not mean he needed to abandon it all together. If Miss Arlen liked him well enough to help his efforts with her lady, did that not accomplish much the same goal he'd had before her offer?

The castle felt far too quiet at this hour. He hadn't seen any servants coming or going from the warm, humid room. Most of the guests had retired to their rooms to rest, he supposed. There were few entertainments to be had in the country on a Sunday afternoon.

At home, his family would rest to prepare to attend evening mass together.

Luca prodded a broad-leafed fern of some kind, trying to

remove his thoughts from home and bring them back to the present moment.

"Mr. Gardiner would be able to tell you exactly what that bit of green is." Miss Arlen's tone sounded as bright and cheerful as ever, and when he turned to face her, he saw that she still wore her cream-yellow gown from morning services, as well as the slippery blue shawl that kept trying to escape her shoulders.

He bowed. "Miss Arlen. Good afternoon."

"Good afternoon, Lord Atella." She curtsied from where she stood, a dozen feet away from him. "Thank you for agreeing to speak with me. I felt certain after our last conversation that things needed to be mended between us."

"Not at all. You merely caught me off guard at the picnic." He took a few steps toward her, then tucked his hands behind his back. "But after some consideration, I do believe you have your mistress's best interests at heart."

"That is always true," she said with a firmness that surprised him. "Lady Josephine is like a sister to me, and the duke and duchess have looked after me as one of their own for many years."

"Your loyalty to them is a high compliment," he murmured, measuring the determined glint in her eye by what he already knew of her. "I wonder, Miss Arlen, if we might begin the conversation on what has brought us both here. You say you have observed my attempts to get to know your mistress. You find them wanting."

She had made that clear enough.

"I am afraid so." Her tight-lipped smile showed her reluctance to embarrass him, as did the way she turned from him. "You will never endear yourself to Lady Josephine by following on her heels. She will only think you intrusive. The best way to win her interest will be to bring her notice to you."

Luca stepped away from her, bending over a potted fern as though to examine its leaves. Hopefully, she did not notice his discomfort with the subject. Growing up among monks and then men at university hadn't prepared him for this. "That is what you believe? And how does a man go about such a thing if he is not already in the woman's company?"

Miss Arlen spoke kindly, but with conviction. "A woman like Josephine will notice a man who is happily himself, a man who is not trying to impress her. She has had gentlemen and nobility alike vying for her attention since she was a girl of fourteen."

Somehow, it hadn't occurred to Luca that she would be used to more eloquent suitors than himself. And from such a young age. "The duke permitted that?" he asked, somewhat at a loss.

"He put a stop to some flirtations before the duchess presented Lady Josephine to the Queen. When he knew about them." Miss Arlen released a humorless laugh. "I know he has also told a few men their suits were not welcome. Nor is he willing to arrange a marriage Lady Josephine will not consent to." Affection colored her words about the duke. "He is a very loving father."

How did one woo a woman who had men from the highest echelons of England seeking her favor and her hand?

For one awful moment, Luca's ambitions wavered. Much of his planned success hinged upon an English bride with a rank high enough to command respect and breeding fine enough to impress upon his countrymen and hers his suitability for his position of ambassador. How had he begun this course without realizing how complicated it would be?

Miss Arlen's hand landed upon his sleeve, startling him out of his bleak thoughts. He hadn't even heard her approach.

"Take heart, my lord." She wore a gentle expression with a softness in her eyes. As though she understood the difficult path he had laid for himself. "I will arm you as best I can for this battle." Then her tone lightened. "No one knows my lady better than I do."

Luca relaxed, then looked down to where her bare hand remained upon his sleeve, contemplating her words. A thought occurred to him—strange, but he did not doubt the impression.

"You are not really a companion, are you? You serve in that place, but there is more to it than that."

She withdrew her hand, but rather than appear offended, she took on the air of someone with a secret. Her chin raised, she turned from him to pace the width of the conservatory. "The important thing is that I have the insight you need. My first instruction to you remains the same. Stop trying to win Lady Josephine's interest by interjecting yourself into her doings and conversations. Her whole life, people have come to her and blatantly attempted to win her favor. My lady will be won by someone who makes her come to him. I am certain of it."

Luca followed her to a padded bench against the glass wall, and after she sat, he took the opposite end for himself. "I submit myself to your instruction, Miss Arlen. What would you have me do?"

"Be yourself," she answered without pause, angling her body toward him. "In company, express your own thoughts rather than seeking after hers first. By all means, listen to what she says, but Lady Josephine cannot stand toad-eating."

Everything she said had made sense until that phrase. Luca stared at Miss Arlen, his mind taking her words and turning them over. Had he understood her correctly? What did eating amphibians have to do with anything? Did anyone he knew eat frogs or toads?

He opened his mouth, closed it, and tried once more to understand the English phrase.

"Is something wrong, my lord? You appear confused."

"Did you say—I apologize—but did you say she does not like people who consume toads?"

Miss Arlen had the grace not to laugh, though she momentarily pressed her lips together before speaking. "I suppose that is not a common phrase in Italian. In England, when someone is a false-flatterer, or pretends to agree with everything someone else says in order to win their favor, we call that 'toad-eating.'"

He stared. Considered her explanation. "I still do not understand what toads have to do with flattery."

She laughed then. "I suppose I'm not certain where the phrase came from, either. But that is how it is used."

He muttered a complaint against the English language in Italian, rubbing at his forehead. "I will keep that in mind. No false flattery or pretended agreement to win favor."

"Good." Miss Arlen folded her hands in her lap. "I cannot tell you how often I have seen men and women both do that to Lady Josephine. She cannot abide it. Another thing you must never do is behave as though you have superior knowledge. I do not know a single woman who enjoys a man acting as instructor over her opinion or activities. Not unless she asks. I have watched men explain things to Lady Josephine that she learned in her infancy. Nothing makes her more impatient than someone setting themselves over her as a master."

Did anyone enjoy such arrogant behavior in others? "I can understand that irritation. When I first arrived in England, many spoke to me as though I had lived in the wilds of a forest instead of civilized society."

"As though a difference in primary language meant a difference in your intelligence. Yes, I am afraid it is the same for my sex as a whole." She waved away the topic. "Now, as I said before, I think if you wish to gain Lady Josephine's attention you need only show yourself to advantage."

Luca leaned forward, elbows on his knees, and put his face in his hands. He muttered between his fingers. "*Sono ridicolo.* This is the most ridiculous conversation. I am not a prize horse at an auction."

"Neither is Josephine," Miss Arlen said, tone even and firm. "You are both people with individual goals, thoughts, and talents."

"*Sì,* I know. I only thought this would be simpler."

Miss Arlen tilted her head to an angle which suggested she well understood that he'd revealed something he had not intended her to know. Perhaps she recognized the desperation in his voice. Perhaps she thought him pathetic. What sort of man needed this much assistance in the early stages of a courtship? A foolish one. He ought to forget the whole thing and take a vow of celibacy. The monks who had educated him for five long years would approve.

NEVER HAD EMMA SEEN A MAN AS OPEN AND VULNERABLE AS the *conte*. Lord Atella had not held himself with the arrogance she and Josephine abhorred in others, but he had been closed and solemn. Here she began to understand why. Somehow, the poor man had never learned the trade secrets of Society. In some cases, that would put him at a disadvantage. In others, such as this moment, it made him most endearing.

It was almost a shame that Josephine had no romantic interest in him. She could only count such openness in a husband to his credit.

Perhaps Emma could keep her word to Josephine *and* help Lord Atella.

If she provided a distraction to him by helping him acclimate to the world of flirtations and courtships, she would do him a service. If Josephine liked what came out of it, she might grant Lord Atella an opportunity, at least.

On his end of the bench, the man's entire posture indicated defeat.

"Surely you have entertained a *tendre* for a woman before, my lord," she said, somewhat hesitantly.

"I am afraid there have been few opportunities for me to exchange more than a few pleasantries with the wives and daughters of other dignitaries. I was educated first in a Sicilian monastery and then at the university in Vienna. Then I lived at the Spanish court, learning all I could about the politics between the Two Sicilies and Spain. There has been little time for anything else."

"You have put aside all personal pursuits for your political passion." The single-minded dedication might be admirable, and it explained what she had already observed. "Which means you do not know how to enjoy yourself in a more informal environment." Poor man.

He lifted his head, glancing at her, then abruptly resumed his severe posture and frown. "I enjoy many things outside of the political arena, Miss Arlen."

"Do you enjoy other people?"

He stared at her. "What do you mean by that?"

"Do you enjoy being near people? Interacting with them?"

"I am an ambassador—"

"That is your position, yes." Emma tried to sound encouraging. "Part of your role is to understand people. But do you enjoy being around others? At social functions, at balls, at parties? Or do you only enter each new situation with a view to how to use it politically?"

She saw when he understood, as his eyes slowly widened in comprehension.

"I—I have not ever—that is to say—" He wiped a hand down his face, and his frustration slipped out in his native tongue. "*Sono ridicolo.*"

Emma regarded him quietly, sorting out her initial impression of the *conte* with what she now knew of him. The new picture she formed of him gave her pause. He needed a great deal of help.

"All right. Let us begin with something simple. The picnic yesterday—you enjoyed it?" she asked.

He nodded but did not speak, his gaze trained on the floor.

"And you enjoy literature, based on our previous conversations. And music."

"*Sì, certo,*" he agreed, quietly.

"Then I suppose you are not a complete monster."

His head finally came up, his wide-eyed gaze colliding with hers. Emma grinned at him without reserve, then laughed when his expression relaxed with his understanding.

"And you do not mind when others jest."

"No. Not when it is in good taste." He gestured to her. "But is this enough for English women?"

"For some. Is it enough for Lady Josephine? We will have to see." She stood, and he hastened to do the same. Then Emma crossed her arms and examined him again, peering into his dark eyes. If only she knew of a lady who would suit him. Then she could turn his attentions and his talents in another direction entirely. "Lord Atella, what is something you do well? Something interesting or entertaining. Do you ride? Sketch? Play an instrument?"

"I ride. And I fence. I sing."

"Sing?" Her eyebrows came up. "That could be useful during an evening of music. Fencing is excellent, too. Simon and Andrew both fence, so there would be opportunity to show that off." Emma tapped her fingers along her arm. "There are races in October, the same week that we have our harvest market."

"Harvest market?" He realized the loose lock of his hair had fallen onto his forehead, for he suddenly began to brush at it. Trying to make it stay upon the top of his head.

"Yes. There are markets every month, of course, but this one is special. His Grace always pays for minstrel shows and hosts the games and races."

"That is generous of him, to pay to entertain the entire community." The ambassador dropped his hand to his side. "You think I should race?"

"I do." Emma's grin grew slowly. "Among other things."

For a moment, the man's eyes widened, and she saw in them some measure of alarm. Rather than reassure him, Emma turned away and paced to one of the young trees kept indoors, away from the changeable weather. Let him be uneasy for a time. Perhaps a little more alertness would help him.

"How will doing these things win the favor of Lady Josephine?" he asked while her back was turned.

Emma stroked a leaf on the tree, rubbing its soft velvety texture in her hand, and considered what she might say and still maintain honesty. "You will draw her attention for the best reason —you will enjoy yourself. In short order, you might invite her to join you."

"Is there anything more...?" he asked, sounding plaintive.

"Yes." She turned to him, pulling her shawl tighter. "You are a handsome man, my lord. But everyone's appearance only improves with a cheerful countenance. You always appear solemn. Is there anything that makes your heart lighter?"

When he did not immediately answer, Emma sighed. "Please think on it. Now, if you will excuse me, I had better return to Lady Josephine." She started to curtsy, but he took a step toward her with a hand raised.

"Wait, Miss Arlen. Please. I am lost in these matters. I am not certain what to do next."

"You aren't?" She blinked at him, surprised. "You are to ignore Lady Josephine and enjoy your time at the castle. That is what is next. And do not fear. I will help where I can." She bestowed a final smile upon him. "Until dinner, my lord."

He let her take her leave of him, appearing almost as confused as when they'd first begun their conversation. "Good afternoon, Miss Arlen."

As Emma walked through the castle, making her way back to Lady Josephine's sitting room, she couldn't help thinking on the man. She chewed her bottom lip as she went, a touch of guilt in her heart.

She wasn't hurting anyone. She was helping. Helping Josephine avoid unwanted attention. Helping the *conte* improve his chances in English society. Truly, he seemed a kind man. Honest to the point of vulnerability. Intelligent. Educated.

But in great need of a little whimsy in his life. Something beyond the manly pursuits that served more as a way for men to measure themselves against each other rather than offer real enjoyment. Perhaps she should apply to Andrew for ideas. She didn't know anyone so light-hearted as her cousin.

Then again, Josephine couldn't really stand more than a quarter hour of Andrew's company.

Emma's smile returned with that thought. Perhaps that made Sir Andrew her best possible resource for assisting Lord Atella.

CHAPTER TEN

Sir Andrew didn't seem at all amused by Emma's request. "You are doing what?"

She had ambushed him outside of the billiard room before dinner. They were both in their evening finery, though he had only just replaced his coat. His hair was mussed, artfully so, and his freckles stood out more than usual after his time in the sun the day before. Her cousin always gave off the appearance of being windblown, in Emma's opinion.

"I am helping Lord Atella become more comfortable in our society," she repeated, one fist going to her hip. It wasn't a very ladylike posture, but her cousin hardly cared. "He is a guest in the duke's household. A foreign diplomat. You must see why this is important."

Andrew wrinkled his nose. "He is a grown man and a politician. I doubt he needs the help of a woman barely out of girlhood."

Emma gasped and punched him in the arm with the fist that had been upon her hip. "How dare you? I am one-and-twenty this December, and I am a great deal more mature than *you* will ever be."

"Then why do you need *my* help, little cousin?" he asked, folding his arms and leaning against the doorway to the billiard room. "If you are the paragon of wisdom and maturity."

She scowled at him but disregarded his mockery. "I do not understand why you are resistant. You care about the duke, don't you?" Emma asked, poking her finger into his chest.

For the first time, Andrew appeared thoughtful. "Yes. I respect His Grace, especially for all he's done for you and then for me when my father died. What does that have to do with anything?"

"I just told you." She huffed and dug the finger a little deeper into his chest. The thick coats men wore likely gave him too much padding to make it uncomfortable. Pity. "We want to give Lord Atella a favorable impression of English Society. We want His Grace to be a successful host to an important foreign guest. Some of our ways are strange to him. Will you help me or not?"

The considering stare her cousin fixed her with made Emma shift away, somewhat uncomfortably. If Andrew knew this had anything to do with Josephine, he would outright refuse his help just to antagonize the duke's eldest daughter. If he suspected it had something to do with Lord Atella finding a wife, Andrew might laugh at her and walk away. He was of the opinion no man should marry before the age of forty.

"Very well. Atella seems a good enough fellow. I'll do what I can during my visit to make him feel welcome."

"Good."

"Why aren't you pestering Simon about this?" he asked, standing upright and brushing off his sleeves. "Shouldn't the duke's heir be the one taking this much of an interest in their guest?"

"I am certain Simon is under his father's direction. He likely is more focused on the political aspects of Lord Atella's visit." And Simon wouldn't humor her the way her cousin did.

"Do you think we could go to dinner now?" Andrew gestured

down the hall. "Or do you intend to starve me by keeping me out in the hall?"

Emma looped her arm through his. "I am not without mercy, dear cousin. Let us go to our meal." They were nearly to the parlor, talking of other things, when Josephine turned a corner ahead of them. She looked beautiful as ever, with her hair piled high and flowers peeping out from her curls.

Andrew stiffened when Josie joined them on Emma's free side, but he didn't do more than nod a greeting to her.

Honestly, these two. Emma refrained from making the comment out loud, but only just. Her two dearest friends always being at odds made it difficult to enjoy herself with them. All she could do was ignore the tense atmosphere they created.

"Has your father finalized his plans for the harvest races?" Emma asked, knowing the subject would please both of them.

Josephine's posture relaxed, and she released a light laugh. "I believe he has spoken to the squire and the innkeeper, and the orders have gone to the kitchens. I think Father enjoys the event more than anyone, given how far in advance he sets the plans in motion."

"Good. I was telling Lord Atella about the events this afternoon."

"Is that where you disappeared to? I wondered. I thought for certain you would want to spend a few hours with me reminiscing on Mr. Gardiner and Alice's wedding." Josephine's eyes brightened at the same moment they passed through the doors to the parlor. "They appeared absolutely radiant with their happiness."

"How long do you think it will last?" Andrew asked, and Emma immediately jabbed him in the side with her elbow. He didn't even give her the satisfaction of appearing affronted, only stepped out of her reach and released her arm. "It's a fair question. They are enamored with each other *now*, but will the level of affection remain at such a high point?"

SALLY BRITTON

Josephine glowered at him. "You obviously know nothing about love."

"And you know so much more?" he countered, smirking down at her.

Emma's head started to ache. She knew all the signs of their verbal battles, and she had lost the patience for them years ago. Rather than stay standing between the two as they exchanged fire at one another, she crossed the room to where Lord Atella stood with his secretary.

"Lord Atella, Mr. Torlonia. Good evening." She dipped a curtsy, and when she rose, Torlonia was already peering behind her.

"Is your mistress upset this evening, Miss Arlen?" the secretary asked, frowning darkly.

"Not at all." She cast an amused smile to Lord Atella, whose expression held curiosity. "My lady and my cousin often spar verbally before a meal. I am under the impression it increases their appetites."

The secretary wrinkled his nose. "The ways of youth, *ci credo.*" He sniffed and gestured to one of the visiting barons. "*Mi scusi, signorina.* I must continue a conversation with Baron Ghellen." He cast a look to the ambassador. "Are you joining me, *Signore?*"

Lord Atella shook his head, his expression firm as ever. "Not at present."

The secretary's frown deepened, but he bowed and departed from them.

"He is most serious," Emma murmured, taking her fan from her wrist to snap it open. The room was quite warm, given that the duke had twenty guests currently inside of it. The duke himself stood in a corner with his mother. "I think your secretary would get on well with our dowager duchess. They have matching scowls."

For one incredible moment, Lord Atella laughed. He quickly

108

strangled the sound with a cough and a gloved fist over his mouth. But the hint of sound had been enough for Emma to decide he ought to laugh more. If only she could inspire more levity in the man.

"He means well," Lord Atella told her, tucking his hands behind his back and appearing as solemn as ever. "But I think he has forgotten we have months ahead of us in the castle rather than days. While it is true we have much to accomplish and learn, we need not rush through the experience."

"I would think your primary aim would mean speaking with those possessing a more direct influence over foreign trade and tariffs." Emma considered Baron Ghellen and the secretary in animated conversation with each other across the room. "I cannot think the baron troubles himself over such things. In a fortnight, Viscount Castlereagh comes to visit. Have you met him yet?" The British Secretary of State for Foreign Affairs wasn't known to visit many house parties. His drop in general popularity made him reclusive, Emma knew, from reading the duke's newspapers.

Only the duke's reputation for fairness could draw out a man used to being mocked in newspapers by caricatures and verse.

She looked up when the ambassador didn't answer at once. He stared down at her, his eyebrows raised. "I have not had the pleasure."

"Given Lord Castlereagh's sympathies toward those nations Napoleon harmed most, I think he would take great interest in speaking to you of your countrymen and their hopes. Especially with the close connection to Spain that your kingdom enjoys."

"You do not think his lack of popularity—as you call it—would make such a connection unwanted?"

"Public figures must weather the worst of a nation's blame and censure." Emma moved to stand shoulder-to-shoulder with him, the bare skin of her upper arm nearly brushing his sleeve. "Those in positions of influence understand this. He still has many friends, the Prime Minister among them."

The *conte* did not speak immediately, but she felt his eyes upon her profile. Emma lowered her head on the pretense of examining her fan as she flicked it closed, then open again. What must he think of her, a little no one in the wide world of politics, offering *him* advice? He—whose entire career revolved around knowing the personal lives and political views of everyone around him—could not possibly care for her opinion on such matters. Even if the duke enjoyed engaging her in debates now and again, that did not mean any other man would take an interest in what she had to say.

"Thank you, Miss Arlen. Your insight is helpful."

Emma raised her head, nearly squeaking in her surprise. "Really?" Then she hastily forced a laugh. "I am afraid I give my opinions too freely, my lord. Thank you for humoring me."

His eyebrows lowered sharply, and he opened his mouth either to protest her words or reassure her. She did not find out which.

"Dinner is served," the duchess's clear voice sung through the room.

Emma tilted her head down again, curtsied, and stepped away from the ambassador. Unmarried and untitled, she waited for the man of the lowest rank to escort her into dinner. Her place at the bottom of the social ladder usually comforted her. That evening, watching as Lord Atella escorted a visiting noblewoman into the dining hall ahead of her, Emma's stomach twisted uncomfortably.

How many times would the lines blur as she tried to keep both the *conte* and Josephine happy? The months stretched ahead of her, longer than before and far more intimidating.

CHAPTER ELEVEN

The mount Luca had borrowed from Lord Farleigh danced impatiently to the side, not fond of the slow pace Luca and Sir Andrew had set. They rode across the duke's lands, up one rolling hill and down another, passing sheep and orchards both. The baronet had invited Luca out to enjoy the crisp fall air, and the trees in the surrounding land had filled more of their branches with orange and gold than Luca had seen in the previous week.

They had spoken little, despite how close they rode to one another. Luca's thoughts lingered on Torlonia's frustrated conversation after dinner the previous evening. His secretary had sputtered indignantly when he'd learned Luca had taken the advice of a *mere woman* over his trusted advisor, appointed by the king himself. Never mind how sound the advice had seemed in the moment Miss Arlen had given it.

Luca paused at the crest of a hill, looking out over farmland rolling away from their location, most of it empty, though some fields bore wheat meant to be harvested later in the season.

Sir Andrew brought his horse to a halt as well. The baronet wore an unusually sober countenance, his jaw tight, as though he contemplated weighty matters of his own.

Riding along in silence, and at a tortoise's pace, couldn't keep up all afternoon.

"My cousin is unusually fond of you."

Luca's horse flinched at the sound of the baronet's voice. Luca nearly did the same.

"Miss Arlen?" Luca spared himself a moment's thought by calming the horse with a pat along its powerful neck. "She is kind to a man who is a stranger among you. I am most grateful." He had no intention of sharing the fact that he had won her help in his pursuit of another lady. What man would admit to such a thing?

"Excessively kind," Sir Andrew muttered, adjusting his seat on the horse. "Did you know I am her closest kin? Her mother was sister to my father. I think, had I not lost my own mother, Emma would've come to live with us when her parents died, instead of joining the duke's household. But my father felt unequal to raising both a son and a niece without a woman in his home."

The personal revelations were unwarranted. Yet, when Luca thought of the vulnerability of his own sisters when it came to gentlemen, he understood. Every gentleman with a female relative ought to do his duty in protecting them. Sir Andrew's invitation came into the appropriate perspective at last.

"You are close to her." Luca spoke gently. "I understand. I must reassure you that my intentions are—how do you English say it?—honorable. I want nothing more than friendship, which Miss Arlen has offered. She pities me, I think."

Sir Andrew's eyebrows shot up. "Pities you? I doubt it. Emma might seem all sweetness and contentment, but that woman has ambition of her own. And a mind sharper than most. If she has befriended you, then I am willing to wager she has reasons beyond friendship."

Although the other man's suspicion likely had root in knowing his cousin well, Luca had to shake his head. "I cannot think what she would gain from helping me that she could not do without our association. Her mind, as you say, is sharp. I have seen ample evidence of this already. If anything, she only wishes to support the duke's efforts to see me comfortable during my stay."

Sir Andrew grunted a grudging agreement. "Perhaps." Then he pointed his horse back toward the castle, which rose high enough on its hill for them to see it above the trees. "Fancy a race back to the stables? Your horse certainly does."

"I have barely kept this beast in check." Luca wheeled his mount around, too. "Lord Farleigh likes his animals spirited."

"Lord Farleigh is competitive and likes to win races." Sir Andrew's countenance lightened somewhat. "Shall we make a wager on ours?"

"I am not a gambling man." Luca made the admission somewhat reluctantly. Every English lord he'd met placed wagers on the oddest things. He'd even heard of gambling books kept in London clubs filled with wagers on everything from drops of water falling down windowpanes to how long a man would court a woman before proposing. Luca's time among the monks had taught him a stricter morality and an aversion to excess that his English contemporaries did not practice.

"A prize, then?" Sir Andrew's horse nickered impatiently, and Luca's mount responded in kind.

That was acceptable. Luca nodded. "What sort of prize?"

"A favor, to be named by the winner and be paid by the loser, at the victor's pleasure. We'll add the stipulation that the favor can be nothing immoral or dishonorable. How does that suit?" The scheming gleam in the baronet's eye clearly relayed his confidence in victory.

The coiled muscles of the horse beneath him, its energy in every twitch of ear and stamp of hoof, gave Luca a matching faith in his borrowed mount. "Very well. I accept your challenge, prize, and stipulations. You may call the start."

"On three." Sir Andrew's open expression as he called out the start was all eagerness. "One. Two. Three!"

The two of them gave their horses leave to leap forward at last, the animals snorting and tossing their heads before stretching their necks and stride into a gallop. The animals were well-matched, with neither pulling much ahead of the other as they dipped into small valleys and up again through the hills. The castle was nearly always in sight.

What had taken half an hour of a leisurely pace they covered again in mere minutes, clods of dirt flying up behind them, the men bent low over their horses.

Freedom from the confines of Luca's former life felt like this. Riding with abandon, the ground speeding by beneath him and the wind tugging at his coat, reminded him to enjoy *living*. At least in that moment.

When they came to the winding drive leading to the castle stables, Luca encouraged a last burst of strength from his mount, shouting in Italian. *"Dai, sbrigati!"*

They pulled ahead of the baronet—and won.

Luca laughed, rubbing the horse's neck while it whinnied and shook its head, its sides lightly coated in sweat.

Sir Andrew didn't appear the least upset by his loss. He wore his usual grin, looking every bit as pleased as if he had won, and congratulated Luca before dismounting. The two of them left their horses in the care of the stables and started the walk up the hill, passing the practice ring and a flurry of grooms as they walked through one of the lower gardens.

The castle was practically its own village with the number of people constantly moving about the estate, working to ensure the duke's home ran as it should, seeing to all things necessary for His Grace and the comfort of his guests.

Gardeners worked on trimming hedges and covering roots with mosses and straw, preparing the delicate plants for winter, while others planted flowers meant to bloom through the autumn and winter. The sheer size of it all made Luca's home feel small by comparison. His family had a small estate on an unremarkable hilltop with a sleepy village at its base.

"Oh, Lord Atella. There you are."

Luca had barely stepped inside, stripping off his gloves and hat to hand them to a footman. Sir Andrew did the same, and he responded before Luca could.

"And where is my greeting, cousin?"

Miss Arlen cocked an unimpressed eyebrow at Sir Andrew. "You probably do not deserve to be acknowledged today. You have a look of mischief about you that means I must be on my guard." Despite her words, she came forward and tucked her hand through Sir Andrew's arm. "Had you a good ride?"

"Yes, until Lord Atella bested me in a race. I owe him a forfeit now."

"Poor you." She turned her wide smile to Luca. "You must take full advantage of having my cousin in your debt, my lord. He is surprisingly useful."

The footmen had left with their things, giving Luca little to do with his hands other than tug at the sleeves of his coat. He likely smelled of horse, though why that should bother him in Miss Arlen's presence, he did not know.

Luca attempted to join their banter, though uncertainty made his posture taut. "Perhaps I will seek your counsel before I decide how best to claim the debt."

Sir Andrew laughed and started walking, guiding them all down the long hall of black and white marble, up to the first staircase. "I beg of you, my lord, do not encourage Emma's tormenting ways."

"Nonsense. I rarely ever torment you." Emma raised her gaze to Luca on her other side. "Can you imagine I have any power over my cousin, my lord?"

Despite his awkward stiffness, Luca had to chuckle. He could picture the petite woman forcing her cousin into all sorts of trouble with nothing more than a few coaxing words. She had a talent, an air about her, that made him think her capable of achieving many feats through will and humor alone.

"I dare not contradict you, Miss Arlen. Nor give your cousin reason to think less of me by agreeing with you."

"Ever the politician," she responded with a dramatic sigh. "Very well. I will not force you to take sides." She pulled Sir Andrew to a halt. "Here I must part ways with you both. I am to wait upon Her Grace, my lady's grandmother."

Sir Andrew released her arm before crossing his own. "Ah, the dowager. What lessons has she to teach you today?"

Luca raised his eyebrows, wondering why Miss Arlen would have an audience with the dowager duchess. She hadn't seemed overly fond of Her Grace when they spoke of the woman. She met his gaze and laughed.

"You needn't worry, my lord. She is not such a dragon all the time. Today, I am to read to her. While this would normally be a duty for Lady Josephine, the dowager says she does not like how my lady fidgets when reading."

Sir Andrew snorted, though whether the situation annoyed or amused him was difficult to tell. "Josephine never can sit still for long."

"I do not blame her. Her Grace's suite has the most uncomfortable chairs." Miss Arlen met Luca's gaze. "And they have vastly different tastes in books. Her Grace much prefers titles written by noble pens. Her current favorite is a French tale, *La Belle et la Bête,* by a noblewoman."

"A fairy tale?" Luca had heard of it. A French masterpiece, popular with the court in the prior century.

She grinned at him. "*Oui,* Lord Atella. In this one thing the dowager duchess and I share our taste. We are excessively fond of stories with wicked fairies and princes in disguise."

"Lady Josephine much prefers modern tales and comedic romances," Sir Andrew said with a grimace. "Give her a silly heroine and she is all the more pleased." He shook his head, then bowed to his cousin. "Good luck, Emma. I hope the dragon finds your reading favorable enough that she puts off eating you for another day."

Miss Arlen waved her cousin away, and he left without caring that Luca remained behind.

The woman looked up at Luca, her smile smaller, though by no means less pleasant. Her expression softened, and she may have spoken had he not blurted his question first.

"Is she unkind to you?" Luca shifted, uncomfortably aware the answer wasn't any of his business. "Her Grace?"

Miss Arlen blinked at him, her expression turning to one of confusion. "Not at all, though she is certainly disapproving of me from time to time. When I was much younger, she accused me of only being kind to Lady Josephine because of my lady's money. She thought I manipulated Lady Josephine to spend her pocket money on me."

That made Luca wince. "An insulting accusation, no matter your age."

"Indeed. I became aware of that accusation, though it wasn't made to me directly, and confronted her. I did feel like I faced a dragon on that occasion."

"How old were you?"

"Thirteen." She shrugged one shoulder, letting the past discomfort fall from her, given the way her expression brightened. "I told her I used my own pin money for everything I wanted, as His Grace gave me a most generous allowance, and that I would sooner swallow a bee than have anyone think I did not love Josephine for her own sake."

"Did she believe you?"

Miss Arlen tilted her head to one side, and a loose curl fell from behind her ear to brush her neck. "She never spoke of it again. I rather hope she was ashamed of herself, accusing a mere child of such a thing. Doubtless there are those who would take advantage of a position like mine, but one would hope she would better assess my character before voicing such horrid thoughts to others."

Luca had faced similar accusations in the past. Many in King Ferdinand's court had supposed him to curry favor of their monarch for his own benefit rather than out of a sincere desire to improve the kingdom for the sake of all its inhabitants.

"That you bear her no ill will after she questioned your honor is commendable," he muttered, thinking of the snide expressions his peers had worn when he'd been made an ambassador. He hadn't forgiven any of them. Only determined that he would stop at nothing to prove them wrong.

"She was not the first to question my position in the household. Nor will she be the last. Until Lady Josephine weds or has no more use for me, I will always face that censure." The flicker in her eyes, the determined tilt of her chin, tugged yet more admiration from him.

Before he could say another word on the subject, she composed her expression to something bordering on business-like. "When I looked for you earlier, I had hoped to arrange a walk with you through the garden. I should like to tell you more about Josephine. But the day is nearly over. Perhaps we may take a walk tomorrow morning?"

"I am afraid I am scheduled to accompany His Grace to visit a member of the House of Commons. A Mr. Hart."

"Oh, I see." Her enthusiasm momentarily dimmed. "Beware of his eldest daughter. She is only sixteen, but she is a most determined flirt. You will take dinner with the Hart family, I assume?"

"Yes." He blinked at her. "Do you know all your neighbors so well, Miss Arlen?"

Her smile reappeared with a crooked bit of mischief to it. "Of course, my lord. Here and in London. People fascinate me, so I make it a habit to study them."

"And me?" he asked, trying her trick of raising a single

eyebrow, but failing to do more than wince with one eye. "What do you find in studying me?"

She took a step backward, tapped her bottom lip with one finger, and raised that single eyebrow with perfect natural ability. "I cannot share my findings yet, Lord Atella. But I will continue to observe and let you know my discoveries another time. As it is, I am late to meet a dragon." She curtsied. "We will have our walk another day."

He instinctively bowed, and she strode away down the long corridor before he could think of anything clever to say.

CHAPTER TWELVE

Emma couldn't decide how best to approach the next step in her plan to lure the ambassador out of his staid and stiff posture. She had caught enough glimpses of his wit and humor to know that he had a spirit more playful than stern. The poor *conte* had obviously been trained by life to act the part of a man several times his own age.

She finally managed to schedule a walk with him a few days into October. That in itself was a feat, considering she never found him alone.

The day's weather didn't prove ideal for such a *rendezvous*, given the icy wind coming down from the north. She bundled up in her favorite winter dress with its long sleeves and added a pair of boots and a lined straw bonnet. For good measure, she wrapped a thin blue scarf around her neck.

Though she might not look the part of a fashion plate, Emma couldn't help but be pleased as she examined herself in the mirror prior to her walk.

A knock on the door interrupted her perusal of her curls. Ought she to tug one or two loose to frame her face more prettily?

Not that it mattered much to anything other than her own vanity. She wasn't trying to impress the *conte* the least bit.

"Come in," she called.

Josephine came through the door, a light skip to her step. "You aren't going outside," she exclaimed. "The weather is positively ghastly. That wind could lift your bonnet off your head."

"I plan to stay in the hedge garden. The shrubbery will take the brunt of the breeze." Emma turned to take in Josephine's comfortable dress and shawl. "I am walking with Lord Atella today, since I know your grandmother intends to keep you on display in the duchess's salon."

"Oh, thank you." Josephine fell into a chair, heaving a grateful sigh. "I cannot tell you how much I want to make my escape, but Mama has noticed my scarcity and says it is not polite to our guests. If she were more insistent, I would think her in league with Papa or Grandmama in trying to marry me off."

Rather than protest—again—that no one had any such designs at present, Emma turned back to the mirror. "What would you rather be doing?"

"Nothing special." Josephine picked at the edges of a cushion, her eyes lowered most suspiciously so that Emma could not see them in the mirror's reflection. Her interest immediately piqued.

"I know you are avoiding the *conte*, quite successfully I might add. But even I am having a difficult time finding you when I wish. Where have you been sneaking off to lately?"

"Sneaking off? Me?" Josephine's voice rose in her innocent denial, which Emma marked as a sure sign of deceit. "I have been nowhere other than where I'm supposed to be."

"Mm." Emma turned and put both hands on her hips. "I know you better than anyone, Josie. You aren't doing anything inappropriate, are you? No meetings with stable boys or gardeners?"

Josephine laughed freely at that. "No! Can you imagine? Father would send me away to a convent—and we aren't even Catholic." She snuggled into the chair, plucking up the cushion to hold it over her middle. "There are no men involved in my secret —and yes, I *do* have a secret. I promise I will tell you all about it soon. I only wish to keep it to myself a little longer."

Although tempted to nettle her friend until Josephine revealed all, Emma let the matter rest with that promise. She trusted Josephine. That would be enough for the time being.

She found her gloves in her bureau and tugged them on. "You had better be on your way. I will only be able to keep Lord Atella at bay for so long, especially given the wind outside."

"You are marvelous in your sacrifice." Josephine stood and dropped the cushion back in place. "I will owe you a thousand favors for this."

"Not at all. His company isn't truly horrible. If it were, I would not be so willing a sacrifice."

Josephine laughed and accompanied Emma out of the room, though they parted ways long before Josephine met Lord Atella at one of the castle doors leading out to the gardens. He had dressed as warmly as she, his elderberry coat of fine wool making her rather envious for a moment. Men's clothing always looked warmer than what women might commission from their seamstresses.

He appeared as skeptical of her costume weathering the elements as she was. "Will you be warm enough, Miss Arlen? We could limit ourselves to the conservatory, if you prefer."

Then they would only have a quarter of an hour in a room where anyone might interrupt or overhear them. No, they must brave the wind if Emma had any hope of keeping him away from the salon long enough for Josie to appear and disappear.

"I will be warm enough, my lord, though I thank you for your concern." She tucked the ends of her scarf more tightly beneath the neck of her coat. "A little wind will do us no harm."

He politely offered his arm to her, which she took with gratitude. The additional warmth of human touch, limited though it was, would be of help.

They left the castle through a side door and crossed the open lawn along a broad pebbled walk. An opening between two hedges let them into the first level of gardens, just below the castle with stone steps taking them down into the rose garden. Here, four different paths met at a small fountain, which they skirted to continue downhill.

They passed beneath trees and hedges both, and the wind that had nipped at their heels tapered off. The *conte* slowed their pace.

"The day began with such promise," he said, looking through the branches above them. "A blue sky, a bright sun."

"That is the way of things in England. The weather is most unpredictable, and one must always consider whether to carry an umbrella." Emma released his arm to check that her bonnet remained correct atop her head. Josephine hadn't exaggerated the effect that the force of the wind might have upon her headpiece.

The ambassador tucked his hands behind his back and looked down at his boot-tips. "Your cousin has kept me company many times the last several days. Do I have you to thank for that?"

Emma nearly denied having anything to do with Andrew's sudden friendliness, but one look at the ambassador's shrewd expression made her give the idea up. "I did ask that he treat you with hospitality. Is he a great nuisance? Shall I call him off?"

"I must admit that I did not care for him at first." The ambassador's lips tilted upward at one corner. "I find that I enjoy his sense of humor. He has a playful nature."

"He does." Emma tied her bonnet ribbons tighter beneath her chin. "He likes people, too."

They said nothing as they turned a corner on the path, passing deeper into the hedges. Emma had prepared herself to offer counsel, but it took her a little more time than she thought it would to arrange the introduction of the topic. Lord Atella said little, though he kicked the occasional pebble out of his path.

He spoke first, delaying her presentation of her idea further.

"I received a large trunk from my family yesterday."

"Oh, yes. I did hear about that." Emma snatched onto this topic happily. "Is your family well?"

"Yes. They are quite content. One of my sisters, the second of the three, is now engaged to be married." His expression softened, from the gentle press of his lips to the light in his eyes. "To a friend of mine I met during my time at the Austrian university. He is a fine man. I think they will be happy together."

"Are you sorry you will miss the wedding?" she asked, lowering her gaze to the walk. "I cannot imagine you could return home soon enough to suit them."

"No. It would not be practical. Instead, I will send them gifts. Many, many gifts. And a letter to my friend filled with the dire consequences he will suffer if my sister is not happy."

Emma's gaze shot to his like an arrow, her mouth gaping, and then she saw a glint in his eye that she had only glimpsed before. The man had made a joke. She laughed, as surprised by his efforts as amused by them. "You are a fierce protector."

He nodded sharply, a smile teasing at his lips again. "Very fierce. A lion in the defense of my family."

"A lion." She cocked her head to the side, pretending to appraise him. "Do lions wear such fine suits, my lord?"

He held out his arms and looked down at his clothing. "I suppose they must. How else do they command the respect of all the other creatures?"

"I generally thought it would be through roaring and gnashing teeth."

"Hardly polite. Not at all befitting an ambassador."

She shook her head. "An ambassador lion would be rather ridiculous."

He chuckled and faced forward again. "I cannot think they have the ability to compromise, which is necessary for one in my position."

"Ah. So you are the first of your kind. A politically intelligent lion. I would not tell the Regent. I have heard he rather likes adding exotic creatures to his menagerie."

Lord Atella's remarkably charming smile rewarded her silliness. Had he finally grown easy enough in her company that she would see more of that expression?

"Then I am even more grateful for the things my family sent me, if I am to be locked up in a menagerie. The trunk—everything in it was like a taste of my homeland."

Of course—Emma bit the inside of her cheeks. It was his family that had put him in good humor, not her banter. The poor man *would* cheer up with word from home. She turned away from him, down a path that went deeper into the trees.

The leaves overhead trembled with the breeze. There was only one place in the garden where they might be completely free of the wind. She led them that direction.

"You must miss your family."

"Very much." He fell into step beside her. "They also sent many things I could give as gifts to those who are my hosts. Seeds from our gardens. Books of poetry. Perfumes made from my mother's roses. Instructions—*ricettas*—for food from our kitchens."

Emma supplied the English word without pause. "Recipes."

"Recipes, *ecco la parola giusta*." He moved closer to her when the wind whipped around them, dipping his head to hold on to his hat. "This is not a day for a walk, *Signorina* Arlen."

"We are nearly at a more protected garden." A break in the trees revealed a stone grotto tucked into the hedges. Emma pointed at the small, dome-shaped building. "The duchess's garden. Have you seen it yet?"

"No." Several leaves fell from above, twisting as the wind snatched them away. "The building is a garden?"

"An entrance. Come." Emma hastened her steps, one hand clamping the bonnet to her head while the other snatched at his sleeve. "Hurry, before the wind dashes us to pieces!" Then she laughed, to assure him she wasn't the least bit worried, and ran forward.

The grotto was artificial, built to look like an old stone hovel with ivy growing up around its sides. They passed through it, the echoes of their footfalls bouncing off smooth walls, and then they came through to the other side. The garden had been created in a natural dip in the landscape, surrounded by a wall covered in vines on the inside and hidden by tall hedges and trees on the outside.

In the duchess's private garden, everything was silent. A tranquility rested within its walls, the wind kept out, and Emma stood still to drink in the moment's peace. She glanced up at Lord Atella, noting with pleasure the shock upon his face. Even in the autumn, when most of the plants and flowers had been put to bed by the gardeners, it was a beautiful place.

"The garden was a gift," she told him, keeping her voice soft. "After the duke and duchess married, she found out that his mother had fashioned most of the estate's gardens to her specific desires. She wanted to keep the peace with her mother-in-law and did not make any changes to a single seedling. Then one day the duke brought her to the walled-in garden and gave it to her to do whatever she wished with it."

He spoke with reverence. "It is a beautiful gift. The duke must care for his wife's happiness."

"From what I have seen, there is more to it than care and kindness. They have a genuine regard for one another, the likes of which those of high birth find so rarely." Emma blinked when his gaze met hers, his expression stern once more.

"Because most of high birth marry for other reasons, yes?"

"Yes." She lifted her head and walked deeper into the garden. Though they were out of doors, the privacy they enjoyed could also be their downfall if she did not keep them in motion. Not that she thought anyone in the duke's household would force anything upon her if they were found in such innocent circumstances. But one must consider appearances.

"I have been thinking about other ways you might impress Josephine." Emma immediately chastised herself for blurting out what she'd been trying to say with more tact. Subtlety wasn't usually this difficult for her. She bit her own tongue and hoped Lord Atella wouldn't think her odd.

THE QUIET OF THE GARDEN HAD SUNK INTO LUCA'S SOUL, easing the muscles in his shoulders and the tautness of his thoughts. Until Miss Arlen mentioned her mistress to him. Yes. Lady Josephine. He needed to impress her.

"But still from a distance," he said, measuring the words carefully. He had kept his distance, as Miss Arlen suggested, not going out of his way to speak to or be in company with the duke's daughter.

"Yes." Her smile returned briefly, and her eyes dimmed as she disappeared into her thoughts. "The race at the harvest market is one place where all eyes will be upon you, even hers, but there are other things we might do. Lady Josephine and I were discussing Sicily and Rome, and how it would be wonderful to travel there one day. She mentioned that she has had the cuisine of your homeland only rarely. French cooking is what most households serve when they wish to impress His Grace's family."

Such a simple thing to note, a detail he might not have picked up himself in conversation, but his mind followed Miss Arlen's course with enthusiasm.

"Perhaps if I provide a Sicilian menu to the duke's cook, we could enjoy an evening feasting on meals from my homeland—"

"Thus putting you at the center of the evening." She finished the thought for him, coming out of her thoughts and wearing a look of such pleasure that he smiled merely to see it. "You said your family sent recipes."

"Sheets and sheets of them." Luca paced from her to a tall, thin-branched tree, looking up into its bright orange leaves. *"Pasta al pesto e pesce.* My favorite meal." He turned to find her watching him. "Other courses, too. I will give them all to the cook, after I speak to Her Grace about taking over her dining table."

When Miss Arlen laughed, her cheeks turned a soft shade of pink. "I am delighted at your enthusiasm. Most men would think arranging a menu beneath them."

"Pah." He made the same sound his mother made when she felt particularly dismissive. "In my country, food is a language of its own. Everyone must speak it, consider it, and enjoy it. Our breads, sauces, pasta. It is important."

She came to stand beneath the tree, leaning against its trunk as she watched him speak. "Does everyone feel that way about it?"

He shrugged. "There is pride in providing food for the table. Only the monks I lived with did not express it so—but even they said that food ought to be prepared with joy and thanksgiving. There are some dishes that tell our whole history." He paused, studying her expression. "I am boring you, *sicuramente.* The English do not care so much."

She arched one eyebrow at him. "I am not the least bored, my lord."

A breeze passed far overhead, loosening the leaves at the top of the tree enough that a few fluttered down, flickering like flames in the air around them. Luca put a hand to one low limb, steadying himself as his mind reached backward to the lessons he had learned at tables heavily laden and those nearly bare.

"When Rome was the capital of the world, so much wealth came from agriculture. From grain, used to make bread. Then Christianity rose while Rome declined, and the Holy Sacrament taught us to see our Lord's sacrifice in the bread we ate to live. Grain is a symbol of prosperity. When my people learned of pasta

—of eating it fresh, of preparing it with few ingredients, and the possibility of drying it for storage and travel—we took it into our lives and upon our tables with enthusiasm. Even the poorest family can find enough flour, a little salt, eggs, and make a meal that will feed their children and fill them."

He caught a leaf as it fell through the air and twirled it idly between his fingers. "There is even a factory in Venice—far from my home, but I have heard of it—that makes pasta in enormous batches and sells it on the streets and exports it to other countries."

"How incredible. I cannot think of any way that we distribute food on such a scale." She came closer, no longer leaning against the tree but peering up into his face with her wide, intelligent eyes. "Pasta is a sign of prosperity."

"Yes, but there is more." Luca opened his arms, his hands gesturing as he spoke—a habit learned from his father. "When you sit at a table in my country, it is a show of trust. No decisions are made between neighbors who have not first broken bread together. When you are invited to eat with a family, it is a show of acceptance. Even affection." He paused with one hand still in the air, looking down into her gaze and finding curiosity and interest.

"Affection?" she repeated. "Food shows affection? The French believe it is an art form, and so do the English. A meal on a well-laid table is a chance to impress others."

He snorted. "I have noticed." Then he realized his mistake and hastily lowered his arms, resuming the appropriate posture of a diplomat. An imitation of an English lord's stance. "Forgive me. I forget myself. I meant no disrespect—"

She made a dismissive gesture with one hand. "I am learning, my lord. You are introducing me to your culture. Is that not what an ambassador is meant to do?"

Luca gazed into her earnest expression, her eyes lively with interest, and leaned closer to her. "You would be amazed at the food upon my family's table, *Signorina* Arlen. My mother, though a fine lady, watches over the kitchen with care. Sometimes, she prepares our favorite pastas alongside our cook."

"Do you know how to make it, too?" she asked, and Luca realized quite suddenly how close they stood.

Close enough that they shared the same breath.

Close enough that if he leaned forward only a little more and if she tilted her chin upward a mere inch—

Too close. They were too close.

He stepped back, confused at his wandering thoughts. She remained silent. Waiting for him to speak.

What had she asked?

Oh, yes. Did he know how to make pasta?

"I have seen it done many times." But he had never done it himself. He had watched in his mother's kitchen as a boy, then watched the monks while he took on the less important kitchen duties that would not dishonor the son of a prominent family. "I could do it, I think," he muttered, rubbing at the back of his neck.

Had he nearly kissed *Signorina* Arlen? The flicker of thought had come and gone so quickly.

Because we were talking about food, he told himself firmly. Somehow, speaking of his native food had brought about a moment of passion. Passion for food. Not for kissing. For tasting the cuisine of his home country. Not tasting *Signorina* Arlen.

What would kissing her taste like?

The sudden curiosity alarmed him. He needed to court Lady Josephine. That could not be done if he entertained ideas of kissing her lady's companion.

"That is a singularly wonderful idea," she murmured quietly.

Luca whirled around. Had he spoken aloud? "Idea? *Che idea?*" He felt the tips of his ears burning and hoped his hair hid them from view. Cursed reaction—he thought he had left that behind in childhood.

"You could make a portion of the pasta," Miss Arlen said with a wave of her hand, her gaze directed elsewhere. "Think of it—you could tell all the duke's dinner guests of how you made it. The traditions behind it. Not only would that be an impressive thing for you personally, but would it not further your goals as ambassador? It would show how you trust the duke, preparing food for his table. A strong political gesture."

"A political gesture," he repeated dumbly. She was talking about pasta. Not kissing. Good. But— "You want me to make pasta?"

"Or at least oversee the process." She faced him again, brimming with excitement given the way she bounced forward on her toes. "Lord Atella, the idea is marvelous. Might I accompany you to watch the pasta be made?"

He considered the request as well as he could, his mind muddled. All the talk of food had confused him. Had he eaten breakfast? Had tea? He couldn't remember. Perhaps he was only hungry. "You—yes. I suppose—"

"Thank you. This will be marvelous. Then I can tell Lady Josephine about it, too. But first you must speak to the duchess, and then the cook, to have things arranged." She shivered and wrapped her arms about herself. "I think that is enough planning for this afternoon. There is no need to rush things."

"No need," he murmured in agreement. "Then ought I escort you back to the castle?"

"I think that would be best. Those clouds look like they wish to make it rain." She pointed upward to the west, where light gray clouds had been replaced by obvious thunderheads.

"Then we had best hurry," he said, and gestured for her to precede him through the grotto entrance. They did not speak again, with the wind snatching away their very breath and the threat of rain imminent, until they parted ways in the corridor, with servants taking their things.

Luca went to his room directly after making his polite bow. He retrieved his book from its locked drawer, opened it to the pages where he recorded his progress with Lady Josephine, and wrote a stern note to himself.

Courting a lady cannot begin by kissing her companion.

He underlined it. Twice, for good measure.

Then he leaned back in his chair and stared at the ceiling, his thoughts melting away until only one concern remained.

"I agreed to make pasta." He groaned and covered his face with one hand. "*Sono scemo.* A complete fool."

And that was the one thing he couldn't afford to be seen as by anyone—a fool.

CHAPTER THIRTEEN

Josephine laughed far too much when Emma revealed the outcome of her *tête-à-tête* with the ambassador. And she laughed again on the afternoon appointed for the pasta-making. To the point that Emma finally threw a cushion at her friend's face. Josephine caught the cushion before it fell to the floor, then threw herself onto Emma's bed while Emma sat at her desk writing a letter.

"You cannot blame me for laughing. You have put the poor man in a horrid position. However did you get him to agree to *cook*?" She giggled and rolled onto her side to stare at Emma with widened eyes. "Can you imagine what an Englishman would've done had you suggested such a thing? You would have been put out of polite society."

Emma scoffed and signed the letter to the new Mrs. Gardiner with a flourish. "They would have treated the suggestion as a jest. Lord Atella seemed genuinely interested in the idea, though." All to impress Lady Josephine. Who only laughed.

The momentary irritation Emma felt toward her friend bothered her. She folded the letter. It would go through the regular post, as the duke did not frank the personal letters of the household—though he certainly could have gotten away with it.

"What is the point of having a national mail system if we are never to use it properly?" he had said on more than one occasion when a member of the family muttered about the expense of sending and receiving letters.

"Do you wish to come to the kitchen with me?" Emma asked, not meeting Josephine's eye, instead folding her letter carefully.

"That would rather defeat the purpose of the event." Josephine threw a pillow in the air and caught it again. "I am entertaining Grandmama and her friends this afternoon in the music room. If Lord Atella wasn't already engaged to *cook*, he would have been invited. Once again, you have spared me."

"He isn't all that terrible," Emma murmured quietly.

"Of course he isn't. He is an ambassador." Josephine tossed and caught the pillow again and again as she spoke, her tone one of boredom. "He knows precisely what to say to be agreeable to everyone in the room. That is the role of a politician, be they noble or gentry, foreign or domestic. They make friends with everyone, ask for favors, and all to further their own interests."

All true. Emma had heard the duke caution his children with similar words as he prepared them for their roles in Society—a society that thrived on connection and favors. Emma knew the lessons, too.

However, all her interactions with Lord Atella had *felt* genuine. Especially the last one, alone with him in the garden, beneath the autumn-wreathed myrtle. Her favorite tree—her favorite place in all the gardens.

Why had she taken him there? To get out of the wind had been the obvious answer at the time. But now she wondered. And fretted. When spring came, the tree would burst with pink blooms before any of its neighbors unfurled their tiny white buds.

She had always liked that particular tree for that reason—it was so bright and glorious while everything around it still slept.

Yet now when she visited it in the spring she would think of Lord Atella, and how she had tricked him into a performance that the one he intended to impress did not care about. Not one whit.

Hopefully, the rest of the duke's guests would be impressed. If Lord Atella still had a political victory from making a spectacle of himself, she need not feel entirely guilty. Which was yet another reason she had to attend to him in the kitchens. It was only right.

And the idea of pasta-making and the preparation of food having such importance attached to it *did* intrigue her.

She left her letter on the desk, trusting the maid to post it, and went to the wardrobe to find an apron. She only wore it on rare occasions—such as strawberry-picking parties. It wasn't at all like what the upstairs maids wore, or the kitchen staff. Her apron was delicate, made of fine white material, with embroidered bilberries and vines all along its edges. Not at all practical for kitchen work.

A very good thing she didn't intend to actually participate. The apron was an accessory—a nod to the work being done.

"How do I look?" she asked Josephine after she had tied the apron around her waist. "Ladylike?"

"I think so. But you should probably cover your hair. Grandmama will have a fit if you come to dinner with flour in it."

"Do you think there's a danger of that?" She went poking about in her bureau for a cloth she might use to cover her hair.

"It is a kitchen. I know nothing of it. There may be danger of falling into a vat of strawberry jam." Josephine bounded from the bed with a wide grin. "Do you remember when we used to watch Cook in the London house make biscuits?"

"Barely." Emma found a long, thin piece of white cloth she had used once as a hair ornament for a ball, braiding it through her hair to create a coronet. "Will this work?"

Josephine took the cloth and put it over Emma's hair, twisting and tucking things into place. "It will do. But here." She twisted out a curl. "Very pretty. Like a milkmaid."

"What do you know of milkmaids?" Emma challenged, narrowing her eyes at her friend.

Josephine tilted her head to one side, appearing thoughtful. "Only what I have seen in classical sculpture and artwork."

Emma batted away her friend, gave one last shake to her apron to make certain it lay flat, then she went to the door. "Wish me luck. The kitchen is as foreign to me as England is to the ambassador."

"Fair sailing and good fortune to you," Josephine sang, then withdrew a handkerchief and waved somewhat dramatically. "Fare thee well, dear friend."

The ridiculous conversation lifted Emma's spirits. She went through the castle humming, making her way to the lowest floor of the house, excepting the cellar.

When she came to the kitchens, she found several downstairs staff standing in the hall, peering through the large doorway to the bright workroom. Though she rarely visited the kitchens, she had always loved the large, curved windows that began above the heads of the workers and stretched upward, easily fifteen feet higher, to the whitewashed ceiling. Chandeliers hung low, too, to keep the interior bright even at night.

As she passed through the doorway, the servants drawing back at her approach, she noticed an unusual quiet in the large room.

In the middle of the kitchen were several tables laden with raw foods, knives, and bowls, and several assistant cooks and kitchen maids stood around the tables as still as stone.

The head cook, a French *chef de cuisine* the duchess had met during a trip to Paris, stood at the center of the room with his hands on his hips. His forehead was deeply wrinkled and his face an unsightly shade of red.

"Already the menu you have changed, why must you also cook? A nobleman—cooking?" He made a strangled sort of sound. "Absurd. Dishonorable. In my kitchens? The staff will not know how to perform their duties with you nearby, my lord."

Lord Atella stood in front of the cook, taller but somehow less imposing than the bossy Frenchman, with his secretary at his side.

"You would dare," the secretary said, chest puffed out, "speak against your own duchess's wishes for my lord to serve her in this way?"

"I dare to think of the sanctity of my kitchen, of the food that must be *la perfection*! If the rest of the meal suffers for the distraction of my staff, it is not my lord who will be blamed, but *moi*, Absolon Dupont. Then what will I do?"

Emma had reached the eye of the storm, and she joined the conversation before Mr. Torlonia could speak again. "Monsieur Dupont, *bon matin*." She addressed him in French, softening her tone to one of respect. *"His lordship respects the importance of the meal, I assure you. Perhaps we could work in the smaller dining room for the staff? No one is eating there at present, are they?"*

He pursed his lips and narrowed his eyes at her, responding in his native tongue. "You think to win me over with your pretty French, eh? Miss Arlen, the kitchen is no place for you or him. This is where we work."

"I promise, we will remain as out of the way as possible." She switched back to English as she put her hand over her heart. "You have my word."

The wrinkles in his forehead smoothed, and he raised his hands with a broad shrug of his shoulders. "Very well." He turned his back and muttered in French, "Even though I am perfectly capable of creating *noodles*."

Lord Atella leaned toward her, keeping his voice low. "I did not mean to start a battle with the French in my quest to improve relations with the English."

It took her more than a little self-control to smother a laugh. "Monsieur Dupont will not view this as an act of war. I'm most certain."

A kitchen boy came forward, his apron as clean as his youthful face. "Cook says I'm to help with whatever you need. I'm Gerry."

"*Grazie.*" Lord Atella opened his mouth to say more, but Mr. Torlonia spoke first.

"Show us to the dining room," he commanded.

The boy nodded and shuffled quickly away to an open door on the other side of the room. Torlonia started to follow first, his expression stony.

Emma winced and fell into step behind him, with Lord Atella following behind. When they arrived in the room with the long table, benches on either side and chairs at either end, Torlonia started barking like an irritable dog.

"Bring flour, eggs, and olive oil. Salt, too. A bowl. A sharp knife." He cast a quick look at the *conte*. "And an apron for the ambassador."

The boys' eyes went large, and he bobbed his head rapidly before scuttling out, obviously used to taking orders.

Emma clasped her hands before her apron and stared up at the ceiling, dreading whatever time she would spend listening to the older Italian gentleman grousing about everything, as he immediately began to do. The room was too dark. How did anyone expect his lordship to work in such conditions? The table too short. The surface not smooth enough. The surroundings uninspiring—

"And why does my lord want to make *pasta?*" He paced the room angrily. "What an idea. You, in the kitchens. What would the king say? What would your peers say? The duke has never cooked in his life, I would lay my life on that!" Then he looked sharply at Emma. "You are not to repeat that."

Her jaw dropped open, but she snapped it closed again quickly. That he would *dare* to presume to order about someone of her station rather shocked her. She had been spoken to dismissively before, by people who did not understand her place, but never had anyone thought they could tell her what to say.

It left her quite speechless.

LUCA HAD NO INTENTION OF ALLOWING TORLONIA TO STAY after his poor show of temper. He took hold of his secretary's arm, fixed him with a hard stare meant to remind Torlonia who outranked whom, and spoke quietly in Italian. *"Thank you for your time today, signore. I think you had better go back to our rooms and prepare the letter of introduction for the duke's nephew traveling to Rome. I will press my seal to it after it is completed."*

The ambassadorial duty would be excuse enough to send the man away without making him lose face in front of Miss Arlen, but Torlonia would not mistake the note of warning in Luca's tone. Not if he wished to continue in his position.

Perhaps Luca had given the older man too much freedom in his speech, that he would think himself capable of ordering people about with such superiority.

Torlonia drew himself away from Luca, his nose tilted up, and he cast one dismissive glare at Miss Arlen before sweeping into a bow. "As you wish, *mio Signore*. I would only remind you before I go—do not forget what it is you are trying to accomplish here." Then he left the room while Luca stood silently watching, clenching and unclenching his jaw.

Miss Arlen slipped closer to him, tilting her head at an angle to peer at him from the corner of her eye. "He must be very good at his job."

Luca heaved a sigh. "When he stays within its bounds, yes." Then he rubbed at his eyes. "I am sorry. I should not speak ill of him. Torlonia is a friend to me."

"Our friends sometimes think they know best," she responded, her tone thoughtful rather than offended. "Do not trouble yourself on my account. I am here as a friend, too. Tell me how you wish me to help."

His gaze swept from her partially covered brown curls down to her dark slippers. Though her dress was not as fine as others she had worn, it was certainly out of place in a working kitchen. Her concession of a finely embroidered apron made him smile despite himself.

"If you do not mind, I will remove my coat. We have work to do, and I must keep my coat clean. I do not want my valet to join my secretary in a mutiny."

"A wise decision." She walked alongside the table while he shrugged out of his coat, putting it on the back of a chair. Then he unbuttoned his cuffs and started rolling them upward to just above his elbows. When Miss Arlen stood on the opposite side of the table from him, she stopped.

He hadn't been so underdressed near a woman since leaving home, and it was hardly the same thing since said woman had been his mother helping him pack a trunk for his trip to Spain. Not that he felt at all indecent about it, given the task at hand. Except he noted Miss Arlen's gaze darting from his exposed forearms away and back again.

The kitchen boy returned, proffering an apron with one hand while juggling a bowl full of everything Torlonia had requested in the other. Luca accepted the apron. "Thank you, Gerry. You may put those things on the table."

The boy did as asked, then stepped back with his arms rigid at his side, clearly awaiting further orders.

Would that Luca could somehow withdraw from the task and save face. But once the duchess had heard him speak of the importance of a meal in his country, she had happily insisted he prepare the pasta, at least for the family plates. Then again, she had shared a rather amused glance with her husband when he'd seemed ready to give Luca a way out of the situation.

Perhaps they were laughing at him.

Except they seemed too kind to do such a thing.

Luca sighed and took up the sack of flour. He undid the drawstring at the top holding it together, then poured a pile out onto the table.

Miss Arlen approached her side of the surface, eyebrows furrowed. "What are you doing?"

"The best pasta is not mixed in a bowl, Miss Arlen. It is formed carefully upon a table." He lightly salted the pile—as he had seen his mother and the monks do—and mixed it carefully in with the flour before forming a well in the grain. The flour was of the finest quality he had ever seen, a subtle testament to the wealth of the duke.

Then he took the eggs and cracked several into the bowl. Three or four? Three whole eggs. Four egg yolks.

"I must remove the egg whites," he said by way of explanation as he cracked one egg in half, then poured the yolk from one side to the other over a small bowl, letting the clear part of the egg drip into the bowl.

Miss Arlen came around the table to stand closer to him, peering at what he did. "I've never cracked an egg. Is that strange to admit?"

The admission sounded almost wistful, and he gave her a reassuring smile. "One of your status would have no need."

"May I try?"

"Of course. Here, take this one. We need only the yolk."

She bit her lip and tapped the egg too gently on the table for so much as a crack to appear.

"A bit harder, Miss Arlen. You *are* trying to crack it."

She narrowed her eyes and gave it a vicious smack, cracking the egg in half while still in her hands, causing the insides to spill both in and out of the bowl, and the broken yolk to coat her fingers.

Luca laughed while she stared at her hand in horror. "Too hard, Miss Arlen."

She raised her gaze to his, abashed. "I am terribly sorry." She started to lower her hand to wipe it on her apron—and he caught her wrist to save the pristine piece of cloth.

"One cannot be a cook without breaking a few eggs. But here, use this." He held up his much darker and longer apron. "We wouldn't want to ruin yours."

She wiped her hand on the hem, and her cheeks turned an adorable shade of pink.

Adorable?

Luca stepped back, clearing his throat. He handed her another egg. "Try again?"

She did, tapping the egg softly against the edge of the bowl, then progressively harder until a crack formed. Then she held it over the bowl and pulled it gently apart. "Then you pass the yolk from one side to the other?"

"That is my method, yes." He stepped a little more to the side, and when she finished and triumphantly held half a shell full of yolk to him, he grinned. "Put it in the larger bowl." He only had to retrieve one small piece of shell.

The olive oil was a different story. How much did he pour into the eggs? It wasn't much. He considered. Then took up a large spoon that had been among the items the boy brought. A spoonful seemed right.

He added the olive oil to the bowl, then used a wide fork to whisk everything together. Once he had a dark yellow mixture, he poured the eggs into the flour well.

Miss Arlen squeaked. "You are mixing it together on the table?"

Luca couldn't help sending her a smile—the sort of smile his mother used to tell him preceded trouble. "As you see. Do you think me a madman?"

She narrowed her eyes at him, her eyes glittering with amusement and a touch of wariness. "Perhaps. I shall refrain from passing judgment until I see the outcome of your strange method."

"Now I mix this into the flour. Like this." He took up his fork again and mixed the sides of the flour well slowly into the eggs. Miss Arlen came closer to peer over his arm, and for a moment the scent of flour mingled with something else—something that was uniquely the woman beside him. Lavender and citrus, perhaps. Something sweet and sharp. Bright. Like her.

He forced himself to speak, to describe what he was doing. "Once the flour and egg has joined to form a dough, we switch to using our hands."

"Your hands?" She sounded confused. "Why?"

"It must be kneaded, similar to bread."

"Oh."

"Would you like to try?" he offered, laying the fork down and gesturing to the lump of dough. "It is not difficult. I did this part with my mother, when I was a child."

Miss Arlen's eager expression returned. "If a child can do it, I suppose I could make an attempt." She waited for him to move aside, then held her hands over the dough somewhat uncertainly. "All right. I just—put my hands in it?"

"On it. You are mixing the dough with your hands. Working it, as you would clay. You have used clay before?"

"A long time ago. It is not my favorite artistic medium." She sunk her hands into the dough and squeezed it together, then apart, then made a face when it stuck to her. "Oh dear. It gets everywhere, doesn't it?"

"It shouldn't." He frowned at the long stringy bits of dough. "It is too wet."

A quiet cough from behind made him glance over his shoulder. Gerry the kitchen boy turned red. "If you please, my lord. Adding more flour might help?"

Ah yes. A little more flour.

He took some from the bag with his still clean hands and sprinkled it over the dough, then when Miss Arlen put her hands upon it again, rolling and turning the dough on the table as she would work to soften clay, he leaned around her to add a little more.

His chest brushed against her shoulder, and something in his stomach twisted; heat poured into his chest where the contact had occurred.

He hastily stepped back. "See. Not so difficult." That time, his voice sounded strangled.

Miss Arlen seemed too intent upon her kneading to notice. "How long do we do this?"

"Until it is smooth and stretches easily. Do you wish me to take a turn at it?"

She nodded and stepped away, holding her hands away from her sides with a wrinkled nose. "Dear me. I have flour up to my elbows." She sniffed and used the back of her wrist to brush a lock of chestnut colored hair away from her face. It had looked lovely, loose and brushing against her cheek, but apparently had become a nuisance.

Luca focused on the dough, rolling it this way and that, smoothing it into a ball and beginning the process over again.

"How long does this usually take?" The English woman leaned her hip against the side of the table, folding her arms carefully and keeping her eyes on his work.

"Truthfully, I do not know." He kept at the work, his mind stretching backward to his mother at the table while their kitchen servants chopped tomatoes and peppers nearby. "I have no way of knowing, except that it will feel right."

"Oh." She kept watching, though he saw from the corner of his eye that her expression had turned thoughtful. "This is not as simple as I expected it would be. Perhaps I shouldn't have encouraged you to undertake this much work."

"I am glad you did." The moment he said the words, he knew he meant them. He studied that thought, the feeling of being in the right place at the right moment. "This is the closest to home I have felt in a long time. The reminder is good for me, I think."

It was also one of the things about home he could think upon without conflicting thoughts or worry. The letters he had received about the issues at home—the king's lack of care for the poorer subjects, the malcontent stirred by the seditious leaders of secret societies—caused him great concern. And he could do almost nothing, as far from home as he was.

The quiet settled around them, the only sounds coming from the kitchen through the doorway. A buzz of conversation, the occasional clang of a pan or laughter breaking free from the steady thrum of whatever work went on in the larger room.

The smell of the dough, the warmth in the room, made peace fall upon Luca's shoulders rather like his mother's shawl had on cold winter nights.

"There," he finally said. "This is how it should feel." He took Miss Arlen's hand and put it upon the top of the dough. "See? It is smooth, and when you touch it—leaving a dent—it springs back. Like the best of feather pillows."

She concentrated on the dough, then lifted her gaze. Her hand was still beneath his. "I see what you mean."

Luca swallowed and forced a smile, pulling his hand away. "Now we cover it and let it rest."

"Let it rest?" she asked, blinking at him. "When we are the ones doing all the work?"

That pulled a genuine laugh from him—the first he had released in some time. "I think I said the same thing when I was a child." He brushed his hands on his apron, then picked up a cloth and covered the dough. "We make it comfortable and let it rest. Then, in half an hour or so, we roll and cut the dough."

"Oh." She stepped back, brushing her hands quickly up and down her apron, leaving only bits of flour behind. She pushed her hair back again, leaving a streak of white across her cheek. "What do we do while we wait?"

"We clean." He gestured to the table.

"I can do that, my lord," Gerry offered happily. "And fetch you refreshment for your wait."

Luca looked to the boy, seeing the child appeared perfectly

willing to perform such duties. "That would be best, I think. Go on, Gerry."

The boy disappeared out of the room again, and Miss Arlen lowered herself to the bench further down the table. He joined her, his gaze straying to the flour on her cheek.

"What shall we discuss for 'half an hour or so'?" she asked, her posture the same as it was in the duke's parlor and duchess's salon. The white-dusted apron and flour lingering on her skin made that strict adherence to propriety endearing. Could she know what a picture she made, so lovely and candid?

Folding his arms, Luca directed his gaze to the row of cups upon a shelf. The servants dined here, their meal schedules whatever made their work for everyone upstairs more convenient. Bruno had taken his meals here, too, and said everyone had treated him with kindness. He had a measure of importance as the valet of an ambassador that meant his position was respected, too.

"Have you ever been in this room before?" he asked.

"When the castle was first opened to the family, I walked through every room." Emma smiled, her eyes growing distant. "We played hide and seek many, many times. I even got lost those first weeks. But I cannot think I have come down here more than a handful of times since leaving the schoolroom. And not much before that, either. The castle is vast, and there are other places I am meant to be."

"Such as the library," he said, thinking of finding her curled up in one of the large chairs, book in hand. "Which room is your favorite?"

"I cannot say. So many are magnificent, and there are those where I am most comfortable. I think my favorite rooms are those with my favorite people in them, usually. Places where I can read or speak with others on the things that matter most. The library, the chapel, and the duchess's private parlor, perhaps." She looked around, taking in all the same details he had, most likely. Her curious gaze finally met his again, and her mouth tilted up on one side. "I thrive on excellent conversation, whether it be about books or matters of state."

"Then we will discuss those things, so perhaps this will be one of your favorite rooms." Something about the way she laughed made his breath catch, and then she started talking about a book she had read, not giving him a chance to think upon the strangeness of the two of them being together.

Gerry returned with a platter of fruits and tea cakes, and cups of lemonade. The arrangement was haphazard enough that the boy had to have done it all himself, but Miss Arlen thanked him as though she had been presented with a perfect array of desserts. Then they talked more while the boy tidied their mess, leaving the dough alone.

When enough time had passed, Luca reluctantly left his seat on the bench and took up a knife. He divided the pasta into smaller portions, setting half of the blocks of dough in front of Miss Arlen.

"Gerry, will you start a pot of water boiling for us, please?"

"Yes, my lord." The boy took off again, eager to help.

Luca sprinkled flour over his side of the table and tasked Miss Arlen to do the same. Then they worked the dough flat with the rolling pins Gerry had brought back with him before Luca showed her how to cut the noodles into strips for the pot.

"We could dry them, of course," he explained, carefully forming loose balls of noodles on a tray. "But fresh is much better, and we will eat them tonight."

"I cannot believe it," she said, her voice a mixture of awe and amusement. "I have never made any of the food I have eaten before. The closest I have come is buttering my own bread or eating strawberries I've picked." She stepped back from the finished work, looking at the table in front of them while wearing a look of such satisfaction that Luca's heart warmed toward her.

This was what his mother said good food did for people. It brought them closer together. He nudged Miss Arlen with one elbow—the only part of his arm or hand not covered in flour. "You did very well. Everything looks edible, at least."

She nudged him back and laughed. "Edible will make me happy enough. I trust if we made any mistakes, Monsieur Dupont will correct them with some sort of special sauce or spice."

They used damp towels to brush off their arms and clean their hands. Gerry took the tray and left while Luca untied his apron and rolled his sleeves down. "Thank you for your help and encouragement."

"You are most welcome, my lord. I enjoyed myself immensely."

Luca spoke without stopping to consider what he said. "Please, call me Luca. We have made pasta together. That makes us good friends now."

She hesitated, her hands at her back to untie her apron and her eyes upon his face. "Luca. I had nearly forgotten your given name."

He picked up his coat and slid his arms into it, avoiding her gaze when he said, "I did not forget yours, Emma." He had written it down in his book immediately after meeting her, beneath his initial thoughts on meeting Lady Josephine.

He froze mid-motion, his coat not quite settled on his shoulders. He had not thought of Lady Josephine even once since Emma Arlen had entered the kitchen, wearing her bright smile and embroidered apron with the air of one going on a delightful adventure rather than seeing to a ridiculous guest.

"Luca. It's a very nice name." She bundled up her apron, not quite looking at him. "I am grateful you consider us good friends. One can never have too many of those."

He relaxed and looked at her, that warmth in his chest spreading outward. "No. I suppose not." His eyes lingered on the smudge of white across her cheek. "And as your friend, I cannot let you go about looking like this. You have flour on your cheek." He held his hand up, nearly touching her face. "May I?"

Her eyes, so large and deep, glittering up at him, made everything feel softer. More peaceful.

She nodded silently and lifted her chin, granting him better access as his thumb passed gently over the streak of flour, rubbing it away. His fingers cupped her jaw, her skin warm against his touch.

Emma's lips parted, then her lashes lowered as she leaned toward him. Luca leaned closer, a word on his lips—her name. "Emma, I—"

A scuff in the doorway sent him into a retreat, his hand gliding through his hair as though it had not lingered upon the softest skin he had ever felt.

"Is there anything else, my lord? Miss Arlen?" the boy asked, bouncing on his heels. "The cook has the pasta in hand, he says."

Emma Arlen walked by the boy, not looking back. "I think we are finished here, Gerry. Thank you for all your help." She made it to the door, and just before Luca could curse himself for a fool, she looked over her shoulder at him and smiled. "Thank you for a wonderful experience, Luca."

Then she was through the door, out of his sight, and Luca's universe burned more brightly.

CHAPTER FOURTEEN

Mooore than a week had passed since working with Luca in the kitchen, and Emma still could not stop thinking about that afternoon. Even on her morning ride with Josephine, dressed against the cold, her cheeks stinging from the wind, she remembered exactly how it had felt the moment he'd touched her.

He had left with the duke the next day to visit a friend at a hunting lodge, along with several other men, and he would not return for another day or two. Despite him being out of her sight, far away from the castle, Emma's thoughts lingered on their time together.

Josephine circled her mare back to meet Emma on the path. "You are morose today, Emma," she accused. "What weighty matters are spoiling the fun of a morning ride?"

Emma stuck her tongue out at Josephine. "I am *not* morose. Only thoughtful."

"Too thoughtful. One would almost think you are plotting something devious. I know Grandmother was severe upon your pianoforte practice yesterday, but we needn't plan her demise just yet, if that is what you are thinking of." Josephine grinned jauntily and brought her horse to ride evenly with Emma.

"I have never planned anyone's demise, thank you very much. I am far too gentle a soul for that. I would rather keep the peace than hire assassins." Emma sniffed disdainfully. "Horrible dirty work, that. I'll leave it to you."

"I cannot even think how one would do such a thing, though I imagine you've read about it somewhere." The duke's daughter looked over her shoulder where a groom followed behind them, several horse-lengths back and incapable of listening as long as they kept their voices low. "Speaking of reading and plots, I think I am ready to share my secret with you."

That made Emma drag her thoughts away from the absent ambassador. "Your secret? The one you have kept more than a fortnight? That must be a new best for you, Josie."

"Do not tease, or I will keep it from you even longer," Josephine threatened, glaring at Emma with false heat. "Do you want to know where I have been going or not?"

"I want to know." Her initial curiosity on the subject coupled with her wanting to banish Luca from her thoughts strongly motivated her enthusiasm.

"Excellent. A race back to the castle, then?" Josephine's eyes glowed with the suggestion, and Emma readily agreed.

A quarter of an hour saw them back in the castle's entrance hall, the groom having taken charge of their horses. The two of them hurried down corridors, giggling and whispering that they mustn't be caught by the duchess or the dowager duchess. Not that either grand lady would do much to hinder their progress. Pretending they were performing mischief produced a heady feeling and recalled for both memories of their girlhood.

Emma followed Josephine down one of the corridors in the guest wing, which was quiet and empty at the moment, until Josephine stopped before a small door made to look like part of the wall. The only thing that gave the door away was the slightest seam in the wall. With eyebrows raised, Josephine pushed the door inward, and a mechanism on the inside made it rebound enough for her to catch the edge of the door and pull it open.

Confused, Emma put her hand on Josephine's arm. "This is a broom cupboard. We used to hide in it when we played hide and seek with Andrew."

And as the door swung open, it appeared the cupboard still held only a rack of brooms, mops, and feather-dusters. A shelf at the rear likewise had a bucket and folded linen cloths for cleaning and polishing furniture.

The closet was wide enough that both women could stand inside, shoulder-to-shoulder, and deep enough to do the same.

"I know what it is. But what it is hiding is more fascinating. Look." Josephine entered the cupboard, holding her long riding skirts out of the way, and reached beneath the tall shelf bearing the cleaning equipment.

Emma did not see any mechanism, but the back of the closet suddenly vanished, sliding into the wall. She gasped and came into the closet, closing the door behind her. Light poured in from the new doorway, making it easy enough to see Josephine's broad grin.

"I found it quite by accident. I ducked in here to hide from your tiresome cousin, and I saw the little rod that controls the door slide. I'm not certain why it's here—though of course Mama would have put it in her designs."

There were a few secret rooms in the castle, but each was only a secret to the rest of the world. The duke even had a study, deep within the center of the castle and accessible only through servants' halls, where secretive meetings had taken place in the years England was at war. There was a room where the children were taught to hide if they heard their parents say a particular word, indicating their lives were in danger. There was a pathway out of the castle the family could access through a door in the old nursery, and governesses and nurses alike had been taught how to protect children who would be excellent targets for those wanting to ransom them for fortunes or strike out at the duke.

"Being a duke's daughter is all very well and good," Josephine had said once, "until you think of all the horrid things other people want to do to you."

Emma followed Josephine up a winding staircase made of stone, too narrow for them to walk together, though not so tight a fit as to make Emma uncomfortable. Light streamed in from fogged glass every few feet, and Emma realized suddenly where they were.

"This is the false tower!" she exclaimed.

Josephine hushed her. "At the rear of the castle, yes. It turns out that it is *not* false." She sighed happily when she reached the landing. "Here we are."

The small landing opened up to a circular room with arrow-slit stained-glass windows facing each of the cardinal directions. If Josephine and Emma touched fingertips in the center of the room, they could then each touch the wall with the other hand with little effort. It wasn't very tall, either. The duke would likely have to keep his head bent to remain upright in the room.

The sun coming through the windows made the air warm, and Emma could see her lady's domestic skills put into practice with two small rugs layered atop each other, a large plump cushion against one wall, and a traveling writing desk in the center of the floor. A small trunk stood open against the wall, with shawls dripping out one side and a stack of cut paper resting neatly on the other.

There was a lamp, too, and a little tinder box. A small mantel-piece clock with a crack in the glass rested outside the box, showing the time.

"A cozy nest," Emma said, folding her legs beneath her. "What have you been doing up here? Besides hiding."

Josephine sat on the cushion and pulled her legs up close, resting her chin on her knees. "I have been writing."

"Writing?" Emma blinked at the paper in the box again. "Writing what? Letters?"

"A book." Josephine made the admission quietly, the way one might admit to favoring a mongrel over a gently bred lapdog. "A book about a gentleman's daughter living in the country."

Emma's mouth opened and shut, the words she first thought to say not suitable for her friend's admission. No one of Josephine's standing could publish a book without being laughed at or ostracized. Her father's enemies and political opponents would use anything she wrote as ammunition against the duke.

"It isn't finished," Josephine admitted softly. "It's barely started, but the words are coming quickly and are better than I expected." Her cheeks took on a rosy hue, visible even in the yellow-blue light of the stained glass. "I have told no one else about this."

Rather than admonish her friend or point out all the ways in which writing a book might prove more painful than fulfilling, Emma forced herself to be cheerful for her friend's sake. "That is marvelous, Josie. I did not know you wanted to be an author. I, who have known you nearly your entire life! How did you keep such a secret?"

"You know how much I enjoy reading novels, and so many of them have endings that I cannot like. Usually because there is someone who does not get their happy ending, or I wish to know more about what happens next. I started jotting down my own ideas in my diary some months ago about how I'd like this or that story to have one more chapter, a slightly different ending." She lowered her eyes to the floor between them, her expression solemn. "Then I started writing more. And I worried someone would find out and tease me for it. Or tell me I had no business writing fiction. I am a duke's daughter. It is beneath me." One corner of her mouth tilted upward, like a sadly curling vine. "But I enjoyed it. And when I found this place, I thought it perfect.

Tucked away and secret, I can write here without fear of discovery. I can almost forget I'm Lady Josephine."

Emma's heart went out to her friend. "Are you going to try to publish your stories?"

"Oh," Josephine laughed, a sad squeak. "I haven't any ambition in that direction. You know as well as I do that my grandmother would have fits, and I cannot think Papa would approve. It is best I keep it to myself. But you are my dearest friend—almost a sister."

Emma reached out to put her hand on Josephine's knee. "Thank you for telling me. If you ever want someone to read your work..." She raised her eyebrows meaningfully.

"Maybe when I finish," Josephine said, her expression more cheerful than before. "Thank you, Emma. It is a relief to tell someone."

"I am glad to finally know. I cannot think of any secret you have kept from me before." They had told each other everything, large and small, for more than a decade.

That knowledge made Emma squirm somewhat. "I might need to speak to you about something, too. Not a secret. But— well." She drew in a deep breath, steadying herself. "The ambassador. I think we may have been too severe upon him."

Josephine leaned back against the stone wall, her nose wrinkling. "I have seen nothing to change my opinion of him. Even that business with the Italian and Sicilian food he presented. Mama thought it charming, but I think he meant to draw attention to himself rather than do the family any kind of honor."

"That isn't true at all." Emma stared at Josephine in shock. "I told you how much it meant to him, to share those traditions with everyone."

"I believe he had good intentions, but really." Josephine smoothed the fabric over her knees, not quite meeting Emma's shocked gaze. "He wanted all eyes on him and all the words of praise that came with debasing himself to cook for his hostess. Most would consider it indecent."

"Indecent? He was most humble and honorable in every word he said. In every gesture. Josephine, you cannot really think that —" Emma broke off at the beginning of her indignant tirade when she saw her friend peering up at her with a narrow-eyed look. She swallowed back what she had been prepared to say, the words of defense that had fallen into line like willing soldiers to do battle on behalf of Luca.

Josephine's eyebrows raised. "Go on. What else have you to say about His Excellency?"

With her stomach plummeting dangerously toward the floor, Emma closed her eyes and gathered her thoughts. "I only meant to say you could be a little kinder to him. He is not an ogre." In fact, Luca possessed a dignity and grace that marked him as a man of honor and true nobility. He was more like a knight errant than an ogre.

"I never thought he was. I only thought him too old and an unsuitable match." The light and indifferent tone did little to calm Emma's unease. "Unsuitable for *me*."

"Only because you do not know him," Emma said, her eyes still closed. Picturing Luca as he had looked with his arms covered in flour up to his elbows, his smile relaxed and genuine...*endearing*.

The firmness of Josephine's reply provided little comfort. "I am not ready for courtship and marriage."

"I cannot like misleading him and making him believe that if he does what I say he may win you as a bride—"

"Why not?" Josephine's tone had changed to one of challenge, and Emma opened her eyes to see her friend leaning forward with a strange expression—a knowing look—in the way she stared back.

Emma wrapped her arms around herself and shivered, though she had been perfectly comfortable in the room moments before.

"Because he is a good man. He is my friend." She had imagined what might happen should Luca learn her ruse. If he discovered how she had agreed to help Josephine escape any and all attachment to him, it would hurt him and end their newly formed friendship. Josephine knew of Emma's plan to distract the *conte* with her pretended help.

"As am I. And I was your friend first. Which is why you ought to confide in me." Josephine flicked her hand dismissively. "There is more to it, Emma. Isn't there?"

"I do not like to lie," Emma insisted, hearing the uncertainty in her voice. "It is dishonorable."

"All right. Stop, then. Give him no more information on how best to win me. I will take care of myself. Does that satisfy you?" The way Josephine asked, her tone, made it sound as though she fully expected another denial to cross Emma's lips.

Instead, Emma nodded tightly. "Thank you." Yet that feeling of sinking, of loss, continued to unnerve her. "He is a good man. He will not press you or be so petty as to let the situation between you influence his work with your father."

Josephine stood and brushed off the skirt of her riding habit. "I think we ought to change and meet Mother for tea. She is always lonely when father is away."

"Yes." Emma rose, too, and looked around again at the little tower. "Thank you for sharing this with me, Josie."

"You are most welcome, Emma. You are my dearest friend." Josephine started toward the stairs, then spoke over her shoulder, "And I hope you will soon share your secret with me."

Emma paused. "What secret?"

Josephine shrugged one shoulder and continued down the steps. "Oh, I merely have the feeling you will have one before long."

Puzzled, but unwilling to continue the uncomfortable conversation, Emma forced a laugh and followed Josephine back down the steps. They only parted ways when they came to their bedrooms, on the same side of the hall, only a few feet apart.

When Emma entered her bedroom, she rang for her maid then went to the window overlooking the gardens. The trees were a riot of colors now, with only a few still green. Most were orange and yellow, red and gold. As the cold crept across the hills and dipped into the valley, autumn meant more than a change to the season. She could feel it but did not know why or what she expected.

She chewed her bottom lip, catching her own expression of uncertainty in the window's reflection. Would he even *want* to keep speaking with her, spending time with her, when he discovered Josephine wanted nothing to do with him even after he had heeded all of Emma's advice?

She rested her forehead against the window's cool surface, uncertainty making her sick with worry. All she could do was wait.

CHAPTER FIFTEEN

Five days spent roaming woodlands and valleys, tromping through bushes, and following barking hounds, ought to have exhausted Luca beyond the point of thought. But there were deals to make while waiting to mount horses, and politics to discuss over brandy, and introductions made and accepted between every activity.

Luca's intellectual reserves were stretched to their limit as he smiled in the face of men who claimed his nation was too new and weak to have much bargaining power. It took all his bureaucratic finesse to remind such men of Rome's age and the cultural greatness of the former empire's lands.

Yet another letter had come to Luca from his father. A letter full of concern for their country, hinting that it might fall yet further from glory. His father had named one of the secret societies. The Carbonari. A group whose leaders comprised the descendants of Italy's most famous citizens.

And despite the taxing of his body and mind, every night when he turned in to sleep in his room—with Bruno in a cot at the foot of his master's bed snoring loudly—Luca didn't immediately fall into his well-earned rest. Instead, he thought of a vivacious woman with dazzling brown eyes and a ready smile.

Not the blue-eyed Lady Josephine, but her companion. Emma.

On the final day of the hunt, when the duke insisted Luca join him in the carriage instead of on a borrowed mount, Luca's thoughts remained occupied by the smudge of flour on her cheek, her laughter, and her kindness. The way she discussed politics and books with such ease and how she held herself with the same grace and dignity as the noblewomen around her.

They had not been in the carriage long when the duke began a conversation with his son, the only other gentleman in the box with them. No one else who had made up the large hunting party was returning to Castle Clairvoir.

"Were you able to talk any sense into Sir Andrew?" the duke asked, arms folded and head tilted back.

Lord Farleigh had kindly taken the rear-facing bench, though Luca doubted the younger man could know of Luca's carriage-inspired weakness of stomach. "He insists he will not discuss the matter with Emma. He says she is of an age to make up her own mind."

Luca's interest stirred, and he forbid his stomach to interfere while he listened.

"That is a shame. I had hoped he would add his influence to mine this Season in London. As much as we all enjoy Emma's place in our home, it isn't fair to her to defer her future to Josephine's." The duke noticed Luca's attention and offered an apologetic smile. "Do forgive us, Atella. I do not mean to bore you with our family's concerns."

"Not at all, Your Grace." Luca ignored a bump in the road in favor of trying to work his way into the conversation rather than ending it. "Your family has taken me in, welcomed me more warmly than I could have hoped. I would never presume to inter-ject myself into personal concerns." Except that was exactly what he was about to do. "Miss Arlen has become a particular friend. She has a very sharp mind. That is the right way to say it in English, yes?"

"Yes, she is immensely intelligent." The duke tapped one finger upon his elbow before gesturing broadly with both hands. "Despite this cleverness, she will not listen to reason when it comes to her future."

Luca tried to sound only mildly interested, not too eager to know more about the woman who had remained in his thoughts for far too many days. "How so, Your Grace?" He glanced at Lord Farleigh, inviting him back into the conversation.

"Her position in our family is more than it seems," the duke said, also looking to his son. "How did you explain it to that friend of yours?"

The young lord shrugged. "She is only a companion voluntarily."

With some confusion, Luca put a hand to his temple. "You must forgive me. Voluntarily? She chooses to be a companion?"

"Precisely." The duke's dark eyebrows pulled downward. "A clever thing, when the girls were much younger. She did not have to answer so many questions, and she helped Josephine learn true and false friends with her ability to be partially ignored by others of rank. But the girls are now women, and even though my daughter insists indifference to courtship, we should not force Emma to do the same."

"I am still confused," Luca admitted, wondering if the pounding in his head was because of the nature of their conversation or the swaying of the coach. Likely the latter, influenced in part by the former.

"Emma—Miss Arlen—is my father's ward," Lord Farleigh said with an expressive shrug of his shoulders. "She is more of a sister to me—and daughter to him—than she is a servant or companion."

"She has received the same education, treatment, and even love from our family as my children," the duke added, looking out the window. "Her father was a dear friend of mine. We grew up together. When Emma's mother and father died, she was left in my care. When she and Josephine left the schoolroom, Emma insisted she take up the role of companion."

Another bump in the road did nothing to lessen Luca's sudden lightheadedness.

Lord Farleigh narrowed his eyes at Luca, a clear challenge in them. "Father tried to tell her it was nonsense. That she ought to be treated according to her station. Her family's lines go back nearly as far as our own, though through the gentry and minor nobility."

The duke waved a hand to silence his son, and he gave Luca a stern stare. "You will say nothing of this to others, I trust. Though I hope she changes her mind, I will respect Emma's wishes on the matter."

"Of course, Your Grace. None of this is my concern." Luca suddenly understood a great deal more about Emma Arlen than he had before. If her position as companion meant she acted as a self-appointed guard to Lady Josephine, it was no wonder she had made a point of inserting herself into his attempted wooing of the noblewoman. She served as a gatekeeper to her friend, keeping the unworthy *out* of Lady Josephine's company and friendship.

An admirable task, and many a conniving person had likely been thwarted by Emma's discerning mind.

Had he been one of those deemed less worthy, and so kept away? Yet Emma had spent enough time in his company, had counted him a friend. When he returned to the castle, what would she say? What would her next move be?

The carriage tilted as they went down an uneven road, and that was all Luca could stand. He wrapped the top of the coach in something of a panic. "Stop the carriage!"

The duke's eyes widened. "Atella, you have turned green!"

Lord Farleigh shoved the carriage door open and backed away, allowing Luca to jump out into the lane and stumble into the woods where he promptly cast up his accounts.

Blasted enclosed carriages. Horrid English roads with their bumps and roots and muddy hills.

Bruno and Lord Farleigh were both on the road when Luca returned, with several of the duke's men on horseback ahead and behind watching Luca emerge from the trees. With handkerchief in one hand and bottle of ginger-tea in the other, Bruno came forward to help Luca.

"Since you were *un ragazzino, Signore.*" Bruno smiled sadly, just as he had when Luca had been that little boy. "And you had to be an ambassador, which requires so much travel."

With a sharp laugh, Luca took the handkerchief to wipe at his forehead and mouth, then he accepted the tea his valet had thoughtfully prepared hours before. It was cold, and didn't delight the tongue, but the ginger would settle his stomach.

"Would you like a horse, Atella?" Lord Farleigh asked, a painful smile in place. "Or a place atop one of the carriages?"

Again, Luca looked at the two carriages—the duke in one and manservants in the other—and the horsemen all staring. Torlonia had his head sticking out of the second carriage, and his expression was coldly disapproving.

Luca sighed. "I would like to vanish into the air, Farleigh, never to be seen again." He took another drink of the tea. "But a horse will do for now."

"Cheer up, man." Lord Farleigh chuckled. "We all have our weaknesses. A poorness of stomach is better than a poorness of character."

"Very true." Luca followed the young lord back to the carriage, and after a few minutes he had a horse beneath him, and they moved forward again. Away from the northern woods and back to the duke's lands.

Once in the fresh air and with the steady gait of the horse beneath him, Luca's stomach calmed and his mind cleared.

Though his ears burned from embarrassment, his mind sorted the facts he had learned before he shamed himself on the side of the road.

Doubtless, Torlonia would spend some time trying to lecture Luca on *that* miserable occurrence. But how did one control one's vital organs?

Better to focus on what the duke and Lord Farleigh had said about Emma Arlen. The protective friend, a duke's ward as well as his daughter's companion, with familial connections to one of the most powerful families in England. In Europe, too, given the duke's rumored wealth and the amount of land he owned at home and abroad.

Though an orphan, her position as the duke's ward made her an enviable match. The perfect wife for anyone with a wish to maintain close ties with those in power.

What really mattered—the thing that made a bud of hope begin to grow in Luca's chest—was that he *liked* her. Perhaps more than liked her, though he could not mentally commit to that. Not yet.

There had been that moment in the servants' dining hall when he had nearly kissed her, when he had forgotten everything about his place as ambassador and a guest in the duke's home. Lady Josephine hadn't come into his thoughts once. Only Emma.

Everything that made Lady Josephine a suitable wife was matched in her companion, but Emma had the added qualities of showing a true interest in politics and other cultures and an understanding of what his duties entailed that had surprised him.

Might Emma be a match for him? A better match than her friend?

By the time the castle came in sight, standing on its hilltop with the setting sun turning it shades of orange and pink, Luca knew he had to speak to Emma. He needed to discover her true opinion of him. And soon.

CHAPTER SIXTEEN

Although Emma ate dinner with the family on the night of Luca's return, she didn't have the opportunity to have a private conversation with him. They barely spoke at all, and when they did speak, he seemed oddly reserved. As he had been when they'd first met. Perhaps she had imagined the way their relationship had shifted from mere acquaintance to friendship.

The day following his return, she lingered in the library, her fingers tracing the outline of countries on the enormous globe.

So many places in the wide world to see, and she had never left the little island tucked up near the European continent. Her world was so small. But Luca had already traveled from a little province in Sicily to Rome, Austria, and Spain. Where else might he go at the behest of his king?

She turned the globe. West to the Americas? She turned the sphere the other direction. Or east, to India or China? Perhaps he would venture to Cairo, in Egypt. Perhaps he would never travel further from home than England. Some ambassadors spent their service in one country for a few years or for the entirety of their lives.

A click echoed through the quiet room as the door between

the duke's study and the library opened. Emma stilled, her hand upon Egypt still, and watched from the corner of her eye as the ambassador's secretary exited the room, his expression one of disgust. He caught sight of her and took several long strides into the room.

"Miss Arlen—what business do you have here? Listening at doors?"

Emma pulled her hand slowly from the globe, fixing the man with a stony stare she had learned from the dowager duchess. "That is not a kind thing to say, Mr. Torlonia."

"Nor should you speak back to your betters. Do not think I have not noticed how you attempt to distract the ambassador from his purpose. While his pursuit of your mistress borders on the ridiculous, his time spent given in attention to *you* is far worse."

Her face blazed with heat even while anger tightened her chest. "Mr. Torlonia, need I remind you that I am under the protection of His Grace, one of the most powerful men in England?"

His nostrils flared, and he opened his mouth with enough of a glare that she expected a rebuke rather than an apology.

The study door opened again.

"Miss Arlen—here you are." Luca came out of the room. His expression was far different from his secretary's—in fact, Luca appeared cheered by the mere sight of her. "I had thought I must search you out to continue our last conversation. Thank you for saving me that difficulty." Then he looked at Torlonia. "You may finish the letter to His Majesty, and I will sign it when I return to my rooms. Good afternoon, Torlonia."

The dismissal in his tone did not allow the secretary to argue or hesitate any longer in the formal library. He met Emma's stare with a dark glare, then left the room, his heavy footfalls communicating his frame of mind quite clearly.

Emma rubbed at her left wrist with the opposite hand,

lowering her gaze to the carpet. "You wished to speak to me, my lord?"

Never in her life had she felt such uncertainty, and she found she hated the feeling. Torlonia's unexpected rudeness had shaken her. Usually when people spoke to her in that way she had but to tell the duchess or duke and that person found themselves in the ducal couple's disfavor.

It was one advantage of people thinking her nothing more than a companion—she discovered the true character of many a person simply by being in the same room with them.

"Yes, Emma. I haven't had a moment yet to tell you how good it is to see you again." He came closer, his head ducked slightly as he examined her.

"What?" She laughed, disbelieving him. The awkwardness diminished somewhat with his use of her Christian name. "You cannot have missed my company when you were among so many important men."

The study door had already closed. The duke was still inside —close, if she needed him—and she and Luca were alone. They had been alone several times before, yet this time Emma sensed a difference. A humming energy in the air.

"Ah, but I did miss it." He lowered himself to sit on the arm of one of the chairs—a casual and comfortable move as though he were completely relaxed. She rather liked it. Perhaps she hadn't lost any ground in their newly formed friendship while he'd been away. "You see, I was surrounded by men with political ambition and interests. All they wished to discuss was the law, and when they were not discussing the law, they were hunting, and when they were not hunting or discussing the law, they were eating."

She stepped closer and tried to forget the reason *she* had wished to speak to *him*. "Isn't that why you came to England?"

"To eat?" he asked with feigned surprised and raised eyebrows.

The feigned surprised in his tone made her laugh. "To speak of politics."

He snorted and folded his arms. "I came to learn, to teach, and to change things for the better for both our kingdoms. Politics is an essential part of that mission, but it is not the whole of it."

With him on the arm of the chair and her standing before him, they were nearly eye-level. The days he had spent in the fall sun hadn't made him appear any the worse for wear. Luca's aristocratic nose, high cheekbones, and dark curling hair were all as handsome as ever.

"Whatever shall we converse about to remove the unwanted thoughts of politics?" She tilted her head to the side, studying him, liking the way the corners of his mouth turned upward when he spoke and in the instant before he smiled.

Had he really missed her? The thought that he spoke the truth, not merely idle flattery, made her flush with pleasure. She turned away from him, lest he see and think her some green girl easily swayed by pretty words. That was not her. It would never be her.

But then why did her cheeks burn and her insides twist in delight with his words? *In the short time he has been away, I have turned into a ninny.*

Somehow they both ended up sitting in the library—he on the chair he had at first treated poorly and she on the couch across from him. She asked him about his time in Spain, and from there they visited a host of topics relating to his travels. When he discussed the differences in language, she laughed several times.

"I stood there, waiting in the hall, saying to my host *pronto, pronto.* I am ready. And he kept asking *when* I would be ready—in Spanish, I was saying 'soon, soon.' He grew quite impatient with me."

"Oh dear." She covered her smile with one hand.

"Yes. But this same man, he must have thought me a fool on many occasions. He also would try to tell me where to go—the word he used was *salir*. In my tongue, *salire* means 'to go up.' I kept asking why I needed to return to my room, because I thought he wanted to take me to meet another gentleman, and he wanted me 'to go up' the stairs. *Salir* in Spanish is to depart. He and I were never sure if we were coming or going together."

Emma laughed, delighted with his easy manner. Not all men would confess to such silly misunderstandings.

"But the first time I realized there was a problem with how closely our languages were related was when I found a mouse in my room at an inn—"

"A mouse?" she asked, wrinkling her nose. "I am not fond of those creatures."

"Nor am I. Which is why I am fond of cats."

Emma stored away that piece of information for later—she knew quite well one of the kitchen mousers was excessively friendly. Perhaps they ought to be introduced. "What happened?"

"I went down the steps of the inn, trying to be calm, and asked the innkeeper if he knew he had *topos*. Mice. But in Spanish, I was calmly asking him if he knew his inn had *moles*." Luca sighed ruefully. "As it was the middle of winter, nothing growing, he told me he did not think *topos* would cause any problems. I insisted they would and asked to change rooms. He thought me the strangest man—changing rooms because there might be moles in his garden."

Emma's laugh was as much due to Luca's dramatic sigh as it was the story, and she tried to smother it with her hand. "Oh dear."

"*Sí*. It was then I learned that not every Latin-based word is interchangeable," he said somewhat ruefully.

"Have you had similar troubles with English?" she dared to ask.

Luca narrowed his eyes at her. "Yes."

She leaned forward in her seat, eager for more from him. "Such as what?"

"Do you know your word, *morbid?*"

"Are you asking if *I* speak English? Yes, I know the word morbid."

"Then if I said to you, Emma, you have a lovely, morbid smile—"

She snorted. "That would cause grave insult, I'm afraid."

"Yes. I only made that mistake once. I told a lady she had captured such a *morbid* mood with her painting of her daughter."

"Oh. Oh, Luca. No." Her sides ached as she tried to keep the laughter at bay. "That is terrible! What on earth did you mean to say?"

Luca narrowed his eyes at her, though that twitch of his lips indicated he wasn't insulted. "Soft." He sighed. "You have a lovely, soft smile, Emma."

That made her sober somewhat, and she avoided his gaze a moment. "I have only a conversational level with a few of the modern languages. French is our specialty, of course. Then a little German, and even less Spanish."

"You would speak Italian beautifully, I think." He sounded certain, and when she met his eyes again, she found him staring at her speculatively. "*Pretendere* is Italian. It means to expect—or demand. The English word *pretend,* it means to deceive."

"That is one meaning, yes." She shifted uncomfortably in her seat, remembering again what she ought to have told him from the first moment they were alone. Did he know? "Luca. There is something I must tell you, and I fear it will harm our friendship. I know that honesty is important to you." She kept her voice steady, her focus on him, so she did not miss the way his brow furrowed or his smile transformed into a perplexed frown.

"You needn't fear on that count, Emma. I doubt you could say anything which would make me regret our friendship." Then he leaned forward, elbows on the chair and hands clasped, his eyes intent upon her. "Tell me, *amica mia.*"

How did she tell him? She had practiced what to say, had she not? In her room, looking in her mirror, she had made it sound as though her withdrawal of assistance to him was of no consequence to either of them.

"It is to do with Lady Josephine. While you were away, I gave it all a great deal of thought. I spoke to my lady, saying nothing that would damage her opinion or knowledge of you, of course. After everything, I believe..." She winced when his eyebrows grew together. "I cannot help you win her, Luca. Please do not ask me to. Not anymore. I love Lady Josephine as I would a sister, and though I find you to be a good man and certainly worthy of her, I do not think either of you would be happy if you succeeded. And she truly is not ready to give her heart to anyone."

Luca said nothing, and his expression gave nothing away. His eyes darkened, but whether with emotion or with thought she could not tell, so Emma sat quietly and said nothing. She waited for him to reply without fear of anger, though. Luca had a temperate nature and would do nothing to make another uncomfortable in his presence. A natural characteristic, it would seem, that lent itself well to his role as ambassador.

He leaned back, the movement slow, and unclasped his hands. He rested one on the chair and ran the other through his hair, ruining the careful style his valet had likely spent more than a few minutes on that morning given how well it disguised the way his hair curled at the ends.

"I understand, Emma. Please know that this does not hurt our friendship. I must confess, during my time away, I thought on our purpose many times. You are right, of course. I will put aside my pursuit of Lady Josephine and focus my efforts on other matters."

Emma relaxed, taking in a shuddering, relieved breath. "Thank you, Luca. For understanding."

His smile appeared, though fleeting. "Of course. I am grateful you spoke honestly. This must have weighed heavy in your thoughts."

"Yes." She rubbed her hand down the arm of the couch, trying to steady herself. Her nerves. She had told him, and he hadn't dismissed her. In fact, he had agreed with her. Luca wouldn't continue his pursuit of Josephine, and Emma would not have to give him up.

Give his friendship up, she corrected herself.

Luca's smile, when it reappeared a moment later, was perfectly natural and unforced. "What else did you do while I was away? We have spent all this time talking of me. How does an English lady pass the hours while the men are away on their hunt?"

The sudden change of topic gave them both permission to relax, and Emma spent the next quarter of an hour entertaining him with stories of her visits to the schoolroom and reading romantic poetry to the dowager duchess, who grumbled about it all being nonsense yet asked for it every time Emma read to her.

The room warmed as morning sunlight shifted into early afternoon, and the distant chime of a long-case clock finally brought Emma to remember her schedule. As she stood to take her leave, Luca seemed reluctant to return to his work, too.

"It is a family dinner tonight?" he asked when she went to the door.

"Yes, only family," Emma confirmed.

"Good. The informal evenings here are among my favorites." Luca walked to the door, standing next to her, looking down. "Perhaps I can bring up Italian love poems and see what the dowager makes of them."

Emma giggled, then adopted an air of disapproval. "That would be amusing for you, perhaps, but if she makes me read Italian poetry to her afterward—"

"Then that would also be beneficial to me," he countered loftily. "Such reading would perhaps inspire you to learn my language. A beautiful language. *Allora ti direi cose bellissime.*"

Emma's jaw dropped. "You cannot do that. What did you say? I insist on a translation, sir."

Luca leaned closer, his hand on the doorknob. "I promised to tell you beautiful things in my beautiful language." Then he stepped back before she could respond, before she could even determine why her cheeks turned warm, and he opened the door at the same moment.

She gave the briefest, most negligent of curtsies, then took the escape route he offered. But no matter how quickly she walked down the corridors and up the steps, no matter how she tried to outrun her feelings, the pleasure curled around her heart purred like a contented kitten.

"Friends," she whispered as she turned another corner in the suddenly too-large castle. She stopped and leaned against the wall, closing her eyes. "He is my friend. I want nothing more."

If she kept pretending that was true, she might convince herself in time. Because she couldn't leave Josephine. She wasn't ready for courtship. So Emma could not be ready for courtship. That was the right thing for her to decide.

Wasn't it?

CHAPTER SEVENTEEN

Luca stood at the edge of Lambsthorpe, riding gloves in hand, watching the crowd gather near the horses. Grooms from the duke's stables kept the horses either lined up along the blacksmith's fence or else walked them in a circle nearby. Men from the surrounding villages and estates had come with their finest animals, including all levels of English Society.

Lord Farleigh stood beside Luca, though he carried on a conversation with Sir Andrew and another gentleman. "There are several new entries this year, so I cannot say for certain which of you will come in second place."

"You cannot mean to say you will take first," Sir Andrew protested. "Even with your new horse, there are finer steeds on the starting line. Our friend the ambassador has an impressive mount, too. How did you come by your mare, Lord Atella?"

Luca turned his attention to the tall mare, a fine bay color with excellent lines, and spoke without looking at the others. "If you mean for me to thank you again for the loan of the horse, Sir Andrew, you ought to be more direct. The subtlety of the English is at times lost to me."

The two younger men laughed, and Farleigh struck the

ground with his walking stick. "Well done, Atella. Put him in his place as often as possible."

Sir Andrew put his hand over his heart. "I am shocked either of you would think I am anything less than sincere. You start to sound like your sister, Farleigh." The baronet jerked his chin toward the line of women standing behind a ribbon-covered rope to the east of the starting line.

Luca turned to search out Emma, certain she would be next to Lady Josephine. His assumption proved correct when he found them both holding on to the rope, wearing their richly colored walking gowns and surrounded by ladies dressed in every shade in the rainbow. Despite the bright tapestry around her, Emma stood out in her gown the color of roses at dusk, pink and purple-hued, with a wide-brimmed velvet bonnet of the same color.

He could read the excitement in her expression and in the enthusiasm of her gestures despite the distance between them. She spoke to a woman at her side, not Lady Josephine, and suddenly tilted her head back to laugh. He caught himself straining to hear her at the same moment she turned her head and caught him watching.

Emma paused and bowed her head in acknowledgement. He reached up to touch the brim of his hat, his gaze never leaving hers.

"...hasn't heard a word we said, has he?" Sir Andrew said, forcing Luca's attention back to the men on either side of him. The other gentleman had gone off to the horses, leaving the three of them alone.

Luca pulled his riding gloves on at last and successfully avoided looking directly at either of them. "*Scusatemi,* Sir Andrew. Farleigh. What were you saying? Is it time to mount?"

"I was saying that Farleigh is as skeptical as his sister when it comes to someone's good intentions," Sir Andrew supplied.

"And I told him Josephine is a fine judge of character, so perhaps it is my taste in friendship that ought to be in question,"

Farleigh added with good humor. "Then we asked you what you thought."

"However, you were ogling the ladies." Sir Andrew leaned around Luca to stare at the crowd. "Anyone in particular capturing your interest, Atella? I could mention it to my cousin. She might be persuaded to play at matchmaking."

Avoiding answering that question would be in Luca's best interests. "What does this word mean, 'ogling?' I have never heard it."

Farleigh twirled his walking stick in one hand, looking at the women himself. Children had joined the throng in the crowd of villagers and the knot of nobility standing behind the ribbons. "To stare at someone with flirtatious intent."

"Ah, a most useful word." Luca pointed at the line of horses, most of which had riders mounted or in the process of mounting. "It is time, I think. Shall we go?"

"Do you intend to wager on your win today, Atella?" Sir Andrew asked as they walked, the three of them abreast, along the line of horses and riders. There were at least thirty participants in all.

Luca clicked his tongue on the roof of his mouth before slanting a look at Sir Andrew. "No. Why? Would you like to owe me another favor?"

Farleigh chuckled. "I'll lay a bet that Atella comes before you."

"Excellent." Sir Andrew clapped his hands and rubbed them as though he relished the idea. "What is at stake?"

Luca stopped listening, though he thought the two spoke of ridiculous things rather than seriously exchanging funds as they kept walking ahead of him to their horses. Bets and wagers were certain to lose a man friends if he won too often.

When he arrived at the borrowed mare, the groom held the horse steady while Luca mounted. The moment he had his seat, he looked again at the crowd of brightly colored gowns and parasols. He found Lady Josephine again, though Emma's rose-colored walking gown and coat were not in the same place. His eyes swept along the rope, searching for her, until the duke appeared on a large black horse, the animal appearing to belong on a battlefield rather than in a quiet country setting.

"Men, welcome to today's Harvest Race," he said, his deep voice booming across the field. The watching crowds hushed as all attention focused on the man whose generosity had provided most of the entertainment the crowds would enjoy that day.

"The course has changed this year, as it will always change, to keep each of you guessing and give no man the advantage his mount and talent do not already provide." He went on to name the roads through which a three-mile course had been planned, with the duke's men along the way to ensure no farmer's cart or innocent child stumbled into the path of the horses. They would go nearly all the way around the castle on tracks primarily used by carts making deliveries to the castle.

The duke raised a pistol in the air, pointing it upward. "As usual, I offer the sternest warning to those who do not conduct themselves honorably. Be you yeoman or earl, if I receive word of cheating or cruelty on the race, you will feel my displeasure." He made that dire pronouncement with a stern glare which lingered on each man in turn. "A prize goes to the man who wins. You will begin on my signal. Come to the line, men."

Someone had scattered chalk dust in a line lightly dug into the dirt of the field, making it quite clear where they were expected to wait for the duke's mark.

Luca steadied his horse. The mare had started to twitch with anticipation. The crowd started talking again, buzzing like a hive of bees. He looked again for Emma, wondering if she had no desire to watch, even though her cousin raced. Even though Luca took part, despite there being no need to impress Lady Josephine.

Would Emma care about him racing? Perhaps not.

Then he saw her, at the end of the line farthest from the start.

She leaned as far over the rope as she could and waved to him. Luca's ambition came back, a competitiveness he hadn't known took hold, and suddenly, he had to win. Because Emma watched.

He bent over his horse, ears pricked and waiting; the duke fired the starting shot, and thunder filled Luca's ears as his and all the other horses pounded forward. The dirt flew, each man pushing his animal for speed to get ahead before the field narrowed to a road where no more than three or four could ride abreast of each other.

Luca had no time to look for Farleigh or Sir Andrew nor to see if he had many other competitors near him. He had been introduced to almost a dozen others who rode that day. But they didn't matter. Only the thought of Emma, delighted by his victory, mattered.

He fell behind five other riders as they came to the road, then had to bide his time to take a curve faster than another man and move into the fourth-place position. The horses snorted, their breathing heavy and fast, their hooves striking the hard dirt sharply before flying forward again.

Up a rise they went toward the castle, the trees a blur on either side, and Luca took third by the time they had made the loop. Halfway, and Sir Andrew rode beside him with the duke's son ahead of them both.

"Atella, watch out!" Sir Andrew's shout saved Luca from the formerly second-place horse and rider stumbling ahead of him. Luca jerked his horse's reins, pulling up enough to dance around the unfortunate rider and horse.

The fallen man's cursing and the horse bolting in another direction at least meant no lasting harm had occurred. But Luca had lost ground between himself and the remaining two ahead of him. Sir Andrew remained nearly even with Luca and his mount.

Luca leaned low over his horse's neck, urging the animal on in his native tongue. "*Forza, forza!*"

The mare kept her legs flying beneath her, and Luca closed

the distance between himself and Farleigh when the end of the race came in sight. A ribbon of bright yellow stretched between two trees, held by boys on either side. He drew even with the duke's son, then surpassed him, but—

The man in the lead, a gentleman who lived near town, crossed the line first.

Luca's horse snorted, carrying him through to the end, then paced and tossed her head as Luca guided her to the field. She stamped and resisted slowing down, but through calming her, Luca calmed his own racing heart. And his disappointment. The duke congratulated the winner, his voice raised as more riders and horses came through to the end.

"Congratulations, Mr. Bydwell. The first-place prize is yours. All who raced may have a drink as my thanks for a race well-run. Please, enjoy the festivities today."

A cheer went up from the crowd, and Luca looked up for the first time. How foolish of him, to lose his head over a woman in such a way. As though Emma Arlen cared one whit about him racing, let alone winning the race.

A dusky rose bonnet appeared, but not in the crowd. Coming toward him instead, with her hand holding her hat in place, Emma wore a bright smile. He dismounted at the same moment she stopped, only two paces from him.

"You were brilliant, Luca. I cannot believe how near you came to winning. I thought for certain you would overtake Mr. Bydwell in those last moments, and that is quite the accomplishment on a borrowed horse." Her smile shone up at him, and her cheeks were flushed pink with obvious good cheer.

Coming second suddenly seemed the best thing in the world.

IN THE PAST, EMMA MIGHT HAVE LAUGHED AT A WOMAN FOR praising a man so much. Especially for something as simple as good horsemanship. But she hadn't wanted to wait to tell Luca what she thought, or to greet him after his near-victory. Luca deserved to know she admired his abilities. A friend would tell him he had done well.

When his lips quirked upward, Emma wanted very much to make him smile more. His broad smiles were too infrequent.

"Thank you, Miss Arlen." He bowed. "You do me great honor and soothe my wounded pride."

"Wounded pride?" she repeated, her free hand going to her hip. "Lord Atella, we both know you did well. I doubt your pride suffered so much as a scratch."

"Well done, Atella," Sir Andrew called. Emma turned to see her cousin approaching, leading his horse while a groom walked alongside them. "You won Farleigh theater tickets at my expense."

"Then I have accomplished my goal," Luca said, his tone dry. "Perhaps if you lose more bets, you will stop making them."

Andrew laughed. "I never wager anything I cannot afford to lose, my friend. That would be a fool's mark." He turned to Emma. "And you, Cousin? Did you cheer for the ambassador rather than your own flesh and blood?"

"Most happily, yes." Emma laughed at his feigned shock. "Do not be too distressed. I have learned that Punch and Judy have arrived and will begin their show very soon. Is that still one of your favorites? It ought to cheer you."

"That might have been my favorite when I was seven years of age. At five and twenty, it is far beneath me to laugh at violent puppets." Andrew put his nose high in the air. "But if there is a group planning to watch together—"

"With mince pies and cider, of course." Emma looked to Luca. "Many of our local friends tend to follow each other about like a flock of chickens at the harvest market. I hope you will join us."

"It would be my pleasure. As I said before, there is much more to my position as ambassador than politics. I must enjoy the culture of the English, too."

The groom successfully took possession of the reins for both horses and promised Andrew to have them ready to return to his estate within the hour. Andrew fell into step beside Emma but did not offer his arm. Neither did Luca, sadly, but she knew well enough why. There was no use in starting rumors about the two of them, not when he intended friendship, and not when he still appeared interested in Lady Josephine.

Yes, she had seen him watching Lady Josephine moments before she had caught his eye as the race was about to start. Although catching him at it disappointed her, Emma pushed aside her feelings to focus on their friendship. She could help him overcome whatever regret might linger.

There were other titled ladies who might take a fancy to him.

Not that she intended to introduce him to any of them.

Ever.

Emma winced as the vehement thought crossed her mind, the silent conviction far too telling.

Luca slowed his pace, with Sir Andrew walking ahead at a rapid speed as he called to a friend. Then the handsome Sicilian turned to her, his voice low. "Emma, are you well?"

She forced her eyes wider and put on her usual smile. "Perfectly well. Why ever do you ask?"

"That face you made—it appeared morbid." Though his expression remained concerned, she saw the twinkle of mischief in his eyes.

Emma laughed, and then brightened when he offered her his arm. "I take it you meant to use that word instead of the other."

"This time, yes." Luca gave her hand one quick press where it rested in the crook of his arm. "But you did appear unsettled. Is there anything I can do to help?"

"You needn't worry. I had a stray thought I did not like." She waved her hand before her to waft away the topic as one might an unpleasant odor. "Have you ever seen a Punch and Judy show?"

"I am certain you mean *Punchinello e Joan*." He narrowed his dark eyes at her. "You English, always taking what you like from others and turning them...well, English."

She laughed despite her earlier disquieting thought, then pointed to the middle of the little town where a large expanse of green marked the place for the community to gather. A hasty theater had gone up, with cheap curtains, and children already sat on the ground looking up as a puppet Punch took charge of the baby while his wife went away.

"We cannot help ourselves, I think." Emma saw Josephine, Simon, Andrew, Alice, and Rupert standing together near the marionette's stage. "Oh, there they are. Come, let us see if Punch gets all that he deserves for his horrid crimes."

Luca took her to her friends, and when she began to remove her hand from his arm he covered it again with his own. Only briefly, his touch so light she barely felt it, but Emma's gaze rose to his with uncertainty. Did he mean for her hand to stay there, the two of them nearly as coupled together as Alice and Rupert?

No, he could not want that.

She slipped her hand away and busied herself with her reticule, finding pennies to pay when Mr. Wheaton, the baker, brought pies and rolls about. Luca bought several sweet rolls and nodded to the children at the front of the audience, instructing the baker to take the treats to them.

Mr. Wheaton's grin grew larger than she'd ever seen it as he distributed the treats to the children—only to be yelled at by Punch for "encouraging little brats to eat things meant for their betters." The audience shouted back their disagreements, and the children laughed when Punch fell over at the fervor with which they shouted him down before taking up the story again.

"I never understood why people like this so much," Alice said from where she stood next to her husband, nibbling at a mince pie. "Punch is horrid, beating everyone with that stick. We would never put up with it in reality."

"I think that must be the point."

Everyone looked at Luca, including Emma.

"What is?" she asked, and had the pleasure of watching that slow, understated smile of his appear.

"Punch acts in a way that is improper, shocking us into laughter, but we can all see that he is the villain of the story. No one likes him for his behavior, and sometimes he is hanged for it in the Italian shows. Sometimes he escapes, but the wife and constable remain happily with the baby. So while he might think himself the victor, he loses everything that most of us require to find happiness."

Emma's lips parted, her agreement ready-formed.

"You learn all of this from a story with wooden-faced dolls bashing each other with sticks?" Andrew's snort wasn't quite derisive, but certainly disbelieving.

Screams of laughter came from the children as Punch mishandled his baby, turning it upside down and trying to feed it through its toes. Emma gestured to the stage. "It's far too ridiculous for anyone to think it realistic, Andrew."

"I agree with Lord Atella." Josephine glared down her nose at the baronet before turning to Luca with an approving smile. "The subtleties are in every story. No child watching this will think it a grand thing to be Punch, when all the world calls for his demise. He's a horrid creature."

Emma finished her baked treat, watching Luca from the corner of her eye as Josephine rained her approval upon him. Luca nodded in appreciation of her agreement, then folded his arms and watched the marionettes.

The others in their little group continued chatting, with Andrew and Simon speaking of the race and the rider whose horse had stumbled. Emma listened to them with half an ear, her eyes upon the stage but her mind on other things. Luca stood between Josephine and Emma, occasionally chuckling at the show, and sometimes pointing out a way in which Punch had been thwarted. To Josephine.

The pie Emma had eaten didn't seem to agree with her after long. She gripped the strings of her reticule and murmured her excuses as she went in search of something cool to drink. Vendors were set up along the principal street in temporary stalls or carts, selling their harvests and handiwork.

At a cart full of baskets of apples, a woman also had large barrels of cider. With no wish to feel tipsy, Emma started to go on, but a hand at her arm stopped her. She looked back, pulling in a deep breath in case she might need to give someone a mighty set down, but her gaze locked with Luca's deep brown eyes.

"You left the show, and you did not seem well."

She winced. "Morbid again?"

His expression softened, concern lingering in his eyes. "Unwell. Do you need to return to the castle, or perhaps sit for a time?" His gaze swung away from her as he searched about, perhaps to find her a place to sit and rest.

"I am not an invalid, my lord." Emma drew away. "I am only in search of something to drink. I think the inn will have tea." She turned away and started walking, her heart in her throat. What was wrong with her? She ought to be glad he had followed. But why? She didn't need his help. She was perfectly fine. Wasn't she?

He stayed with her, though he remained silent until the moment she ordered her tea. They entered the already crowded inn together and went to the long countertop where the innkeeper cleaned cups and served people. Before she could open her purse strings, Luca had paid for two cups of tea and then steered them to chairs in one corner.

"Luca," she whispered as he pulled the chair out for her. "I really am quite well."

"I am glad to hear it. But I will take tea with you, of course, and return you to your friends when you feel better than 'well.'" He seated himself across from her and folded his arms over his chest, wearing an expression that meant she would encounter an argument if she tried to dismiss him again.

"This is ridiculous," she scoffed softly.

"What would the duke say if I let you wander about on your own? Even if you are only in search of tea."

"He would not mind in the slightest, since I am an independent woman in his employment," Emma said with a wave of her hand.

Luca's head tilted back. His expression changed rapidly from confusion to disappointment. He lowered his gaze to the table. "His employment? As Lady Josephine's companion, you mean."

"Of course." Emma studied the woodgrains in the table between them, the dark lines and a single knot worth the lingering observation. She shouldn't remind him of her low place in Society. Daughter of a gentleman, but still a paid companion. But then, it was for the best. A man of his standing would not wish to risk anything by courting someone who supposedly held such a low position in Society.

But she could tell him—she could mention the other position she held in the family. A ward, the duke her guardian, the duchess as much a mother to her as the one she had lost as a child. If she told Luca those things, would it change things?

Would he wish to be more than her friend?

The innkeeper's daughter brought the tea and left it with a small service upon their table. Emma removed her gloves to pour out the tea. She put milk and the smallest lump of sugar in hers, then did the same for the *conte*. When had she learned they took their tea the same way?

She put her hand around her cup—it was the old-fashioned kind, without a delicate handle that would be likely to break in the rough usage an inn must surely see from time to time.

Luca's gloveless hand curled around hers.

"Emma. Once more, you appear distressed." Luca kept his tone too low for others to hear, and almost too quiet for her to make out his words.

"I have a lot to think upon, is all." She studied his hand,

enjoying its warmth, how large it was compared to hers, how strong it must be given the shape of his fingers—narrow except at the joints.

His fingertips brushed across her knuckles as he withdrew it, taking his own teacup in hand. He said nothing else while they drank their tea. The room around them provided enough noise to make their silence notable. Though Luca said no more, she knew he kept his gaze upon her, studying her.

Something troubled her. Something she did not want to examine or admit to. The tea granted her a few moments' peace to fortify herself again. The unexpected wave of emotion she had felt at the Punch and Judy show had been sad and bitter both, and she knew at last what name to give it. Jealousy. Josephine had given Luca no more than a little kind attention, the same sort she would give anyone, and Emma had wanted to keep Luca all to herself. Like a spoiled child.

She would do better. She could share her friendships. The lapse had been strange, but she recognized it now, and all would be well.

Emma smiled around the rim of her teacup. "Is there anything in particular you wish to see today, my lord? The market is not grand, but the people are very enthusiastic about their wares."

Luca's smile seemed forced. "I will go wherever you lead, Miss Arlen. You must be my guide."

They left the inn without any further discussion on her thoughts, and Emma found their party had lost interest in Punch and Judy and had begun to wander freely through the stalls. They went from one to the next, with the ladies purchasing ribbon and thread, apples and buttons. The men with them spoke to one another of the race, of the price of a good horse, and occasionally consulted with the ladies about their purchases.

Rupert Gardiner showed himself an attentive husband, always ready with a word for Alice when she looked for it. Their obvious care for one another made Emma smile, relieved her friend had found such a wonderful match. Not everyone had such luck.

They finished with the market, and despite the amount of time they had wandered about, decided to walk back to the castle instead of taking one of the duke's carriages. He had several guests staying for a large dinner party, including the Gardiners.

They walked through the shortcut with Simon and Andrew leading the way, while Alice and Rupert took up the middle position, and Josephine, Luca, and Emma made up the rear of the party. Luca took responsibility for removing troublesome branches from the path, holding them aside as a footman might open a door or hold a curtain.

Josephine kept a steady stream of words flowing as they went, talking as much to the people ahead as the people with her. "You need to visit for a day of painting, Alice. We can ask for Isabelle and Rosalind to join us. They miss you terribly already. I know no one with as much talent as you when it comes to drawing."

"You are too kind. I happily accept your invitation. When shall we arrange it?"

"Tomorrow, of course. You are staying the night, are you not? My father said you were welcome." Josephine sounded eager, but Alice shook her head.

"I am afraid we are leaving again tomorrow morning. Rupert has business with a beekeeper he will not miss."

"It is fascinating—the beekeeper is preparing the hive for the colder weather. His methods are entirely unique to any other I've heard of," Mr. Gardiner said with obvious delight. "Alice accompanies me to help with notes and sketching."

"Sometimes he is too caught up in the moment to actually write anything down," Alice said, sounding as though this was an endearing trait in her husband rather than a wearisome one.

"It sounds as though you are a well-matched pair," Luca said, surprising Emma out of her quiet disinterest. She hadn't realized he'd been paying much attention to the conversation, either. "You both have an interest in science, the husband in insects and botany, the wife an artist and student of both. What does that mean for your work, Gardiner?"

"It makes it a greater joy than ever," Mr. Gardiner said immediately, slipping his hand around his wife's. "I accomplish more than I ever thought possible with Alice's help, and she lends her talents to my studies with a generosity of heart that makes me most grateful. You have seen her sketches? Her ability to capture color with no more than pencils and a few watercolors?"

"I have. Your talent is impressive, Mrs. Gardiner."

"Thank you, my lord." Alice blushed prettily.

Emma glanced at Josephine to see what she made of the conversation, but her friend appeared as cheerful as ever.

Luca didn't allude to the fact that a duke's daughter and ambassador would complement one another in marriage, did he?

Stop it, Emma. She squashed the confusing storm of emotions again. "I cannot think of many couples better matched," she said aloud. "Lady Josephine and I used to speak of how well-suited Alice and Mr. Gardiner would be, given their mutual enjoyment of the outdoors and Alice's unnatural tolerance for things like spiders and frogs."

Alice laughed, and the conversation turned to the early days of Mr. Gardiner and Alice's acquaintance, with the couple teasing one another as they went.

Emma slowed her steps, watching Luca and Josephine walk side by side.

Hours later, tucked up in her bed after a long evening of entertaining the duke's guests, Emma fiddled with a tassel on one of her bed cushions and stared up into the semi-darkness of her bed.

Perhaps she had been too hasty to give up her attempts at redirecting Luca's interest away from Josephine. But then, Josie hadn't seemed to mind conversing with him in such a casual manner all that day. Had she given up avoiding him, or had she such confidence of deflecting an offer of courtship that she no longer cared?

Emma hugged the cushion to her chest and rolled over, staring at the narrow slit in her bedroom curtains which allowed the faint light of the moon to enter her bedroom.

Luca had behaved perfectly, of course. Not showing too much interest in Josie. Not even flirting with the duke's daughter. He had only been friendly. And not as friendly as he was with Emma.

Why had he insisted on following her about? Why had he covered her hand while they took tea, that earnest look in his eyes? Perhaps she had appeared more haggard than she thought, if he felt the need to be demonstrative in his friendly attention to her.

Emma blushed and put the pillow over her face, thinking over every conversation they had shared since his return from the hunting lodge the week past.

She and Luca had bumped into one another in corridors, taken tea in the conservatory, and sat near one another at meals. They had spoken of books and what he read in the newspaper. She had shared one of his Italian poetry books with the dowager duchess and told him of the esteemed woman's rather emotional reaction to one poem that Emma barely understood. He had translated the tragic love poem for her, then hadn't laughed when she'd wiped away a tear.

They had spoken of the Arabian fairy tales again, comparing wishes they might ask of a djinn and how they would avoid being tricked.

Come to think of it, she had spoken to Luca every single day, at least once privately and then several times in a room full of other people.

Each time they parted, all she had thought on was what they had discussed. And she had yearned for their next meeting, so they might speak again.

He talked to her as though she mattered and her ideas mattered. He treated her with such an open affection that she wished, very much, that it meant more than mere friendship.

Emma groaned and covered her head with the pillow, trying to focus on her frustration instead of the way her eyes filled with tears. A horrible realization had formed, and the truth of it wounded her deeply.

Never had Emma intended to fall in love with Luca, but that was precisely what she was in the middle of doing.

CHAPTER EIGHTEEN

"Sir Andrew," Luca said, storming into the other man's guest room two weeks after the race. "I am calling in that favor."

The baronet rose slowly from his chair and looked at the clock on the mantel. "At this hour? Please don't tell me you need a second for a duel. It's already one o'clock in the morning, and that would give me only a few hours to gather the essentials."

Luca froze in the middle of the room and blinked. "A duel? No. Are those not illegal?"

"They are highly illegal, but that doesn't seem to stop anyone." Sir Andrew dropped back into the chair and stretched his legs out before him. "Have a seat, Atella. Might as well be comfortable when you collect on favors."

"I am sorry it is so late." Luca looked at the clock. He hadn't realized what he was doing when he left his suite of rooms to search out the baronet. But he'd worked himself into something of a frenzy in an attempt to determine what he had done *wrong*.

"Usually, people in this country knock before they enter another person's bedchamber." Sir Andrew hunkered down in his chair again, folding his arms over his chest and directing his stare into the fire.

Luca went to a chair and sat, then rubbed at his face. "I understand, and I apologize. I have not been thinking clearly since dinner ended."

Sir Andrew came and went as a guest nearly every week, which apparently no one found unusual. As far as Luca could tell, the baronet was considered as much a part of the family as Emma. Emma, who still hadn't told Luca the full nature of her relationship to the ducal family. Emma, who had taken to avoiding him, going so far as to unexpectedly enter a room if she saw him approach from the other side of a long corridor. Emma who—Luca strongly suspected—had used secret passageways to completely disappear from his sight.

She had been all politeness in company but had ceased to even try to hold a private conversation with him.

"I have done something wrong," Luca said, hardly aware of how long the two of them had sat silent before the low-burning fire in the hearth. "But I do not know what."

A laugh and then a hasty clearing of his throat was Sir Andrew's first response. "And you think I can help? Why? I am not involved in politics at the same scale as you are. My advice holds little weight. The duke would surely be a better advisor."

The end of the month drew near, and October had grown cold and damp. The hiss and crack of a log in the fire momentarily stole Luca's attention as he tried to form his explanation. "It has nothing to do with politics."

"What, then? You will excuse me for saying so, Lord Atella, but you are well-traveled and highly educated. What problem could you possibly face that I would be suited to solving?"

"I have done something wrong," Luca repeated, but raised his head as he added, "and I need your help because Emma is involved in the situation."

Sir Andrew's gaze swung from the fire to meet Luca's, a sudden blaze of interest in their depths. He sat up in his chair, his feet squarely beneath him, and narrowed his eyes at Luca. "What do you mean, Emma is involved? What has my cousin to do with anything?"

There was no mistaking the protectiveness in Sir Andrew's tone, and that did more to reassure Luca than he could express. He had come to the right person. "Whatever I did has caused Emma to withdraw her friendship from me. To some degree. She isn't the same as she was before the harvest market."

"Why are you calling her Emma? Did she give you leave to use her Christian name?" Sir Andrew demanded.

Luca leaned back in his chair and rubbed at his temple where a fierce tempo began to beat, threatening to drown out rational thought. "Yes, I have her permission to use her Christian name. We are—or were—friends. Friends with enough in common that proper address felt strained rather than necessary. Sir Andrew, please do not look as though you wish to commit murder. It is disturbing and makes explanation difficult."

The baronet didn't appear repentant but grumbled instead. "This is the first I've heard of your friendship. Though my cousin did seem concerned for you when you first arrived. She even asked me to help if you needed anything."

"She did?" Luca couldn't keep the cheer out of the question. "That long ago?"

"A month is not that long, Atella." Sir Andrew rose and took up a log in the curved bin beside his fireplace, then added it to the low blaze. "You need to start at the beginning, I think. If you and my cousin are such *friends*, why are you here claiming wrongdoing?"

"Because she will not speak to me," Luca said, trying not to sound too pathetic. "We have always spoken freely to each other, on many subjects, but for days she has avoided me. Are there secret passages in this castle?"

Sir Andrew quirked an eyebrow upward in a manner very similar to his cousin. "Secret passages? You think Emma is using secret passages to avoid you? Have you heard the term *irrational* before, my lord?"

Luca threw his hands up and rose from his chair. He paced the length of the carpet before the hearth. "I am in earnest, Sir Andrew. I grew close to Emma. We spoke of things in a way I have never experienced with another person." He kept pacing, though his steps slowed, as did his words. "She is a woman of remarkable intelligence. She grasps new concepts with speed, and her conversations are always agile. Fluid, in fact. She has a natural understanding of topics, and the ability to discuss an opinion with reserve even if she disagrees with it."

Quiet descended, the only sound Luca's footfalls and the snapping fire.

Until Sir Andrew muttered, "Confound it, Atella. You're in love with my cousin."

Luca stopped his pacing and turned slowly on one heel, pivoting to face the baronet. Sir Andrew wore a look of mingled shock and amusement. While Luca could appreciate the latter, the former made him draw up proudly. "A man would be a fool if he didn't see all that is good and lovely in Emma Arlen."

Folding his arms again, Sir Andrew leaned against the mantel. "You love her. Admit it." He sounded less shocked now and more entertained by the prospect. "And I thought you were after Josie when we first met."

Heat crept up Luca's throat, but thankfully the darkness and cravat would hide that telling reaction. "I admired Lady Josephine, I will not deny that. Yet it did not take long for Emma to gain my full attention. I have debated for some time what to do about it, but this last week has made everything more difficult. If her feelings have changed, and she no longer wishes to consider us friends, what am I to do?"

"Why do you think you've done something wrong? It could just be a female thing. One hears how changeable a lady's mind can be." Sir Andrew shrugged, his concern having apparently melted away once he realized Luca posed no threat to his cousin's well-being.

Shaking his head, Luca took up pacing again. "This is not that."

"Then you need to ask her directly what you've done, and I would suggest you apologize for it."

"Ask directly? How? When I cannot even speak to her alone..."

"I might be able to help you with that." A devious smile spread across the other man's face. "If Emma isn't in the usual public rooms, or the personal suites that belong to the dowager, the duchess, or Josephine, she's in the duchess's Japanese garden."

Luca rubbed the back of his neck, remembering the way those garden walls had protected them from the stiff wind. Despite the chill in the air, she might be comfortable in such a place. Especially while the sun shone to warm the stones.

When he asked, he no longer cared that he sounded desperate. "When is she normally there?"

"Every morning when Josephine is taking lessons with her grandmother. I would think around eleven you would find her, if the weather is dry enough."

"Thank you." Luca's shoulders fell. "I will try to find her. I am sorry to have disturbed your rest."

"Not at all. I look forward to seeing how things play out between you." Sir Andrew walked Luca to the door, far too cheerful for Luca's liking. "I really did think you meant to pursue Josephine. Nearly everyone does, you know. I cannot think that Emma has ever had a suitor. Most men aren't interested in the companion."

"Most men are stupid, then," Luca muttered as he stepped out the door. "Good evening, Sir Andrew."

"I hope so, Lord Atella."

The door shut behind Luca, leaving him in darkness. He made his way back to his own quarters and fell into bed, planning what amounted to ambushing Emma. While planning a confrontation wasn't exactly what he wanted, it would be for the best if he could clear the misunderstanding between them and determine if they might continue in their friendship—or possibly make it into something more.

THE JAPANESE GARDEN, TUCKED AWAY FROM THE WORLD AND protected by its stone walls, perfectly suited Emma that cold autumn morning. She wore her favorite chocolate colored spencer, with her gloved hands tucked deep into a muff, and she followed the path that looped around the edges of the garden. The exercise refreshed her, and the quiet allowed her to think without distraction.

Most of the time.

She had made only one complete lap when Emma became aware of another person in the garden. The one person she had wished to avoid. The ambassador from the Kingdom of the Two Sicilies.

He had already seen her and paced toward her, his long stride quickly halving the distance. She briefly contemplated climbing up the wall to escape, but she was no longer a child of ten capable of such ludicrous behavior. Best to stand still and smile, she knew, and have whatever discussion he wished to have with her.

Even if it proved unpleasant and focused on Josephine.

Luca's approach set off a reaction inside her she had yet to grow used to—it felt as though she had swallowed dandelion puffs, which then fell to pieces and floated about inside her causing all manner of disquiet in her stomach.

"Emma, I have searched for you all over the castle." He wore a smile as he spoke, as though performing such a task had proved a delight rather than a bother. "Your cousin told me I might find you here."

Oh, he had? She would deal with Andrew later.

"Yes, well. The day is fine, and this is one of the best gardens during the fall. Even if it lacks its usual color." She gestured to the trees which had lost most of their leaves. She spoke quickly. "The icy wind stripped the Japanese magnolia of everything, making it almost impossible for one to imagine how beautiful the tree will be in the spring when it sprouts its pink blossoms again. It is my favorite tree in all the gardens."

She hated when she babbled, but Emma couldn't stop herself. "The duchess is certain that the fascination with everything from Asia will grow in popularity. Now it is all Indian shawls and Chinese silk, but the beautiful plants will follow. She planted this tree the same year she married the duke."

Luca's expression had gone from open to confused, though he dutifully studied the tree every time she waved her hand toward it. "Fascinating. And it is your favorite?"

"Yes, my very favorite."

"The color—is it like the dress you wore to the harvest race?" he asked suddenly, his gaze fully upon her.

Emma swallowed her surprise and shook her head. "No. Lighter. Almost like cherry blossoms." She tucked her hand securely in her muff with the other, clasping them tightly together. "You ought to talk to Mr. Gardiner about the subject. He is fascinated with the idea of transplanting species from one side of the world to the other."

"Perhaps I will. But Emma, I didn't come out here to speak to you about trees." He came closer, his gentle smile returning.

Her heart fluttered along with her stomach. Dratted dandelion puffs.

"Oh? Have you something in particular you wish to discuss?" Emma neatly stepped around him and started forward on the path again. Toward the only escape route through the grotto.

Luca kept pace with her easily. "I do. I am wondering if I owe you an apology."

She laughed, the sound almost hysterical. "An apology? Whatever for? No, Luca. You do not owe me any apologies."

"I have not offended you?" he asked, confusion upon his face. "Then why—? Emma. Emma, please stop." He put his hand gently on her arm. So gently she could have ignored him and kept walking. But she stopped as requested, though she refused to meet his gaze. She kept her eyes on the stickpin in his cravat. It was lovely. A stylized silver lion with little blue gems for eyes. A masterpiece by an artisan, of course.

"You haven't offended me," she said to the lion. Its eye winked back at her in the sunlight.

"You say that, yet I find no relief in your words." He released a very eloquent and disappointed sigh. "You will not even look at me."

She stole herself against allowing more lions to disturb her and raised her eyes to his. "There. I am looking at you. You have done nothing to offend me, Luca." She tightened her jaw and smiled.

Luca held his hand out to her, palm-up. "Do you promise?"

What could she do but lay a hand in his, as though to seal her agreement? "I promise."

The instant her palm touched his, he closed his hand around hers and drew closer. Too close. Almost as close as they had stood together in the kitchen when he'd taught her how to make pasta.

"Emma." Her name upon his lips was like a caress, and it drew her gaze to his mouth. She had always loved the hint of his accent in his words. Had anyone else noticed how the accent grew stronger when he spoke on subjects that had nothing to do with politics? The shift was subtle, but she always heard it—and always knew when he spoke on a matter which genuinely interested him.

"Yes, Luca? Now that you know we are not at odds, is there anything else?" She peered up at him from beneath her bonnet brim, trying not to expose too much of her feelings through her eyes. "Perhaps you wished to speak of Josephine again?"

He blinked, then slowly shook his head. "Why do you think that?"

"You have a very earnest look about you," she observed, keeping her tone soft. "As though you are on a deeply personal mission that has little to do with politics."

His lips twitched in that way that made her want to coax them into a full smile. "You already know me so well. Yes. I wish to speak of something personal."

Personal? Could he wish to speak to her about the difference that she sensed between them? If he had noticed her change in demeanor, he was clever enough to guess what it meant.

No. To get her hopes up at that moment would prove foolish. And yet.... "Very well. How may I help you?" Because that was what friends did. They helped one another. And he said it was not to do with Josephine. He had given her up.

"You understand why I wish to take an English bride," he said suddenly, without warning, diving deeply into the subject she least wanted to discuss.

Her mouth went dry. The way he held her hand, looked so seriously at her—he could not mean for her to be his bride, surely? "Of course. It would cement your relationship with England and prove to everyone that you are here permanently, as well as facilitate your desire to connect our kingdoms through more than just trade negotiations." Her interest in politics made her a bit of a realist when it came to political matches.

His smile appeared, though relieved rather than broad. "Yes. That is part of it. But marriage is not something to enter in lightly, especially given the way Catholics are treated here and Protestants are treated in my country."

"That could pose difficulty, yes." And she had done enough research in the matter to know that an Anglican could never marry in a Catholic church, though a Catholic might marry under the supervision of an Anglican priest, and with exceptions made by higher church authorities. She had looked into the matter when

Luca had first mentioned the differences between weddings after Alice and Rupert wed.

Her heart started racing.

She had no great hope of seeing such a wedding performed. Or being part of one. Not at all. Unless. What if Luca wished to speak to her on the matter because he needed to know if Emma would consider such a marriage?

Luca still had hold of her hand. "Then as we are friends, and you know me so well, how would you advise I pay court to an English woman who must necessarily join herself to my cause and my life?"

Her heart sank all the way down to the ground beneath her feet. Perhaps even further, given how cold she felt in its absence. He wanted her advice to court another woman. Not Josephine. Then whom?

The words stumbled from her, tripping and tumbling form her tongue. "I-I must think on it. Marrying into such a situation is no small thing. The woman you chose would need to dedicate her life to helping your position and your work." Why had her voice betrayed her by quivering?

She stared at their joined hands, blinking back tears. "Let me consider the issue. Then we may talk of it later."

She couldn't look at him; she kept her head turned slightly away.

"Thank you, Emma." His voice had a strange quality to it, too. It sounded deeper, almost making her shiver. And then he leaned in close to her, unexpectedly, and his lips pressed gently against her cheek.

She closed her eyes, memorizing the sensation despite its brevity. It took her by surprise, the warmth of his lips, how his heat transferred into her and ran through her entire body before she went cold again, and how much she wished to turn and press her lips to his.

She nodded tightly. "You are most welcome. Good day." She

made to leave, moving faster than before, and he called after her, sounding bewildered.

"Emma? But where are you going? Wait—I do not think you understand."

Another voice shouted for her from the grotto at nearly the same moment Luca caught up to her.

"Emma? Are you in there?" Josephine stepped out into the sunlight, bundled up against the cold, her cheeks rosy and her eyes sparkling. "Oh, good. I found you."

Why did everyone know where to look for her? Emma would have a word with her cousin, and it would not be a cheerful one.

The footsteps behind her faded. Luca had stopped following her, and Emma did not look back at him. He would not continue his conversation on courtship or English brides while Josephine was present. She immediately looped her arm through Josie's and dragged her friend back through the grotto.

"Emma, whatever is the matter?" Josie asked, her voice echoing on the stone before they were out the other side.

"Nothing," Emma said, marching quickly away from Luca and all his talk of marrying someone. Someone who wasn't her. Then kissing her as a brother might kiss a sister. Her eyes burned, and the path blurred.

"Something is wrong," Josie insisted, hurrying to keep up. "Have you a cold?"

"No," Emma snapped. "I do not have a cold." Then she tugged Josie behind a hedgerow and stopped. "I am sorry, I only wished to get away from Lord Atella so we might have a private conversation."

"Oh." Josie's blue eyes conveyed her confusion. "Has he displeased you?"

A sad laugh escaped Emma. "Why does everyone think that?"

"You have avoided him of late. I would think avoiding me, too, except I know I am guilty of hiding in my tower far too often." Josie folded her mittened hands before her and studied Emma, her gaze far too perceptive. "He has upset you. But you are not angry. You're hurt."

Why did they have to be as close as sisters? Could not Josie pretend for even a moment she didn't read every emotion on Emma's face as others read books? "I am perfectly well, thank you, and I do not wish to speak of Lord Atella. I thought that attitude would suit you."

Josephine's eyebrows drew together sharply. "Why?"

"Because you dislike him."

"I like him well enough," Josephine said, voice quiet.

"Not well enough to let him court you." Emma's thoughts and feelings spiraled together inside of her, making her unwise in her words. "And if you had never minded such a thing, I would not be in this predicament. He is talking of courting another English woman. Even after I proved of no use to him where you are concerned, he had the audacity to ask for my assistance."

Josephine's soft "oh" barely entered Emma's consciousness.

"First you wanted me to help you by distracting him, then I offered him my guidance to woo you, and then everything was better when I said I had rather not bother with it at all. He is too good a man to deceive or trick, Josie. He is honorable and kind, and there is so much gentleness to him. I think he does not know how much life he has missed, how much joy the war stole from him. He did not have a childhood like ours, where he knew he was safe and kept close to those who cared for him."

Emma's tears fell, and she knocked them away with the back of one hand.

"That sounds terrible," Josephine said quietly. "I did not know. His circumstances seems to have affected you deeply." The wind whistled through the hedges, making them both shiver, but Josephine was good enough to not suggest they take the conversation indoors. "Now he wishes to court another woman, and that upsets you?"

"No," Emma said, drawing the word out slowly. "Or perhaps...

yes. He deserves someone wonderful, Josie. Someone who sees him for all that he is trying to accomplish, and for all the wonderful things he could do. If only you had shown some interest—" Emma broke off, looking up at her friend. "He could make you happy, Josie, I am certain of it. He is the sort of man who would put the person he loves before anything else. He would spend hours in conversation with you about your writing, if you wished it."

"Would he?" Josephine smiled, though the expression struck Emma as amused rather than intrigued. "But I am not looking for a husband."

"Someday you will want one," Emma argued, hearing how ridiculous she sounded and not caring. "Why not *Conte* Atella? You would be a countess—an Italian *contessa*, in a new kingdom."

"Emma, listen to yourself." Josie placed a hand on each of Emma's shoulders, her blue eyes sparkling with mirth. "You said he would put the person he *loves* before anything else. I think you must marry him."

"Me?" Emma squeaked the word out. "No, not me. He needs a woman of high rank, someone well-connected—"

"Like the ward of a duke?" Josephine asked.

Emma shook her head in denial. "That isn't the same. Besides which, he doesn't know that—"

"Tell him, then!"

"But my circumstances shouldn't matter. If he doesn't want me when I am only a lady's companion, then I shouldn't tell him."

"That is silly. You know as well as I do that as beautiful as stories of love between classes may seem, they are unlikely and improbable. Even if he fell madly in love with a milkmaid, a man of his station couldn't marry her without being stripped of everything he holds dear. Especially the respect of his peers." Josephine gave Emma a little shake. "But that doesn't matter because you are *not* a poor relation forced to take work. You are a well-connected daughter of a gentleman, with more than a few pennies to your name, and the full support of the Duke of Montfort."

Everything Josephine said was true. Yet Emma shook her head. "He doesn't want me, no matter what I am."

"How do you know?"

"Because if he did," Emma shouted, "he would not ask me to help him find a wife!" Then she tugged out of Josephine's grasp. "I am sorry, Josie. I cannot speak of this now. Please, you must excuse me," she begged. "Tell everyone I am ill. I must think."

Josephine's eyes were wide as the moon and nearly as blank, and Emma recognized her friend's confusion. She felt much the same herself. All ability to discuss the situation rationally had fled with the touch of Luca's lips to her cheek—a touch that still burned upon her skin.

Emma needed to leave before she made a greater fool of herself.

She left her friend in the garden and entered the house by a servants' door, then climbed the hidden steps to the second floor and her bedchamber. She secured the door with a twist of the key, grateful for the expensive locks the duke had installed in all the family's personal rooms. He took their privacy and security seriously, as he did every responsibility of his position as the head of the family.

Emma fell into the chair beside her hearth and covered her face with both hands. Her cheeks burned beneath her touch, the humiliation of the day staining her. In the space of half an hour, she had insulted the duke's guest and his eldest daughter. Both people she counted as her friends. All because she could not bridle her heart and keep hold of her affections.

What a mess she had made of *everything*.

CHAPTER NINETEEN

In the guest wing the next morning, Luca sat at the writing desk in his retiring room, adjacent to his bedchamber. He stared at the writing implements, the penknife, the blotter, though he didn't actually see them.

All he could see, in fact, was the empty place at the table the night before. Only after Lady Josephine had explained to the family that Emma felt unwell was the place cleared away. A footman had swept toward the table and packed everything from cup to plate away onto a tray, while another removed her chair.

As it had not been a formal dinner with others present, no one had lamented an unbalanced table. But Luca had looked at the empty place more than once. Sir Andrew had seemed concerned at his cousin's absence and shared a significant look first with Lady Josephine, then with Luca.

In the drawing room after the meal, Luca had tried to speak to Lady Josephine—to ask her about Emma—but the woman had deftly brushed aside his inquiries, then joined one of her younger sisters at the pianoforte to avoid him the rest of the evening.

Luca took out the little notebook he'd kept with him since his arrival in England. He turned the pages, not even smiling when he reached all the strange phrases the English used. He found the page he had started when he had determined to take Lady Josephine as his bride.

How ridiculous he had been to think gaining a wife would be as simple as making a list. The concept of courtship and attraction had infinitely more complexities than the trade negotiations he had studied for hours on end that week.

Part of his difficulty was that he had gone about looking for a wife the wrong way. What he had thought of as important had nothing to do with what would be of lasting happiness. *Well-connected or noble*, he had written. Preferably both. Pretty. Young. An excellent hostess. All such qualities would be important in a wife, but he knew now that he needed more than a woman to look lovely upon his arm and preside over social functions.

He turned to a blank page and wrote at the top: *An ambassador's wife needs several qualities. She should be capable of setting others at ease, understanding politics, respecting other cultures, and possess a natural curiosity that makes her want to learn more. She must have a sense of adventure and be kind-hearted. She ought to enjoy speaking of books and art, past and present, and converse well on challenging topics. She must be more than a political partner, but a friend to her husband.*

Luca needed a wife that fit this new list. In truth, he needed Emma.

He dropped the pencil and pressed the heels of his hands into his eyes, rubbing at them but unable to dismiss his concern.

She had misunderstood him in the garden, but he couldn't be certain how to repair the damage. Not until he spoke to her. And she had successfully avoided speaking to him alone for nearly a week.

A knock on the door leading to Torlonia's room made Luca mutter a less than appropriate word. The monks would've been horrified he even knew such language. He winced and sent a silent prayer to heaven for forgiveness. Then he called, "Enter."

Torlonia came into the room between both of theirs, dressed for the day as impeccably as ever. Frowning as darkly as ever.

"*Mio Signore*," he said, speaking rapidly in their native tongue. "The ambassador from Austria is in London, and we have received word of his attempts to paint our kingdom as unstable and unworthy of English trade." He shook a piece of paper in the air as he spoke, his eyes wide and wild. "There are all the usual claims made, that Austria must have sovereignty over the whole peninsula, and Metternich is pressing for a meeting of nations."

Metternich, an Austrian diplomat with more to do with Napoleon's rule than anyone liked, had shown far too much interest in Italy of late. The man had helped engineer Napoleon's second marriage, tried to control the outcome of the Congress of Vienna in 1814, and made his first visit to Italy the following year. He had been part of every important committee in Europe for a decade, having the ear of more than one monarch at vital moments.

"I thought he was to return to Austria after the Congress of Aachen," Luca growled, reaching for the letter. He had a counterpart at that congress sending him letters and newspapers as representatives from other nations discussed what to do about the allied troops in France.

"Not until December. He is coming from Brussels—the congress there is ended—and will spend Christmas with the tsar in Venice. You know how it will be. He will spend all the time gathering information to present against unified Italian states." Torlonia started pacing while Luca read the report. "We must go to London."

Luca's head jerked up. "London? Parliament is not yet in session."

"I know that," Torlonia barked. "I am not a simpleton. But communication is easier there, and faster. I have it through my sources that Matternich will send a representative to begin the work of convincing the British to call another meeting with Spain, to speak of forcing King Ferdinand to change the constitution or give up his rights to his Austrian cousins."

Luca dropped the letter on his desk. It contained the suppositions Torlonia shared, as well as information that the Prussian court supported Austrian rule over all of Italy.

"It cannot be as dire as you seem to think," Luca said, frowning at the paper. "We have heard nothing distressing about Austria's claims from our own court. Things move slowly. There is time to understand more."

"Time?" Torlonia froze on the spot. "You speak of time as though we are wealthy with it—but do you remember how quickly France swallowed most of Europe? Of course not—you were a mere boy. Hiding with monks in the country." Torlonia shook his head, his shoulders falling. "We must go to London, at once. We can leave now and have our luggage sent after. The duke will understand. In London, we will be better positioned to keep watch over this situation."

"It can wait," Luca repeated, though without conviction.

"His Majesty the King would not want you to sit idly in the country when you could move forward, when you could take action. Parliament will not convene until January, yes, but there are members who are there *now*." Torlonia took on a pleading tone, then reached into his coat and withdrew another folded piece of paper. "And there is this."

With misgiving, Luca took the paper from him and opened it. "What is this?"

"This is a letter from a friend in Ferdinand's court." Torlonia lifted his chin into the air. "There are questions that have arisen about your suitability for your role."

"Why would such questions come about?" Luca asked, reading a list of rumors about himself that made his temperature rise. "They say I do nothing? That I am spending my time as a youth—frivolously wasting the king's coin?" Luca lifted his eyes to Torlonia. "Who would dare say such lies? I have worked every day since my foot touched English soil to see to our country's needs."

Torlonia said nothing, but there was a gleam in his eye. He had triumphed, Luca realized, presenting the argument that would most efficiently make Luca see things his way. The secretary had been present when men of greater standing had questioned Luca's suitability in the role of ambassador due to his age and his lack of experience in the political arena of their nation.

If the same men continued to vent doubts when Luca was not there to defend himself, the king might well decide to recall him.

"We must go to London," Luca murmured, a weight pressing upon his chest. "I will inform the duke—"

Nothing could have delighted Torlonia more, given his sudden and rapid speech. "I have already told him and sent for your horse. Bruno is preparing your things now."

Luca looked up, meeting the secretary's eyes. "You did what?" he asked, standing. "You would presume to do such a thing before you even informed me of the circumstances?"

The older man's cheeks turned red. "I knew how it would be. You are young, *Signore*, but you are not stupid."

Something felt wrong about the circumstances, about rushing away, and it was not only the knowledge that he must leave Emma behind.

Leaving her with such uncertainty between them could well end everything—their friendship and the potential for so much more between them. Torlonia had overstepped, and Luca would make his secretary and himself look foolish if he did not leave that very day. Torlonia had seen to that by announcing their departure to all in the castle.

"I must write a letter first."

The door to Luca's room opened, and Bruno came out, holding a saddle bag over one arm and Luca's riding clothes over the other. The elder man moved with haste, his face pale. "È tutto pronto, mio Signore."

Torlonia gestured to Bruno. "Yes, get dressed at once. You may write your letter in London. I will dress and meet you in the grand hall. I am certain His Grace will be waiting to bid you farewell." The secretary, all pomposity restored, turned and left the room, slamming the door behind him.

Luca could not keep the duke waiting. He looked to Bruno, noting the sheen of sweat on the other man's forehead. "What is happening, Bruno? Why the haste?"

The valet shook his head. "It is nothing. Here, let us hurry to have you ready."

Rather than distress the old man by making him wait, Luca dressed with his help. He kept composing a letter to Emma in his head, but there were no simple words for what he felt—for what he must explain—and how he hoped she might come to see things between them as he did. What could he possibly do—how could he convey everything to her in the midst of this uncalled-for haste?

Why was Torlonia so insistent they leave right away? The secretary had thought visiting the duke would demonstrate status and elitism. Surely he had to know that Luca's friendship with a high-powered member of the English nobility meant good things for their kingdom. Practically fleeing the duke's hospitality would cause the opposite.

Luca finished dressing and took out his notebook. He carefully tore the page out upon which he'd written his new hopes, his new ideals for a companion of his heart. A wife.

"To Emma," he scrawled at the top of the torn page. Then, at the bottom, he wrote: "I must leave today—though I do not understand the need for haste. Know that I regret leaving before we could speak. Emma, write to me. Please. There is much I must tell you. I hope these words will make a beginning. You must know, they describe you perfectly."

It was as bold a statement as he could make on paper. He rushed from the room, saddlebag over his arm and paper in hand.

Torlonia waited in the hall. "Finally. Come, we must go down at once."

"No, I need to deliver this letter to Miss Arlen." Luca turned toward the long hall which would eventually take him to the family's quarters, where he knew Emma's room lay.

"She will likely be downstairs to bid us farewell. Come." Torlonia started walking at a fast clip, and Luca followed. He didn't know where Emma's room was. He had only been in the family wing once. It made sense that she—as a member of the household—would be present to say goodbye.

Except Emma wasn't there. Only the duke, Lord Farleigh, and Sir Andrew stood at the door. Luca stopped before the duke, confusion swirling in his heart and thoughts.

"We are sorry you must leave, Atella," His Grace said, his expression friendly enough. "I hope we will see you in London after Christmas. You must come visit us at at our house in Mayfair."

"The moment I can, Your Grace, I will call upon you there." Luca still clutched the letter in his hand, and he knew he had only one option left to him if he wished it to find its way to Emma's hand. "Your Grace, though I leave you in this rude manner, I have a great favor to ask of you. Would you grant me permission to write to Miss Arlen?"

He heard Torlonia's sharp intake of breath.

The duke's eyebrows raised, but it was Sir Andrew who spoke.

"To what end, Atella?" He wore a wide, almost mocking, grin. "After our last conversation, I was under the impression she hadn't any particular desire to spend time in your company, let alone receive your letters."

Luca glared at the baronet, wondering why anyone liked the man and his constant jests. "You know precisely why."

"I am not privileged with this information," the duke said, his deep voice measured and certain. "Why do you wish to write Miss Arlen?"

"I hope to continue our friendship while I am away," Luca replied, meeting the duke's gaze squarely. He and his daughter shared blue eyes, but while Lady Josephine had never seemed to give Luca a serious thought on any matter, the duke's gaze was probing and quite solemn. "And hopefully grow it into something more. If it pleases you, Your Grace."

The duke considered Luca, then gave one slow nod. "Very well. You may write to her."

His heart stuttered, then he turned to Sir Andrew. The man wore a smile as smug as anything Luca had ever seen. "Will you see to it your cousin receives this note?" He held the folded paper out to the other man, then gritted his teeth when he realized Sir Andrew might well be the sort of person who would read it before delivering it.

"I will." Sir Andrew took the folded paper and tucked it into a pocket. "And I will promise not to read it, in case that's what made you frown like someone stepped over your grave."

Although the English phrase made Luca hesitate, Torlonia cleared his throat, and Luca knew he had spent enough time on the matter. His secretary felt an urgency Luca did not understand, but everything set in motion for his departure could not come to a halt now.

"Thank you again, Your Grace. I hope you know that the time here at Castle Clairvoir has meant more to me than I can say, and that you will always have a friend in me." He bowed, formally taking his leave, and then Luca and Torlonia were out the door and on horses.

At least it was horses and not a carriage.

Luca heaved a disappointed sigh as they rode away, casting one last look over his shoulder at the castle before he set his sights forward. To London.

England had a reliable mail system, at least. Emma might well send a letter after him that would arrive before his luggage did. The thought alone made him content.

⁂

Tucked up in her bed, playing the part of an invalid, Emma turned Luca's note over and over again in her hands. She said nothing, only stared at the blankets on her bed. Josephine sat in a chair, arms folded, glaring at her friend.

"I hope you see what playing at being ill has caused," Josie said. "We could have been downstairs when he left, but no. You had to plead illness last night and illness upon waking. You could have seen him, could have looked directly in his eyes and—"

"And what?" Emma asked, voice soft. "It is not as though he would make a confession of love in front of your father. Or anyone else. If he even intended it."

"Of course he intended to," Josephine argued, gesturing to the letter. "You are everything he wants. He said so himself."

With a disappointed shrug, Emma unfolded the note in her hand and read it again.

To Emma:

An ambassador's wife needs several qualities. She should be capable of setting others at ease, understanding politics, respecting other cultures, and possess a natural curiosity that makes her want to learn more. She must have a sense of adventure and be kind-hearted. She ought to enjoy speaking of books and art, past and present, and converse well on challenging topics. She must be more than a political partner, but a friend to her husband.

I must leave today—though I do not understand the need for haste. Know that I regret leaving before we could speak. Emma, write to me. Please. There is much I must tell you. I hope these words will make a beginning. You must know, they describe you perfectly.

- Luca

"He mentions being a friend. That is not a declaration of love." She handed the letter to Josephine. "And an ambassador's wife? Josie, I couldn't do that. Not without more than friendship."

"First of all," Josie said, reading through the letter, "you would make an excellent ambassador yourself. If women were permitted to be such things. So I think you are perfectly suited to be the wife of an ambassador. Second, he says there is more he wants to tell you. What else could it be but a declaration of love?"

Emma shook her head and closed her eyes. "In the garden, he said he wanted to discuss finding an English bride with me."

Shaking the letter at Emma with some violence, Josie spoke sternly. "Did you ever stop to think that he meant *you* for his bride, you ninny?"

With alarm, Emma's eyes popped open, and she reached for the letter, afraid her friend would harm it by shaking it about. "For a moment, I hoped he did. But I convinced myself it could not be so."

Josephine released the paper into Emma's hand. "You are behaving foolishly, which the poets and playwrights lead me to believe means you are very much in love with the ambassador. Because you are never foolish, Emma. You are the most clear-minded person I know."

"I haven't felt that way in a long while." Emma put the paper down on the table near her bed, then took up a cushion to hug to her chest. She ought to get up. With Luca gone, there was no reason to feign illness. She had only done so to avoid answering him about helping him gain an English bride.

"Papa gave you permission to write to him." Josephine rose and pointed one elegant finger at Emma's writing desk. "You must begin at once. I imagine it will take you many drafts before you are happy with whatever it is you wish to say. I suggest you take him to task for misleading you, then forgive him, and tell him how you feel."

Emma's cheeks heated. "Certainly not."

Josephine glowered. "What are you going to say then?"

"I don't know." She looked at the paper on her table, the single ragged edge that meant he'd torn it from a book where some other soul had carefully sewn it together. "I need to think about things. Perhaps wait for another letter from him explaining why he left in such haste."

Although Josephine frowned in disapproval, she did not say anything else on the matter. She changed the subject instead, and rather abruptly. Perhaps she knew that the more she pushed Emma, the more Emma only wished to push back.

Matters of the heart could not be decided through *letters*. Luca hadn't confessed his feelings to her. Indeed, he had provided a list of things he wished for in a wife and stated she fulfilled those qualifications. It wasn't quite a declaration.

Perhaps his next letter would help her understand what he really wanted from her and if she was capable of giving it.

CHAPTER TWENTY

A fortnight in London, and Luca had not received a letter from Emma. What he had received, in terms of mail, amounted to a large stack of papers locked in his temporary desk drawer. Temporary because the house he had leased to set up as the embassy was under minor construction. So he stayed in a hotel near St. James's Court.

Eventually, he would move into Davies Street, where number 14 Three Kings Yard would host him and future ambassadors at a most reasonable rate, considering the fashionable address. But at the moment, it wasn't livable, with men-of-all-work coming and going at all hours.

As it was, he only visited the site that day and stood in the room meant to be a reception hall and ballroom. It was large enough to host a fashionable number of couples, and the floors were in a fine state, but the walls were atrocious.

If only he could ask Emma about them. Her opinion on decor was the only opinion that mattered to him. Unfortunately, with no encouragement to write to her, there was no way to know what she would wish. Luca had chosen a silk paper with ivory pillars and curling vines that reminded him of his home.

SALLY BRITTON

Torlonia was at the hotel, too. Busier than ever with his letter writing, and gaining invitations for the both of them to fine homes. The man was in something of a frenzy about the work. Something Luca didn't understand.

The pounding of hammers in another room made Luca's head throb, but he walked through the house slowly anyway. His papers would keep, and he needed to make decisions about the house. And about Emma.

Did he dare write her a second time?

A young man dressed in the clothing of a well-paid servant appeared in front of Luca, his expression earnest. "Lord Atella? Your Excellency?"

Luca blinked back to the present and offered a brief nod. "I am he."

The servant held out a piece of paper. "I tried to find you at your hotel, Your Excellency. This is an urgent letter that came to my master's house by mistake. He apologizes for the misdirection."

Luca looked down, seeing the laboriously beautiful script had left quite a few margins for error in delivery. The only clear thing in the looping, formal handwriting was his name. "Thank you." Luca slipped a coin into the young man's hand, then opened the letter.

As he read the words written by a firm, sweeping hand, and signed with a flourish and kingly seal, Luca's stomach turned. It was worse than being in a closed carriage. He read the letter again, then put it in his coat and hurried out of the house. His horse waited for him, held by a boy who received more pennies than he'd likely ever held in his life.

Luca pulled the horse's head around and dashed through the streets as fast as he could, without causing incident. He arrived back at the hotel and hurried to the suite of rooms he and Torlonia had taken.

Torlonia was in the common room, writing a letter at the desk near the window. He jumped when Luca slammed the door behind him, then stood. Luca remained near the door, knowing if he approached the other man he would certainly lay hands upon him. He seethed in silence, every possible start to the conversation he wished to have something that would shame him to say.

"My lord." Torlonia edged away from the desk. "You seem disquieted. Was something wrong at the future embassy?"

Luca's hands curled into fists, then uncurled. "I received a letter while I was there. A letter from Ferdinand's secretary."

The other man paled. "All letters are supposed to come through me—"

"This one was misdelivered and came directly to my hands." Luca stalked forward, and Torlonia backed up against the window. "And a good thing, too. This letter, it demands an answer. From me. Directly. Because our king grows tired of hearing *your* accounts of my *inadequacy*. It would seem that you, Torlonia, have been writing the court *weekly* with reports of my failures."

"That—that isn't true. How would you even know—?" Torlonia lifted his chin, affecting his usual haughty expression. "What proof do you have of such lies?"

With a violent speed, Luca tore the letter from inside his coat and threw it to the table in the middle of the room. He didn't dare take another step near the dishonorable man. "This letter, signed by the king's secretary and bearing the royal seal. It demands that I answer the accusations against me—accusations made by *you*. What have you done, Torlonia?"

"Nothing." Torlonia sniffed and cowered. "These are lies."

"No. This is not a lie." Luca pointed at the paper. "*Sei un bugiardo. You* are the liar. I know you disapproved of me. My lack of experience. But we have worked together all this time, and I have valued your counsel. Why would you tell our king that I mock him to his political enemies?" He pointed an accusing finger at the paper. "That I disregard what is best for our people, that I am slothful?"

Torlonia drew himself together, like a man preparing for an attack. "They were supposed to recall you. Not send *another* letter after I told them you discarded the last. Then I would stay here, the ambassador in your place." His gaze turned icy, his words dripping with venom. "You are a disgrace. You are not even true nobility. Your family was nothing before Napoleon, and it will be nothing again. I am descended from the greatest Italians—from Michelangelo, from the princes of Rome."

Luca released his breath in a hiss. "Carbonari."

For a moment, Torlonia seemed surprised by the word. Then he smiled. "You can prove nothing."

The door to Luca's room opened. Bruno came out, looking between both men. "*Mio Signore*," he said, his voice shaking. "Please. He has said he will hurt the family—your sisters—you must stop him."

"Traitor," Torlonia barked angrily. "I believe in a free Italy," he shouted, his calm gone again. "And as ambassador to England, I can make certain that happens. The connections, the power, would strengthen our cause. Do you not love your country, Atella? Ferdinand is nothing—he is not Italian, he should not be our king. He is nothing more than an Austrian puppet, and he will run our people into the grave—"

"Silence!" Luca stalked forward, and Torlonia backed up. "You are under arrest, by my order, and charged with treason."

The traitorous man balked, but puffed his chest out one last time, like a rooster. "No one will believe you. And when you send me back, my friends will see that I am free within hours."

"We will see," Luca warned. "Bruno, send for the constables."

Bruno bobbed a hasty bow. "*Sì, mio Signore*."

"I have friends everywhere, Atella." Torlonia glowered as he spoke, and Luca wanted nothing more than to place a fist through the man's horrible face.

Luca loomed closer, glaring down at the shorter man just before he took Torlonia's arm in a tight grip. The monks had a phrase they'd said, time and again, to encourage Luca's caution when he entered the world once more. *"Non ci sono amici tra i serpenti.* There are no friends among snakes. I will give my king your scent, Torlonia, and he will set the hounds loose. They will find the den, and that will be the end of your *friends."*

In less than an hour, Torlonia's escort to prison arrived. Luca spent the remainder of the day going through his former secretary's letters, with Bruno's help, and contacting every citizen of his kingdom in or near enough London with the news and asking for more information. And help. He needed testimonies to add to his own, and he had a great deal of explaining to do in his letters back to Ferdinand's court.

Always in the back of his mind, and settled in his heart, were thoughts of Emma. Could she have written him and Torlonia concealed the letter? He found nothing of the kind in the other man's notes and books. The longer he worked at sorting through the mess, the more he realized the precariousness of his position as ambassador.

If the king didn't believe him, Luca would lose his position. He would return home to his family's modest holdings and be nothing more than a landlord of a small village for the rest of his days. If that happened, he could offer Emma nothing. And she deserved everything—all that was good and beautiful in the world, all the adventures she wished, all the experiences that she had read about and yearned to make her own.

He closed his eyes in the early hours of the morning, and he tried to let Emma Arlen go.

CHAPTER TWENTY-ONE

Emma sat in the library, on her favorite couch, staring at the duke's globe. The late afternoon sun barely peeked through the clouds, creating the barest smudge of color through the stained-glass windows. The colors were more sickly shades of yellow and green than the usual vibrant hues she loved. But that was how the end of November usually was. Pale. Dull. And cold.

The next day would mark the first of December, and still no word from Luca. No explanation for why he had gone or what the paper he left had meant. She wanted to cry, or scream, but both of those things would only be her pretending to be the scorned heroine in a novel.

The reality of the situation, she knew, was that she had waited too long. If she had written him right away, a letter full of all her questions, she would feel less agony. Instead, she had put the burden upon him, without his knowledge, and all that did was leave her a lonely, miserable heap of a woman.

A soft click made her turn, looking to where the door to the duke's private study opened. The duke himself exited the room, his eyes immediately on hers, and his eyebrows raised.

"Emma. What are you doing in here all alone?" He came out

into the room, and she started to rise. "No, please. Sit. It has been some time since the two of us have had a moment to speak to each other." His eyes crinkled at the corners as he sat in the chair nearest hers, and Emma's heart tightened.

Her own smile was far too forced. "I am afraid I do not have much of interest to discuss, Your Grace."

The warm, fatherly expression he wore barely changed, but she could read the concern in his eyes. "Emma, my dear child, I cannot think that is true. I am very interested in you. In everything you do, as if you were one of my own daughters. You know this."

She bit her bottom lip and looked down at her lap, lacing her fingers together. "Yes, Your Grace. I do. Thank you for that."

"Has this been a happy home for you, Emma?" the duke asked, his voice as gentle as she'd ever heard it. The same tone he'd used when she was much smaller and still afraid of the dark.

"It has," she answered truthfully, the pain diminishing for the moment. "I love it here. I love being a friend to Josephine, and I love when Her Grace, your mother, clucks like a worried hen over my upbringing. And the duchess is always tender and kind toward me."

"I am glad to hear it. We all care for you, Emma. In fact, every member of this family cares about you so much that each and every person has been to see me with a most serious thing to discuss." He paused until she looked up, curiosity compelling her to look while he explained what this meant. "They wished to speak with me to express concern for you, Emma."

She blinked at him. "For me? But—nothing is wrong." She forced a laugh. "I'm perfectly well."

The duke settled into his seat a bit more, then leaned forward with his elbows resting on the arms of the chair. "My wife mentioned it first. Cecilia said you seemed unhappy of late. Then my mother mentioned that you have been far too quiet and unwilling to debate her in matters of poetry."

Emma's eyes teared up a bit at that. The dowager had noticed? Had cared enough to tell her son?

The duke continued. "Simon and your cousin Andrew spoke to me together, and Andrew offered to go to London to fetch a certain ambassador back to Clairvoir Castle."

Emma looked down again, her cheeks burning.

"Then James, young as he is, said you weren't nearly as fun as you used to be. Isabelle and Rosalind asked if you were ill. But it was Josephine, of course, who was most persistent. She asked if I would write that ambassador your cousin mentioned, and when I said I would not, she asked if she could do the honors instead."

"Oh no." Emma raised her head. "Josie didn't say a word about that to me—and you wouldn't let her. Would you?" She winced.

The duke slowly shook his head, his eyes full of compassion and understanding. "The only one who ought to write Lord Atella is you, my dear. Have you answered that note he shoved into your cousin's hand? His last act before leaving, you know."

Now thoroughly ashamed of herself, Emma lowered her voice. "No, Your Grace. I haven't written him. It's been a month. I think —I think I must have lost my chance." Her voice broke a little, but she cleared her throat and clutched her hands together tighter, trying to keep everything she felt inside. Then she started talking, the words coming too quickly and accompanied by all her fears. "He cannot care for me; he thinks I am only a companion. And I cannot entertain him as a suitor because Josephine is still at home. I promised I would be her companion until she settled on her future. Leaving her now—that would be an act of ingratitude for all the family has done for me."

"Emma," the duke interrupted, firm and kind. "That is nonsense. You are part of this family, not a servant, and you owe us nothing. I have long wondered if I was wrong to give in to your requests to act as a companion, and I have never allowed you to be treated as anything less than family. We all want your happiness, especially Josephine. If that means marriage—no matter if it is tomorrow by special license or years from now—I want that for you. Your father and mother would have wanted it for you."

Then the duke did something he hadn't done since she was a little girl. He left his chair and kneeled before her, offering his handkerchief so she might dry her eyes. "Your father was as dear to me as a brother. Everything I have done for you has been out of love for him, and then love for you. Dear little Emma. Take up your courage and follow your heart."

Emma sniffled and smiled through her tears, then dabbed at them. "Thank you, Your Grace." As another obstacle formed in her thoughts, she twisted the handkerchief in her hands. "But there is one thing I do not understand. Lord Atella—I care deeply for him, though I never meant to. But I know he must wed a woman of high standing. He thinks I am only a paid companion."

"Ah." The duke winced and shifted from the floor to the seat beside her. "I am afraid that isn't true."

"It isn't?" Emma studied the duke, trying to make sense of his words. "I never told him otherwise."

His Grace appeared sheepish for a moment. "Simon thought —after seeing you and the ambassador together—that he might form an attachment to you. But from what I had seen of Lord Atella, I knew him to be a man of honor. He would never make overtures toward a young woman he didn't think he could marry. As his position demands he marry a woman of some standing, I thought discreetly revealing your status as my ward would remove the only barrier to his affection." The duke sighed. "Perhaps I ought to have been more direct."

Emma opened her mouth, emitting a pitiful sound of distress before hastily closing it again. Then she stood and paced away to the window, turned and rushed back. "Your Grace, when did you tell him?"

"The day we came back from the hunting lodge," the duke

said, staring at Emma with raised eyebrows. "Did you notice anything different about him afterward?"

"Yes." Thinking through their week of friendly exchanges and conversations, of Luca's more relaxed manner and easy smiles, her heart thudded with excitement. "But not a very great difference. He seemed only more at ease. As though he did not guard himself as carefully as before."

The duke's knowing smile returned. "Then it is as I hoped. His knowledge gave him permission to care for you freely."

As Josephine had said before, she and Emma might read stories of romance and enjoy tales of princes and paupers, but they lived in a world where the highborn gentleman could never wed the dairy maid. An ambassador on a royally appointed mission could never wed a paid companion and keep his place, and his wife would not be accepted into higher society functions.

An Italian count and a duke's beloved ward could marry without negative consequences or shame attached to the union.

She sat down next to the duke abruptly. Then stood again, worrying the cloth in her hands. Then sat. "Then he might care for me."

The duke laughed, though not unkindly. "Emma, write to him. I'll even frank the letter."

Her mouth popped open. "But you never frank our personal letters—"

"This one is a matter of state, I think, since it's regarding the future happiness of His Excellency, the ambassador from the Kingdom of the Two Sicilies." He gave her a kiss on the forehead, then stood and walked to the door leading to the corridor. "I hope this means you will find reason to be your usual cheerful self at dinner tonight."

Emma nodded, though she still harbored some fear. If Luca knew everything, if he did care, why had he not written her again? She needed to write to him. At once.

That decided, she left the library in a rush, practically running through the corridors to get to her own room where she took up pen and paper. She opened her drawer and removed the letter from him, propping it up against her desk so she might read it again before writing her response.

To the Ambassador

Dear Lord Atella...

CHAPTER TWENTY-TWO

The echo of Luca's footsteps across the newly polished floors was the only sound in the ballroom. Finally, the embassy was complete enough for Luca to move into the grand house. But apart from the furnishings that came with the lease, the building remained empty.

There was no use in putting a personal touch in any of the rooms. No reason to hire servants and staff. Not until he knew what the King would decide about his appointment as ambassador. Another man might well be master of the house. Another couple, husband and wife, might enter the master suite of rooms to retire from a long day of political conversations and social engagements.

The letter in his coat pocket, sweet as its presence was, also reminded him of all the reasons he must wait to move forward with his plans. Emma had written him. He had received the letter only three days previous. She had spent half her words in apology —for waiting too long to write, for misunderstanding his intentions, and for her confessed role in aiding Josephine to avoid Luca from the beginning of their acquaintance.

He had to laugh at himself, and at the two of them, while he read. Had there ever been two such inept lovers?

As he walked the length of the ballroom, studying the way the light picked up the silver threads in the wallpaper, he wondered.

Luca hadn't written a reply yet. He'd tried. Numerous times. Either he stared at a blank sheet of paper, or he started to explain all that had gone wrong. Even though a few of his fellow countrymen had come forward to add testimony to his of Torlonia's duplicity, he waited upon the pleasure of the king.

Luca went to one of the windows overlooking the back garden. The plants were starting their winter sleep, leaving the grounds to look dull and gray. The garden, large by London standards, stretched back farther than he could see to a stable block shared by the other grand houses on the street. The whole of it would be beautiful in the spring. Yet all he could think of when he tried to picture a garden full of color and life was the autumn leaves of gold surrounding Emma's lovely form.

He leaned his forehead against the cool glass and offered a prayer—one of many, pleading for mercy shown to him for his foolishness, and asking that no matter the outcome of his circumstances, that Emma find happiness.

A soft tap on the ballroom floor made Luca straighten, fixing his coat by pulling on its hem. A workman might have returned. Or perhaps Bruno had come searching him out.

He turned, chin up and expression set to one of solemnity.

The figure on the opposite side of the room didn't belong to a man at all, but to a familiar woman. He knew her at once, dressed as she was in a deep green traveling gown with pink flowers wreathing her hat. She took another step, hesitant in the room lit only by the late-morning sun.

"Luca?"

He took one step toward Emma, and then another, and then he crossed the room with as much speed as he could. She met him halfway, her face turned up to his with roses in her cheeks. He extended his hands, and she placed hers in his without hesitation.

No matter his misgivings, there was only one correct response to her sudden appearance.

Luca drew her gently to him, hands clasping hers, and bent to kiss her. Emma met him halfway then, too. Her lips were soft as petals, her scent fresh as a spring rain, and it took everything in him not to wrap her in his arms and keep her there forevermore. When they parted, it was only for him to dip his head to kiss her anew, at a better angle than before, with a deeper token of his affection given.

She sighed and leaned into him when he tried to move away, and what could he do but give in a third time?

They had to part, though. Emma didn't know the mess of things. She needed to know the precariousness of his position.

"The duke had a letter," she said, staring up at him with her gentle brown eyes. "Torlonia betrayed you."

For a moment, he stared at her in disbelief. Their first words to each other in over a month, he realized, were not what he would have expected. "Then you must know what that means for me. For us."

The gentleness turned into frustration. "Luca, I'm not going to give you up. Do not ask me to."

"How did you come to be here?" he asked, ignoring the unpleasantness for the moment. Touching her cheek with one hand. "I only received your letter three days ago."

"The day after I sent my letter to you, the duke received word from a contact in London. His Grace said you were in a difficult position, and I asked if we could come to offer you our support." Her cheeks turned a deeper shade of pink. "I still cannot believe I asked such a thing of him. He's the Duke of Montfort, for goodness' sake."

"Your guardian," Luca said quietly. "Who loves you, I think."

Her smile returned. "Yes, he does. I imagine my own father

would have done the same for me. But you must see, Luca—with His Grace's word added to yours, your king will understand. The duke has written to our king, lodged a formal inquiry with Parliament, written your court, and has invited you to dinner this evening."

The last of the list made Luca laugh. "This evening? Is the whole family with you?"

Emma shook her head. "Only Simon and Josephine. And me. The rest will come after they have packed up the house for the Season. Luca, everything will turn out as it should. I know it."

She touched his cheek, her gloved thumb near his lips. Her eyes took in his. "I still have to help you find an English bride, you know."

Luca laughed and leaned down to rest his forehead against hers. "I think I have already found one. If she will have me."

"Englishwomen like to be courted properly before agreeing to marriage," she said quietly.

"Oh? And what constitutes a proper English courtship?" he asked, his lips hovering near hers again.

"The usual things. Walks in the park. Morning calls. Dancing. Oh, and most importantly...pasta making."

His laugh barely escaped before she kissed him again.

"I love you, Emma. I hope you have felt the truth of that now."

"My darling ambassador, I love you, too. With everything I am."

They left the ballroom to find the duke waiting in the entry hall, along with Simon and Josephine, Bruno standing quietly to one side. He must have brought them to the embassy to find Luca.

"Your Grace." Luca greeted the duke with a formal bow. "I would like to request permission to court your ward, Miss Emma Arlen."

The duke turned his attention to Emma. "I will approve the courtship, Lord Atella, though I will be honest with you. Emma has ever been her own woman. It will be her decision if she keeps you or not."

Emma looped her arm through Luca's and leaned her head against his shoulder, the open display of affection rather perfect. "I very much expect to keep him, Your Grace."

They did not leave the embassy until Luca gave them a tour, the duke offering suggestions for security as well as where to find the best-trained staff. Everyone acted as though Luca's position was assured, and for the first time in weeks, he felt hope that they were right.

"You ought to move forward with all your plans, Atella," Lord Farleigh said when they stood once more in the empty ballroom. "Hold a ball. Act as though you intend to be here a very long time. I think a statement like that would go a long way to showing both the English court and King Ferdinand's that you are the right man for the position."

Luca listened, then gave a slow nod. "That is sound advice. I must consult with my chief advisor, though." He looked down at Emma, who watched him with one raised eyebrow. "What do you think, chief advisor?"

The smile that lit her face and beamed at him through her eyes enlivened him, heart and soul. "I think you ought to listen to Simon. He has a good head for politics. Nearly as good as mine."

They all laughed together, and Luca felt himself drawn into the family. They loved Emma, and by extension, they cared for him, too. With the Duke of Montfort and his family supporting Luca, his time as an ambassador would prove long and fruitful. He had to have faith in that.

With Emma on his arm, Luca could hope for the best, and expect it, too.

Two months after her arrival in London, Emma entered the ballroom at the embassy. This time, it blazed with light from several chandeliers hanging above, their crystals throwing the light even farther. The whole room glowed with warmth and life, with couples dancing and members of parliament standing along the walls with their families and friends.

Luca escorted her, with Emma tucked close to his side. "This is stunning, Luca," she whispered so only he could hear. "It is magnificent."

Her handsome Italian chuckled and bent to murmur in her ear. "You only say that because I followed every single one of your suggestions for the evening."

Emma wrinkled her nose at him. "You ought to have asked a married woman to be your hostess, you know. That is how it is done."

"But not how I will do things. You are the only woman who will ever plan a ball, or a social, or a picnic, in this embassy. Or any of my houses, for that matter." He took her hand and led her to the ballroom floor.

Tonight they would announce their engagement, turning the ball into a celebration of love rather than a political gathering. She couldn't ask for anything more wonderful.

They took the lead position and other couples joined, the foremost among them Lady Josephine on the arm of some young lordling who did not have any chance of claiming a second.

"Do you think anyone will mind that we are going back to the castle to be married?" Luca asked as the music began.

"I don't care," Emma responded. "I have dedicated my life to you and your role in everything but this."

The way he smiled at her, broad and happy, free of worry, made her wish they were alone instead of at the center of a ballroom.

Spring couldn't come soon enough.

EPILOGUE

The first blooms of spring always appeared in the duchess's Japanese garden. The magnolia tree adorned itself in flowers of pink and white, wreathed more gloriously than any lady at court. Emma had invited only a few others to join the family there for a picnic the day before her wedding.

She sat next to Luca beneath her favorite tree, leaning against him while their friends surrounded them. Mr. and Mrs. Rupert Gardiner sat together, he examining the drawing she had sketched of a fallen bloom. The duke and duchess sat a little further away, and the dowager near them in a chair brought out at her demand.

Rosalind and Isabelle were chattering about the wedding and which flowers Emma ought to wear in her hair. "I still think roses would be prettier than wisteria," Rosalind said. "I shall have roses when I wed."

"Of course you would, but I want wisteria," Isabelle said. "And Emma will have the magnolia blossoms."

James played with his new dog, a little pup meant to live in the kennels, but the animal somehow ended up in the boy's room more nights than not.

And Josie sat on Emma's other side, under strict instructions to avoid bickering with Andrew.

"I want you both to get along for a day or two, as a wedding present," Emma had asked a mere hour before the picnic.

"That is a horrid present. Let me give you a better one. I have ordered the entire collection of *Arabian Nights* for your new library. Even the books my father said we had no business reading."

Emma had been hard-pressed to remain firm in the face of such a thoughtful gift. But she had managed. "That's lovely, and I thank you for it. But still. No bickering."

Luca's arm stole around Emma, and he leaned back against the trunk of the magnolia tree. "*Sono in paradiso, amore mio.*"

Even being under the dowager's watchful eye couldn't keep Emma from snuggling closer to him. "It is rather heavenly, isn't it?" She released a contented sigh. "Even still, I look forward to tomorrow. When I become Lady Atella. I so wish your family could have come."

"We will go to them soon enough." He pressed a kiss to her temple. "Perhaps this summer, when the fields are green, and then my mother will cook for you."

Alice gasped suddenly, making everyone look at her. Though she was not what one would call large yet, the slight protrusion of her stomach well communicated that they would add a little one to their nursery that summer. Expectant women suddenly gasping would make anyone nervous, Emma decided.

The entomologist's wife took off her spectacles. "I nearly forgot. I have a gift for you both." She pointed to the basket near her husband. "Rupert, if you would?"

He took out a rolled sheet of cream-colored paper, tied by a pink ribbon. He reached across the blanket and handed it to Luca. Luca leaned back against the tree while Emma sat forward to untie the ribbon. He unrolled the paper to reveal a sketch of her, in repose, staring dreamily away from the viewer.

"*Bellissimo*," Luca murmured. "It captures Emma perfectly. When did you draw this, Mrs. Gardiner? I feel I have seen it before."

"You really must call me Alice," she said with a dismissive wave. "That was on the day of the boat race when Emma seemed terribly out of sorts. Except, of course, when she spoke of you."

Emma's cheeks warmed, and she stared at the picture a little closer. "Perhaps I was already falling in love, even then."

"Were you?" Luca asked, masculine pride deepening his voice. "Thank you, Alice. We will frame it and hang it in our personal quarters at the embassy."

"Yes. Thank you." Emma watched her soon-to-be husband roll the paper up carefully, and she tied the bow back in place.

Tomorrow, her life would begin anew. No more longing for adventure or waiting for change. With Luca, Emma would see the world, and learn everything about it she could. Someday, they would teach their children to approach new things with curiosity and a sense of adventure.

Emma was quite certain the next day would be only the beginning of her happily ever after.

SIR ANDREW, THOUGH A MERE BARONET, HAD BEEN PART OF the duke's family in practice if not in reality for most of his life. Watching his cousin nestle happily against her chosen gentleman, and surrounded by people who had known him since infancy ought to have been a peaceful situation.

Instead, he kept shifting his weight. First he leaned back against his hands, then crouched forward; he tried kneeling as well as sitting with legs crossed. But he was too unsettled to remain still for more than a few moments.

When Lady Josephine caught him squirming like a youth in church, she gave him a withering glare. He fully expected a tart remark to follow, but instead she heaved a put-upon sigh and smiled at him. "Would you like to walk with me a moment, Andrew?"

Sensing a trap, he agreed anyway. If he had to sit and watch his cousin exchange doe-eyed glances with her betrothed, he might well say something that would earn him a set down. Not that he begrudged Emma any happiness. But he hated the change.

They strolled away from the group at a leisurely pace, the two of them silent for a number of steps. Andrew watched Josephine from the corner of his eye, noting the way her expression changed with her thoughts.

"You have been remarkably quiet today," he noted.

Josie shrugged one shoulder. "Emma said not to enter any battles with you today."

He chuckled. "So we are incapable of having a conversation without argument? That makes us seem like spoiled children."

Her lips twitched. "Precisely what I was thinking. It is rather awful of us, isn't it? Can we not agree on anything?"

"I am certain we agree on many things. I just like to torment you by offering counterpoints." He grinned broadly when she glared at him. "But if my cousin has decreed no arguments today, we had better adhere to her wishes."

With a regal nod, Josie faced forward again and tucked her hands behind her back. "I will miss her terribly when she leaves with him, though I am happy for her. Emma has been with me as long as I can remember."

"You two were rather like twins all those years ago." Only five years Emma's senior, Andrew could well remember the early years when his cousin had first come to be with the duke's family. "Whatever will you do with yourself, Josie?"

She narrowed her eyes at him. "You aren't supposed to call me that, you know. I am far too grown up. And so are you. Only my family calls me that."

That stung. Andrew forced a smile. "Forgive me, my lady. I overstepped."

She huffed. "Don't you dare—"

"No, I insist upon offering my deepest apologies. I, a lowly baronet, presuming to use a familial pet name—it is inexcusable." He bowed deeply to her, flourishing his hand as he did. "I must owe you a forfeit for such a breach in etiquette. Or else you may name a champion to duel me for your besmirched honor."

"You are ridiculous, Andrew." Josephine put one fist on her hip and glared at him. "Why do I even bother trying to interact with you at all? You are nothing more than a little boy who has outgrown his leading strings." She turned and went back the way they had come, marching with shoulders stiff, straight as a soldier.

Andrew chuckled to himself as she went, then turned his attention to James and the dog. He shrugged. If she thought him a little boy, he might as well enjoy himself like one.

He went to play with the boy and dog, pretending not to notice whether Josephine looked his way again. Someday, he'd best her in their continual battle of wits and wills. Once and for all, he'd win their friendly little war.

If you enjoyed this gentle tale of love, and you're wondering about Sir Andrew and Lady Josephine's on-going battle of wits and teasing, you ought to know that the next book in the series is all about them.

Sir Andrew and the Authoress, available Autumn 2021, can be ordered now.

You can also keep up with Sally Britton's release dates and other work by signing up for her newsletter.

AUTHOR'S NOTES
OR "WHAT IS REAL AND WHAT I MADE UP."

Castle Clairvoir is largely based upon the real-life Castle Belvoir (pronounced Bee-ver), the seat of the current Duke of Rutland. The history of the family who built the current castle (as several have existed in the same spot before) inspired the history of my Duke of Montfort and his family, with a few notable exceptions. The inspiration for the gardens came from following Castle Belvoir on Instagram. You should take a peek if you want a good feel for the setting of this book.

The Kingdom of the Two Sicilies was quite real. That's the first question readers have asked about this book. It existed for a brief time in the 19th Century. It was a fascinating time in Italian history—Italy as we know it today was divided in two, between Austria and Spain. Secret societies formed in an effort to unify Italy under its own flag, or to take it back to its original city-states. England and the Kingdom of the Two Sicilies had several treaties and trade deals, so it would not be entirely hard to believe an ambassador from the fledgling country would spend a lot of time in England.

All the books and titles mentioned in this novel are real, and they would have been available at the time this story takes place.

My female characters are often frustrated by the lack of rights they are given, and their lack of voice. At this period in time, women were working harder than ever to be understood. By the mid-nineteenth century, this became the suffragette movement. Prior to this, there certainly were women who worked behind-the-scenes in the political world to influence change.

The pasta-making scene was my absolute favorite to write. While I hope it provides entertainment to readers, please do not use it as a guide to make your own pasta. My cooking experiences never end well, so this scene was written with input from those with more experience and a LOT of online videos.

Italian dialects are all quite different. Rather than try for historically accurate Italian or (likely more appropriate to the hero) Sicilian, I chose to use modern Italian.

As with any work of fiction, there are a few liberties taken with historical nuances. I try to stay as accurate as possible and welcome emails from readers who have questions or comments. You can email me at sally@authorsallybritton.com any time.

ACKNOWLEDGMENTS

Thank you to my loving family. They bring me tea and lunch, they talk to me about where my story gets stuck, and they make all the off-time so worth everything else. They are my greatest joy.

Thank you, as always, to my dear writing friends who keep me going. The Society of Obstinate, Headstrong Girls is one of my favorite groups. They know who they are. They are incredible women with the most beautiful words.

I must express my gratitude to the Jenny and Emily at Midnight Owl Editors. Jenny always sets my stories to rights, and working with Emily to proofread my novel was wonderful.

Thank you also to Marilee, for correcting my Italian and suggesting much better phrases than I could come up with on my own.

My fantastic friend and designer, Shaela Kay of Blue Water Books has outdone herself on the artwork of the cover, and helping me make the inside of this book beautiful as well.

I don't talk about it often enough, but I'm also grateful to Jacob of DabbleWriter.com who created the absolute best writing app that I have ever used. It's allowed me to keep track of this series and everything else I've published so far.

Of course, I must also thank my readers. All of you keep me going. Thank you for joining my groups, following me on social media, sending me fun questions, and sharing your reviews! You make this work a joy. Thank you.

ABOUT THE AUTHOR

Sally Britton, along with her husband, their four incredible children, and their dog named Izzie, live in Oklahoma.

Sally started writing her first story on her mother's electric
typewriter when she was fourteen years old. Reading her way
through Jane Austen, Louisa May Alcott, and Lucy Maud Mont-
gomery, Sally decided to write about the elegant, complex world
of centuries past.

Sally graduated from Brigham Young University in 2007 with
a bachelor's in English, her emphasis on British literature. She met
and married her husband not long after and they've been building
their happily ever after since that day.

Vincent Van Gogh is attributed with the quote, "What is done
in love is done well." Sally has taken that as her motto, for herself
and her characters, writing stories where love is a choice.

All of Sally's published works are available on Amazon.com
and you can connect with Sally and sign up for her newsletter on
her website, AuthorSallyBritton.com.

Made in the USA
Middletown, DE
23 November 2021

53279214R00156